Justice Be Told

by

Sheeba Eeswaramoorthy

The Conrad Press

Justice Be Told
Published by The Conrad Press in the United Kingdom 2024
Tel: +44(0)1227 472 874
www.theconradpress.com
info@theconradpress.com
ISBN 978-1-915494-95-5
Copyright ©Sheeba Eeswaramoorthy 2024
All rights reserved.
Typesetting and Cover Design by:Levellers
The Conrad Press logo was designed by Maria Priestley.
Printed and bound in Great Britain by Clays Ltd, Elcograf S.p.A.

'Never mistake law for justice. Justice is an ideal, and law is a tool.' – *L. E Modesitt Jr.*

Chapter one

MATTHEW

'Arrest me... I need help... I've hit my missus,' I blurted the words out in a rush.

I slumped over the desk, one arm stretched out in front of me. Exhausted, my heart beat loud and quickly. I could not hear anything else around me.

I was drenched with rain and nervous sweat. I patted the back of my matted hair. My shirt hung lopsided out of my trousers in parts. I snatched my soaked cap away, and swiped my forehead with it before returning the sogginess to my wet head.

I pulled myself back and looked hard at the thick-set sergeant, 'I'm sorry, it's crap out there.'

I was the hedgehog in the way of an oncoming car.

The desk officer stared at me in bewilderment and took my details. He was a round man with a face to match. I doubted it was an everyday occurrence for people to stroll in and hand themselves in. Not that I had strolled in, but still. He wore his white crisp shirt, black tie, black trousers combo with pride. I made an outward attempt of matching his confidence, but it fell flat.

'Matthew Barnett, thirty-two, my date of birth is January the nineteenth, nineteen eighty-four and I live at 83 St John's Street,' I said. He instructed me to take a seat and told me that someone would come out to talk to me.

It was a makeshift police station. It housed the

desk sergeant alone, who busied himself manning the place. There were no windows. The grey walls steeped in stories of violence, crime and gruesomeness. Cold, harsh, and miserable within the four walls. A couple of posters hung morosely; one about domestic violence and the other about drink driving. I guessed it was seasonal.

There was one other adolescent male sat there with me. He looked far too young to be here. I wondered where his mum or dad were. He wore a baseball cap and kept his eyes to the ground. Someone should have been with him, someone who cared about him and what was happening to him. A flashback of my outstretched palm striking Kel's left cheek darted through my mind.

I rested my head in the supports of my bent arms, arms sat heavily on my knees. What had I done?

It was a few days after Christmas, and I had fought the ice, wind and rain to get here. Kelly and I had been together for about two years and had lived together for six months. It had been good, but things got too much tonight. Kel's face full of fear still etched in my mind. Why couldn't she have let it be? I shook my head, but the memory lingered on like a pungent odour.

I didn't know where it came from. I was the bottle of exploding pop. Had that explosion come from me? Kel shook me so much that there was no avoiding the explosion.

'Matthew Barnett,' yelled the desk sergeant breaking my thoughts. 'Where the hell did you go, mate, do you know how many times I called out your name?

If I lose my voice, I know who to blame,' he joked.

'Erm… sorry, I didn't hear…'

'PC Thomas is coming for you now and will take you through.'

'Okay, am I under arrest?' I finally mustered.

'PC Thomas will speak to you and let you know what will happen next.'

I only noticed the door as it opened, and PC Thomas strode in.

He was an older man with an air of seriousness about him. The marked crease lined his face from his forehead to the top of his cheek. A permanent reminder of some war story or another. He stood tall and was well built. His bald head in direct contrast to his facial hair that more than made up for the lack of head hair. Kel's soft, pale cheek reared up again and her self-soothing palm glued in shock to her face. Then there was the other thing.

'Matthew Barnett. Can you come through with me?' PC Thomas boomed, more by way of order than question. It jolted me back to reality.

I followed behind him, my legs joint-less, suddenly. He took us into a little room, with nothing more than a desk and a couple of chairs either side. It pressed down on me and there was no escape. He pointed me to a chair, whilst he took the one door side. He yanked out his notepad and pen, 'So what is all this about?'

'I've hit my missus.' My breathing had returned to a steadier pace, but my heart still hammered the walls of my chest. My hands had been wrung dry with how much I had put them through the mangle.

'Right, before we can go any further, I need to let you know your rights. You have the right to...,' and my mind blurred and fogged over. I didn't hear much of what he said but I got the gist. I had been here before, I was a lot younger then, my mates and I were drunk and disorderly.

They offered me a duty solicitor. 'I'm not sure,' I replied.

'Well, you know, you came to us, it seems to me that you wanted to talk to us.'

'Mmmm... but maybe a Solicitor would be good.'

'It's your call, but if you want us to arrange that, there will be a delay. The other option is to get on with it. You get off your chest whatever you want, and you will be done and dusted.'

'Yes, I came because I have done wrong.'

'There you go, I can get the interview set up, to get on record what happened.'

'But I'm not sure, I know how these things can go. Yeah, I want the Duty,' I determined.

It had been a mistake, a god-awful mistake, but a mistake, even so. Something involuntary had overcome me and brought me here. Now though, whatever had possessed me eased away. What I wanted and needed, was help.

They placed me in a holding cell. It was even worse than the waiting room, the bitterness of the suffocation. Oh, how I wished I were back in the waiting room now. This was a tiny chamber, with three tired white walls and dark angry bars on the one side. There was a small single bed with grey coarse material for a sheet. An acerbic smell of a graveyard of crushed souls all around.

I sat there and waited. Alone.

The duty had finally arrived and so I returned to the same interview room. The room was gloomy. My eyes darted around the room searching a distraction from the thoughts in my head. The only item of interest was the black and white clock that hung on the wall. It moved like the internet with connection issues. There were times that it seemed to go backwards. I had not had anything to drink or eat. My stomach churned with a mix of hunger and nerves whilst my throat was too dry from the thirst and adrenaline.

Nevertheless, I continued to wait. Alone.

An Asian woman slim build, short strode into the room and sat opposite me. She looked young and I worried about how much experience she had had. I kicked myself for not having got this over and done with sooner. I'd be out by now or at least know whether I was under arrest or not.

PC Thomas had accompanied her and told me 'This is your duty brief,' and then left us, closing the door behind him.

The lawyer waited until the door had shut before saying 'Hi Matthew, my name is Serena, and I am here to represent you. I want to get the best outcome I can for you. Does that sound okay, so far?' The fruity scent of Serena's perfume misplaced in this cold, sweatbox of bad plumbing, festering bins and unwashed socks. 'Okay,' I said, still unsure.

'Do you need a drink or a bite to eat before we go on?'

'A drink would be good,' I replied and a coffee with plenty of sugar was soon in front of me.

'So, here is what we will do. I am going to go and find out everything that PC Thomas knows. Then I will come back in here to discuss that all with you and get your side of things.'

'Yeah, but don't you want to know what happened?' I asked.

'Of course, but first I need to know what the police know and then I will let you tell me your side of things. Is that okay?'

'Sure,' still hesitant, I was unsure about this Serena, who headed out before I could get another word.

Alone, again.

SERENA

Matthew Barnett sat opposite as I walked into the interview room, a giant ant in the darkness of a hollow cave. His deep hazel eyes set back behind the folds of the corners and sacks underneath. He seemed tall and able to take care of himself. Tufts of dark chestnut brown hair poked out under a cap, which Matt hid himself under. He pulled the cap away whilst his other hand smoothed his rough hair in self-comfort, I guessed. His hands patterned with sporadic scratches. It was hard to miss how he wiped his right palm on his jeans as if cleaning it away somehow. It was an odd habit, but it took all sorts. He spoke gruffly and shortly. I wondered what he was about and what they had on him.

It was quite early for a night duty rota; I got the call at eleven at night and managed to get here within the hour. I was with my book before sleeping. All part of my usual night-time routines, the only action my bed had seen in a long time, which suited me down to the ground.

My bedroom was my safe haven. Photos of my favourite people scattered around me. A couple of pictures hung on the walls to create the sense of peace I aspired to. I loved spending time here and had worked hard to make it perfect for me. Luckily the duty call came as I had started reading. I put a quick suit on, powdered my face, a touch of lipstick, grabbed my duty bag, headed out and here I was.

I sought out PC Thomas in the custody block to learn what this was all about. What I soon learnt was that this man had handed himself into the police. There had not even been any report of a crime until he turned up and admitted to hitting his partner. What the heck!

I mean in my fifteen years of lawyering, I had never come across someone owning up to an assault. I had dealt with thugs, thieves, predators of all shapes and sizes but never had I faced a situation like this. I looked around the dreary interview room.

'Yup, you've definitely got Einstein in there,' PC Thomas joked and broke into my thoughts.

'Good job, there ain't any of those out here, in that case,' I retorted. 'All well suited, I'd say!' I jibed back but was unsure what this Barnett man was about.

How badly had he beaten his partner? How much had he disclosed and tied himself up already? Why had he confessed? Was this a repeated pattern of behaviour or a one-off? Why had he beaten his partner, not that there was ever any justification but there was often a complex back story? So many questions, so many thoughts circled.

'Mmm… say, what you like, but this one is bang to rights, Serena and there is no legal wrangling that can untie this one.'

'We will see, you know, I like a challenge. I am the queen of legal wrangling!'

'Usually, I'd worry about that, but the lad has strapped himself up and not even your magic can Houdini this one away!' PC Thomas said. The truth was I agreed with him. My job was to find a way to mitigate against the disaster my client had created for himself.

The man came in and handed himself on a platter to the police. My mind worked overtime. This man disclosed an unreported crime and I needed to work around that now. He hit his partner but still deserved a defence.

The police did not have any other information for me other than Mr Barnett's antecedents. He had one caution for drunk and disorderly when he was eighteen. He had come in at around nine in the evening and had been in the cells for a couple of hours. As far as the police could tell, he seemed lucid and not under any influences. All of that was manageable. The issue was understanding this man and his thought processes. He did not seem a big talker, so I knew I had my work cut out.

PC Thomas agreed that I have time to consult with my client. They would then conduct a taped interview with him. They would process him and decide whether to charge him.

I needed to consider his position carefully with him. We had to choose whether he responded to questioning or went no comment. All that depended on what he would tell me.

I returned to the interview room where Matthew Barnett was waiting for me. He looked up at me in a curious way. His raised eyebrows and opened palms gave way to a furrowed forehead and clenched fists.

I sat down, took out my Counsel's notebook and explained the next steps. 'The police have explained what they know and now I need to understand what happened in your own words. First, I need to explain that I cannot mislead the police or allow you to mislead them either. Does that make sense?'

'I think so, what did the police say? Am I under arrest?' Matthew rushed out but I got the feeling that he had not followed what I had said, so I tried again.

'Hold on one second. I need to make sure you understand what I am saying. So, if you tell me something that is likely to hurt your case, I cannot lie about that, nor can I let you lie about it. Whatever you do tell me, we must work with that and prepare for that to come out at some point. So, if there is something you do not want the police to know, you need to think before you tell me. Does that make sense now?'

'Yeah, yeah, I get it, I need to know what is going to happen to me now' he replied. He sounded surer but with a growing frustration. I was ready to take his instructions about what had happened that evening.

'Okay, so I am going to ask you to explain in your own words what happened. There may be times that I ask questions. Usually, to clarify a particular point or to understand the situation a bit better.'

'Right.' Matt said tersely, but I was well versed in difficult clients.

I focused on my job of protecting him, despite the horror he might have inflicted elsewhere. Every story had hidden layers and Matthew Barnett was the story I had yet to read. We spent more time grappling over the boundaries of working together. Then, I let Matthew tell me his story.

MATTHEW

I was a little taken aback with this Serena woman, here to represent me. She was so small that I expected her to be quite timid. Serena was in a black skirt suit and looked the part, but I didn't think she had any oomph about her. She seemed inexperienced and I figured that I was on my own with this one.

'So, what exactly have the police told you?' I questioned.

'You already know,' she replied eyeing me suspiciously.

'Well, I hit my girlfriend, didn't I.'

'Right, and?'

'That's it,' I snapped. This woman grated on me and I had no time for her. I wanted to get this interview over and done with.

'Matthew, it's not going like that. You will tell me the full story. I will then tell you what you should do. So, let's try again, what happened before you hit your girlfriend?'

'Listen, I'm not your lackey. I've told you everything and that's that.' My voice filled with tension. Heat rose inside me.

'That's fine, I have all the time in the world. I'm going to have a cup of coffee with PC Thomas. You let them know when you are ready to talk some more.' She swung out of her seat and whooshed out of the interview room.

'Whaaat?' She was gone.

Left to my own devices again.

I did not like this Serena woman at all. I was annoyed with myself for having asked for her and waited around all this time. I worried about Kelly and wanted to find out how she was, how Andi was, how everything was. I still did not know how much damage I had caused. Not the physical damage, but the damage to our relationship. The damage to the family we had talked about and all that I had dreamt of. I had never had a family like Kel's before and never would after tonight.

I paced one way and then the other in that tiny cubicle, with Kel's face reverberating in my mind's eye. Those dark chocolate eyes filled with shimmering tears stared in fear at me. Her small, snowy hand curled in comfort against her cheek and her body, frozen in stunned trance.

The room filled with greyness. A piercing light from the lone bulb hanging forlornly. Stickiness floated in the air from decades of criminal investigations. In amongst all this, Kel's last words echoed around my head, and it took all my strength to push it back down.

I pounded against the solid door. The thickness of the door turned the crashing punches to muted, cushioned taps.

PC Thomas appeared, and I grunted at him that I was ready. He said he would get Serena but returned alone saying she needed a bit more time to finish her coffee!

I kicked the door when PC Thomas slammed it shut. The tuner of the door turned my angry boot to a quietened blow. My foot, and hand, though, felt the pain.

That woman was taking this too far. I could fire her and handle this on my own. Urgh, I hated this, but it was what I deserved.

'So, ready to talk,' Serena said as she strolled back into the room.

'What the hell are you playing at?' I roared.

'That might work with your girlfriend, it doesn't with me. So, quieten down and let's get real,' Serena replied in a steely way. 'I have had much worse than this, I suggest you tell me what happened with your girlfriend.'

'She was nagging at me, I lost it and lashed out.'

'That's all you're giving me,' Serena asked with searching eyes.

'I don't know what else I can tell you. I slapped her and came here.'

'Matt, I am here to protect your best interests. I can only do that if I know everything but if that is all you are going to tell me, so be it.'

'Fine,' I said.

'What about anything in your history that I should know about?'

'You already know, so let's stop with these games and get on with the interview.'

'I only know what the police know but how about family background, anything there that I should know?'

'No disrespect, this is about what I did to my girlfriend. We need to get this done now.' My family was off limits.

'Fine, well I recommend you do a no comment interview. The police only know what you have already told them. You have already said more than you should have, and they can decide whether to charge you, on that basis.'

'Nope, that won't work.'

'What is wrong with you. You are on some collision course.'

I shrugged. She had no clue in her ivory tower and silver spoon what life was like for us.

Serena spent some time repeating her earlier advice. She explained that I should go no comment in the interview, that that would be my best chance to get out of this mess. 'They have to punish me, Serena,' I replied.

Serena shook her head side to side but said, 'So, first you hit a woman, then you develop a conscience. Fine, well we still need to do the best we can to mitigate that damage. You might want punishment but trust me, you don't want prison.'

'I will take whatever is coming to me.'

'Prison is not coming your way if you work with me. Trust me, living with this will be its own punishment if you are sincere in your remorse.'

'I don't care what you think, get this done.'

We settled on preparing a statement together. With all the other questions, I would respond no comment. I wanted to tell them what had happened. What I didn't want was to be outsmarted.

When we were ready, PC Thomas and a female police officer, PC Shaw joined us. A small rectangular, cold table between us. The room felt closed and stiff with the fluorescent light marking me out. PC Shaw switched on the tape.

We had our introductions, followed by PC Thomas' recital of the right to keep silent. Serena had already broken it down for me that I could reel off the caution myself.

Serena explained that I would not be responding to any questions put to me but that I would read out a statement.

'I live with my girlfriend, Kelly McInley and her four-year-old daughter, Andi. We have been living together for about six months. Kel and I have been in a relationship for about a year and a half before that. We have been getting on great and generally don't even have a cross word between us.'

I pressed on, 'Tonight, we had an argument over something stupid about seeing her family and I lashed out. Andi was in her bedroom upstairs. I have never gotten so angry like that before. I don't know what happened to me and it scared me. I slapped her across the face, and she fell back into the sofa. I am disgusted with myself and rushed out of the house immediately. I made my way here because I know I need to be punished and want help so that this never happens again.'

That statement seemed so cold. It did not explain the family I had ruined and lost, the family I never had. No one cared about those details, or the terror in Kel's tears, her self-soothing gentle hand, or those last words.

As my brief had warned me, the police didn't leave it at that. They probed and prodded. As I had practised with Serena, I kept repeating 'No comment.'

I had to block out what PC Thomas asked because it would have been so easy to respond. For instance, PC Thomas said, 'Well, you have pretty much told us everything we need to know. We need to check that we have understood your Statement. You said you had started living together, six months ago?'

'No comment,' and so it continued.

What an outsider eavesdropping the conversation would have made of it all, I don't know. I followed Serena's instructions to the letter.

I would have answered those questions if Serena and I had not rehearsed as much as we had. It was so easy to fall into the trap of answering what seemed straightforward questions. I forced myself to stop listening, which was the only way I could get through it. I parroted, 'No comment,' and it eventually came to an end.

It was after two in the morning and the police wanted to keep me in until they had spoken with Kel. They said that they would go over first thing in the morning and as it was so late, they kept me in the cells.

I was back in that horrible little cage, the guard rattling the keys around in his hand as he locked me away. It was cold and bitter. I lay down on the hard mattress, with the abrasive grey blanket scratching at my neck. The caustic air pressing down into me.

Kel meant everything to me. She was my perfect. I couldn't explain it any better than that. She was simple, quite plain looking by everyday standards, but gorgeous in my eyes, caring and a home girl. She had long, dark auburn hair that I loved falling loose below her shoulders. She was short to my tall. She had grounded me and given me a place to be safe. I don't mean the place where we live, I mean her.

Seeing the pain engraved in Kel's face was unbearable. She seemed so disappointed and that was harder to face than the anger. I had become a stranger to her within seconds. I had become a stranger even to myself. 'You are your father's son,' she had whispered that I almost missed it. Now so loud in my head that I could not silence it.

SERENA

I was shattered by the time I had driven home, and it was close to half past two in the morning. Sleep took hold of my eyes. I rolled down the window for the winter air to slap me awake. Luckily, I lived near the station.

I stumbled through the lounge in darkness, knocking into bits of furniture. I felt my way as I was still familiarising myself with this, my new home, and headed straight upstairs for my bed.

I unbuttoned as I walked and was soon in my comfy pyjamas before I knew it. I settled into bed with my laptop for company. I quickly inputted my notes from tonight's police station interview.

Matthew was an interesting one. He had slapped a woman, something quite atrocious. Set against that, this guy had something about him. The agonising guilt was intrinsic to this man, and I felt for him despite his abrasiveness. He projected such hostility but there seemed more to the story.

I wanted to do what I could to help him. I was used to the perpetrator pleading innocence. That was easier to work with when you have any kind of moral compass. This, though, was a conflicting experience and difficult to reason away.

Tired, I focused on my notes, there was no time to analyse or over analyse as I was prone to. At times, my papers looked like they had centipedes crawling all over them. Sleep. I needed sleep.

Having the right people around had been crucial and was something I had taken my time over when I started up Smart Law Solicitors. Our receptionist, Janet, was a miracle worker. She had an excellent telephone manner providing a warm but professional welcome. She organised me and was my second-hand woman. She was a walking diary, case manager, debt collector, stock taker, cleaner, superwoman and concierge all in one. She was not a two for one but at least a ten for one or more. I would never get anything done without her.

Then there is my Trainee, Tara, a smart girl, measured and thorough. She was still learning. Whilst quick picking up ideas and practice, she was slow at getting things right. She had incredible potential and was useful with research and preparatory work. I quickly summarised the Barnett case to her. I tasked Tara on finding out all she could about the different assaults, the sentencing bands and mitigation points.

Events would now move swiftly for Matthew, and I needed to be ready to get him the best deal. I made a start on my list of calls.

Matthew had given me his parents' number and his brother's. I put in calls to them but only managed to speak with the dad, the brother lived with him and his wife, in any event. 'Hello,' came the gruff voice from the other end of the phone.

'Hello, my name is Serena from Smart Law Solicitors. I represent Matthew Barnett and am looking to speak to a family member.'

'Right, you are? What has he done?'

'Can I check whether you are Matthew's brother or father?'

'I'm his dad, so?'

'Right, well he has assaulted his partner and turned himself in.'

'And?' The dad did not even skip a beat as if all this

was routine.

'The police are holding him overnight until they find out more and make a decision on whether to charge him.'

'Listen, Miss, can you get to it?'

'Matthew will need a bail address if charged.'

'Fine,' he snapped and with that he said his goodbyes and ended the call.

Mr Barnett was forthright. That said, he was able to provide what I needed from him right now, for his son, a little begrudgingly, I suspected.

By midday, I finally had the call from the police station asking me to head over there. I grabbed my lunch of black tea in my travel cup, my coat and headed out.

PC Thomas greeted me at the police station and took me back through to the custody area. We were back in the consultation room, and he explained the outcome of their enquiries. 'So, we've been to see Kelly, Barnett's missus.'

I nodded him on, 'She refused to provide any statement and said that she did not want her partner to be in any trouble.'

'Right, so what happens next?' I replied in quite a matter-of-fact way but inside, my head was flip flopping. Something they never taught at university or College of Law – the art of nerve control. Lessons drilled into me during my training; never letting the other side or court see any emotion. Inside, though, all sorts of instinctive urges were clashing with each other. What on earth was going on here? The victim does not make a statement and the perpetrator has confessed. This was all upside down, inside out.

'We are charging him, and he'll be released with bail conditions until court.' PC Thomas confirmed.

It was inevitable but that did not stop me making representations against it. It was disproportionate, given the injured party did not seek any retribution. Barnett had never had any trouble with the police. His voluntary and unforced admission was a credit to him. These would also be some of the factors I would put up for mitigation eventually.

A referral had also been made to Children Services, which was path of the course. Hopefully, mother would show that this was a one-off incident. Care cases were my forte. I stayed on the duty rota for police station interviews to pick up that extra fee income.

PC Thomas gave me time with Matthew. He had a surface calmness but, I could sense a fear beneath it. We stepped out to the custody sergeant's desk for the formalities. They would impose conditions to keep him away from his partner and his home with her. That was where his parents' address would come in use.

'Matthew Barnett, you are charged with assault occasioning actual bodily harm.' I was taken aback as I assumed it would be common assault, actual bodily harm was the higher charge.

PC Thomas must have seen the flicker of my eyes and filled in the gaps, 'She had reddening to her face and... she is five months pregnant.'

Chapter Two

KELLY

I loved this time of the day. The quiet. The stillness. The peace.

The icy coldness hung in the air, battling the central heating that had kicked in. My fluffy, loyal onesie hugged me, but the stinginess of my left cheek remained. It had flared up overnight and felt swollen, but it might have been my imagination.

The backlash of Matt's fast and hard palm struck at me. I was at the kitchen table with a mug of coffee, steam still floated from the rim of the cup. My hands warmed around the comfort of the mug.

Although it was Council accommodation, it was my home. I had spent time, money and heart making it home.

The redbrick houses with black tiled hats strung together as an unbroken chain. It might not be to everyone's taste, but it worked for me. I sipped at the hot coffee that radiated my throat as it scorched its path.

I placed the cup back on the circular wooden dining table that I picked up from a second-hand shop. This table, woven with stories from families gone past, was my favourite place.

I had one child from a previous relationship, which had broken down, immediately Andi was born. I was now five months pregnant. That was what made all this even more frightening.

I couldn't do it alone again.

I wanted and needed Matt with me.

I couldn't quite believe what had happened last night; I had never seen that side of Matt before. He had always been so gentle and loving. He was like no one I had ever met before. He was the holding doors, hugging me in his coat when we were out in the cold, the coffee maker while I lay in bed kind of guy. He was not the cheater and woman beater of my past and yet somehow, here I was again.

The left side of my face branded in one sharp movement. Matt's open palm stung as it struck my cheek. That comfort blanket of a hand had turned to my face swatter.

'Mamma, don't cry,' Andi said as she crawled into my lap.

I rocked her, 'I'm okay, we are okay, ssshhhh. It's okay.'

'Where is Matty?'

'Matty was naughty,'

'Is he on a time-out?' Andi interrupted.

'Yeah, something like that.'

'Matty is naughty, mummy.'

I stroked her hair, damp from my quiet tears. 'Sweetie, you need to get ready for bed. Go brush your teeth and I'll be with you in a bit.' I was sure Andi would have even more questions for me today.

I wondered where Matt went last night. Where had he slept, his parents?

I had frozen with numbness last night as Matt's palm thundered towards me and hit me squarely in the side of my face. I had stumbled a little but more from the shock of it than the force. My eyes watered over, and tears flowed.

It seemed that I still wore the cloak of numbness even this morning, even if my eyes had dried.

There was a knock on the door, whilst I was still amid my reverie. I jarred into action. I felt my body tense and heart pounded. I felt a coolness rush over me as I got up to walk to the door.

I knew that Matt had left his keys, when he shot out of here last night, but I thought I would have had more time. My mouth became sticky with dryness. I went to answer the door and at the same time, heard Andi calling for me. I shouted up to her to stay upstairs and that I would call her when breakfast was ready.

It wasn't Matt, instead two police officers stood in front of me.

My heart rate doubled. My mind was a whirr of thoughts and activity. After a few minutes of fish like mouthing expressions, I asked them to start again.

They introduced themselves to me, PCs Shaw and Thomas. My hands were at my side, gripped into my thighs. I was sure that I would falter otherwise. I was worried that Matt had got himself into trouble after he left home last night. I escorted them into the kitchen. All the while, I watched their every move, every facial gesture, for any sign of the news they had come to deliver.

'Kelly, we are here because Matthew Barnett has told us that he slapped you yesterday.' PC Shaw explained. What had he done?

'So, we need to take some information from you, is that okay Kelly?' PC Shaw continued.

'I'm not sure,' I replied.

'That's okay, I will ask a few questions and you tell us what you know,' PC Shaw assured.

'Mmmmm, I am not sure.'

'We will go slowly, at your pace, Kelly.'

'I don't know, I don't think now is the best time,' I hesitated.

'The sooner we get the details, the better, whilst everything is still fresh in your mind,' PC Shaw explained.

'I don't know... What if I don't want to say anything?' I asked.

'What do you mean?' PC Shaw replied.

'Well, I don't want to say anything right now,' I felt a little braver.

'That is your choice to make but no one has the right to hurt you. We are here to make sure it never happens again,' PC Shaw pressed.

'But you can't make sure of that, can you? Yes, you might be able to prosecute but that might make things a whole lot worse. I don't know that I want that at this stage.'

'Mummy,' Andi called out as her tiny feet hit the stairs and she headed down.

'Andi, please stay upstairs.' I rushed to the bottom of the steps and chased her back up them.

The tete a tete with PC Shaw continued for a while.

PC Thomas chimed in and gave it a go to persuade me to tell them what had happened last night. They wanted my statement, but I did not know what I wanted. I stayed firm that I was not giving a statement. I kicked myself for slipping up about the pregnancy but tried to brush it aside.

For the first few years of Andi's life, it was only Andi and me. Her Dad disappeared. It was a struggle a lot of the time. I remembered well the times that Andi cried endlessly.

Brushing my own teeth by midday was a huge achievement back then. I often cried alongside my little Andi.

Then there was the small matter of keeping her warm, clean, fed and watered all on state benefits.

A lot of the time, I couldn't even look at myself let alone look anyone else in the eye. Somehow, we dragged ourselves on, Andi and me.

I had written Andi's dad off but as Andi started at school, he and his parents suddenly became interested. I was not sure what had gone on in those missing years, but I wanted Andi to have a dad. My own dad meant so much to me and was my hero. I wanted my sweet girl to have that too and so despite everything that had gone on before, I never stood in the way.

Last year, Andi was with her dad for Christmas and this year it was my turn. It was the first time that we had Matt with us, and it was the family unit I had always craved. It was not a let-down, like it can be when you have looked forward to something for as long as I had looked forward to this. It was everything I had hoped for.

It seemed so normal but now, well now, I didn't

know any more. We had had one of the best Christmases and now it had become one of the worst.

MATTHEW

I had had a sleepless night on the awful mattress of a prison bed. A cold slab of nails with the smell of grunge all around. It did not matter which way I turned; it was relentless. It was no more than I deserved after what I had done to Kel but God, I wanted out.

I returned to the custody block, and I saw Serena standing by the desk. She looked even younger and smaller through my ever-weary eyes than she had last night. She was suited and booted but I was fast losing faith. I imagined that she had her admirers, her triangular face with dark chocolate eyes. I remained on the fence about whether she was an effective lawyer.

'Morning,' Serena greeted.

'Yup.'

'Okay, let's get this sorted.'

There was a murkiness to the air, the custody suite and cells seemed hidden underground. There were no windows. It was sparse and although I had never been in a mortuary, it had that sense about it.

I carried a hangover, without having had any of the fun of it. They charged me but then something weird went on with Serena and the custody sergeant. I didn't care and wanted out of this place. I felt like I had not seen a shower for weeks. I wanted to get home.

As much as I wanted to head home, I was also apprehensive about it. I wondered whether Kel wanted to even look in my direction, let alone be at home with me. It dawned on me that maybe I had to stay away. Kel needed time and space but if I left it too long, I would lose her forever.

My thoughts turned to Andi too, the poor kid wouldn't have a clue what had gone on. I don't know if she heard any of what went on last night.

Then there was our baby. I desperately wanted to be the father that he deserved but I wasn't good enough.

'You must attend Stafford Magistrates court tomorrow at 10am,' Custody Officer said.

'Yup.'

'Your bail conditions include staying away from Kelly McInley and to stay at 25 Croft Road.'

'Uh-huh.'

'That's it... you're'

'Hold on a minute, 25 Croft Road, what do you mean, 25 Croft Road. What are they on about Serena?'

'You can't live with Kelly, Matt.' Serena explained. 'Your parents have said you can stay with them, and you'll have to be there until the court action is concluded.'

'What?'

I walked in my shoes but somehow was outside of myself. A cloudy fog of smoke numbed me.

Serena told me to meet her at her office in an hour. She handed me her business card and we separated ways. As I was on foot, I made my way there.

I found a café nearby and went in for a quick coffee. It felt good, the taste of a freely bought coffee. The aroma of the steam soothed me, and the sharp bitterness hit my head awake. The heat burnt my tongue and pricked at my throat. It was exactly the trick to sober up from my hangover of catastrophe.

Serena's office was surprisingly small. I imagined Solicitors having lavish offices, but this was anything but. It matched Serena. Clean, cheerful and functional.

Serena came and took me to her room, again very modest. Framed certificates and a picture of some faraway place hung on the white walls.

'Impressive but still not able to get me home,' I remarked nodding at the paper credentials.

'Oh those, all Solicitors have them and getting you home starts now.'

Serena took down my personal details and found out more about my relationship with Kel. I told her about the pregnancy and that, although not planned, the baby was very much wanted.

I explained about Andi and how I helped with taking care of Andi where and when I could. Kel dealt with disciplining Andi because I did not want to step on any toes. I wanted Andi to know that I respected who her parents were but that I still loved and cared about her too.

Children Services had been called and would be visiting Kel to assess the situation.

I sank into myself with clashing thoughts and questions. My chest was heavy. I rubbed my clasped hands one way and then the other but not breaking the hold for fear I would fall apart. I did not understand what all this meant and worried for Kel and Andi. I wanted to be punished for what I had done. Now they were being penalised for my wrongdoing.

I could not sit still any longer and rose out of my chair. I saw Serena instinctively push her chair back in alarm.

I paced one way and then the other in this cage. 'I'm not going to do anything,' I spat out.

'Well, maybe you could sit back down so we can continue talking.'

'Keep talking,' I retorted.

I hammered the same inches over and over whilst there was a humming from Serena. I wished I could reverse time. I gripped onto the fantasy of a happy ever after even better than before. The reality, though, was a much more bitter pill to swallow and what we would all now have to live.

The heady mix of anger and worry dissipated with every step I punched out. I returned to my chair. 'Do you follow?' Serena queried.

I nodded but something gave me away and Serena said, 'You weren't listening were you! Serena explained again the difference in charge. So, they had charged me with something higher than the most basic of assaults. The mark on Kel's face combined with our pregnancy, merited the higher type of assault.

I didn't care. I deserved everything coming to me. I felt my cheeks warm up as Serena spoke, especially when she mentioned the pregnancy. Kel had tried to protect me despite everything.

'At tomorrow's hearing, the court will need to hear your plea. I recommend that you plead not guilty,' Serena advised.

'But I am guilty.'

'Of assault, but not ABH, Matthew.' Serena stressed.

'I'm guilty. I have already admitted it and want to take my punishment.'

'Listen,' Serena pressed, 'Please listen to me. I am here to tell you what is in your best interests. I will try to persuade the Prosecutor to lower the charge. If he does, then yes, I agree you should plead guilty but if not and they stick with ABH, then you need to go not guilty.'

'I don't know,' I hesitated.

'They need to show you were guilty of causing actual bodily harm; some sort of injury.' Serena explained.

'But I did do that.'

'No, you slapped her, yes and that was completely wrong. But did you cause actual injury? I'm not sure and how will they prove it? There is no medical evidence, and it doesn't look like your girlfriend wants to help them.'

I did not want to shy away from what I had done with some legal trickery.

'You've got a solid case, or at least, as solid as it can be,' Serena insisted.

KELLY

After the police had left, I sorted Andi out with breakfast and getting her dressed. It was punctuated with Andi's inquisitiveness. 'Who was that mummy?'

'What did they say?'

'Where is Matt?'

'Is Matt coming home soon?'

Her questions merged with my own. I dodged the interrogation as best as I could, though I could not bat away the very same inquest in my own mind.

I eventually had Andi settled in self-entertainment of her dolls. I tidied around and packed up a few of Andi's things. She was going to her dad's for a few days.

I was five months pregnant, and we found out a few weeks back that we were having a baby boy. We had not planned on finding out and wanted it to be a surprise but when we were there, we couldn't help it. We wanted to know as soon as the nurse knew. We couldn't keep ourselves in suspense any longer.

Matt lit up, like a little boy feeling his way around wrapped presents, as we had the scan. His eyes sparkled with excitement, and he was open mouthed in wonderment. At the time, he was both gentle and protective all at once. Matt had been positive from the moment he found out we were pregnant.

I began to think that it had all been one big act. I struggled to make sense of it.

I spoke to Matt's mum, Elaine and she told me that Matt was in court early tomorrow. He had bail conditions to stay away from me.

'Kelly, I don't know how things have gotten so bad.'

'I don't know,' I squeezed out.

'He is a fool but believe me, I will be having words with him.'

'I'm sorry,' I gasped, 'I have to go' and rung off.

I had always been uneasy around Matt's parents.

Matt's dad seemed silently authoritative. Elaine was his shadow but abrasive when he was not around. I did not enjoy any time around them but here I was, now entirely reliant on them. They were the lifeline to my own family, and I forced down any discomfort. I was even more lost wearing this sudden life jacket of Matt's mum and dad.

Whilst all these confused thoughts throbbed, I had to keep up with the day-to-day practicalities. All the while taking care of Andi, my unborn and myself.

I sank little by little.

At around midday, there was yet another knock on the door. This time it was Social Services.

I gripped the edge of the door, the internal wall of my chest was hollow, as I tried to stay grounded. I stayed quiet and fought to hear what they said above the noise of the scared voice in my head.

A small Asian woman, with short black, bob style hair stood in front of me, with a white, middle aged chubby woman. They introduced themselves and showed me their ID cards around their necks. I only caught the Asian woman's name as she did most of the talking; Naeed Kaur.

I let them in, and we gathered in the lounge. They both sat on the two-seater sofa, whilst I sat in the armchair and again, I marshalled Andi back up to her bedroom.

Naeed explained that they had had a referral from the police about what had happened last night. As there was a child at home, and another on its way, they had to come out to investigate the children's welfare. I could not hold it in any longer and broke.

I was in floods of tears. I barely heard what the social worker said. I answered her questions in gulps, in between sobs I sniffed. Naeed took the basic details of the family. My name, date of birth, parents' names and addresses, siblings' details. Then we went onto Andi's details, her father's information, and his family background as far as I was able to tell them.

As I spoke, I regained composure. They had the background of what happened with Matt and as with the police I did not want to say much more.

'Kelly, can you tell me whether anything like this has happened before?' Naeed asked.

'No, never. We don't even argue let alone anything like this. I mean, sure, we disagree about stuff, but we are both such easy-going people. Nothing ever bothers us enough to argue over.'

'It's normal for couples to argue,' Naeed tried to tease.

'Yeah, I know it is,' I snapped. I managed to catch myself, 'but I'm not that kind of person and neither is Matt. I don't understand what happened last night.'

'You understand that it is likely that Matt will have to stay away from you until things get sorted.'

'Yeah, okay.'

The Social workers went up and spoke with Andi too. When they came back down, Naeed told me that Andi had told them about what she saw between Matt and I last night. She explained that although Andi seemed unaffected now, she would have been frightened. This was the issue and they needed to make sure that Andi was not exposed to this.

I understood but became worried about where all this was headed. 'Should I get a lawyer?' I asked tentatively.

'No, I'm not saying that. I'm letting you know we need to understand the situation and to work out what is needed for Andi's best interests.' Naeed explained, 'As I said, we are here to look at the children's safety because of the incident last night. We need to learn about your relationship a bit more and how that impacts on Andi and your unborn child.' I nodded and so she went on, 'We want to work with you to make sure that the children remain safe. Does all that make sense?'

'Yes,' I murmured.

'How does Andi get on with her dad and his family?'

'Yeah, good. She loves them and they dote on her, well the grandparents do.'

'We need to speak to them too.'

'Why?' I knew that they would pounce on this, and things would become very hostile between us. They would find a way to use this against me and make things nasty again.

'Well, dad has a right to know.'

I fell to pieces once again and I'm not sure what happened next, but the Social Workers somehow left me.

I curled up in the armchair in a ball of tears. Andi had crept down and was on top of me, hugging me and repeating, 'Don't cry mummy, don't cry.' I scooped her up into my lap and held her for a while, with quiet tears streaming down my face.

MATTHEW

We arrived at the courthouse at half past nine in the morning. Serena found us a consultation room, where she left me waiting, whilst she went to speak to the Prosecutor.

This consultation room was kinder than the one we had had to use at the police station. It was bare but the wooden flooring gave the room a unique sense of warmth. The archaic court building retained the severity of law and order.

Serena wanted to persuade the Prosecutor to lower the charge to common assault. I didn't care; I was pleading guilty to whatever assault charge they put to me. I had tried telling Serena, but she didn't hear me, or didn't want to hear me.

The corridors of justice seemed depressing. There were lots of defendants, their families and friends lined up. It was rundown and bleak. The modern interview room I was in was at odds with the rest of the aged building.

Serena returned to the room. She explained, 'The prosecutor wants time to look at the evidence. He will then consider whether to change the charge.'

'Right, okay.'

'So, like I said before. When they read out the charge, you confirm not guilty.'

'Uh-huh.'

'Matt, are you hearing me?'

'Yeah, not guilty.'

'Right, I know you want to take responsibility. You will but not yet. I'm sure they will lower the charge and then you can plead guilty.'

'Right.'

We had to wait a while before we got called on. I sat with all the scallies. There were chairs lined up against the walls like a doctor's surgery. The usher would come out periodically and call out the defendants one at a time by our surname. Serena went off to chat to another lawyer whilst we waited. They stood side by side and were in earnest conversation.

It was illuminating watching people around this outdated place of authority. The court ushers in their witches' black cloaks flew about like ravens. The defendants, some cocky in sharp contrast to the quiet first timers biting their nails. Then there were the sharp suited lawyers with their heads in papers or in animated conversation with other suits. The guy Serena was with towered above her. They seemed to be sharing a joke and Serena had a distinctive cackle of a laugh.

Finally, the usher called out my name and Serena and I headed in. Serena directed me to behind the front table and she was behind me at a longer table. The guy she had bantered with moments before, stood to the right of Serena. They both sat down, and the court clerk read out the charge to me and asked how I pleaded.

Without a blink, I pleaded guilty.

I heard a sharp intake of breath emanating from

Serena. She asked the Magistrates for time to take further instructions.

I insisted that this was my plea, and I was not changing it. The Magistrates did give Serena time and she dragged me out of the court room.

'What the hell was that?'

'I did tell you,' I muttered.

'This is crazy. You could have got away with common assault and now you have made things a hundred times worse. Why would you do that?' she barked out at me.

'I did hit Kel and I need to take my punishment. I need to move on from this as soon as I can, and I can't do that with this hanging over me.'

'But it will hang over you regardless, because you will have to wear the conviction everywhere you go. Let me do my job and we can get the charge reduced. The rank of conviction matters.'

'I am pleading guilty. Do your job with that,' I retorted.

'I don't understand you.'

'You don't need to understand me, but you do have to do what I tell you.'

'Listen, Matthew, I am here, doing the best I can for you.'

'I am pleading guilty.'

'Fine, if that's what you want,' Serena said.

'It is.'

'Fine.'

I repeated my earlier plea and this time there were no more outbursts.

The chair Magistrate said some things that I didn't follow. They said I'd have to come back a month later for sentence.

Serena told me that probation would be in touch to prepare a report for the court. We didn't spend long dissecting what had happened and parted ways.

I headed back to my parents' home. I had biked it to court this morning and jumped on it to head off.

The grey clouds gathered above as I pumped my way, but the rain held off until I got back. My one slice of good fortune for the day. When I arrived at my parents', my mum warmed some lunch for me, which I soon gobbled down.

I was having the small back room whilst all this was going on. I couldn't believe I was back here again. It was no longer home.

My brother, Tommy, had agreed to go over to Kel's to pick up some of my stuff. Tommy was the person I was closest to from my family. He was the only one of us kids that was still at home with mum and dad. He was older than me, I was the baby of the family, and he was the one above me. We had shared interests, football, PlayStation and the same taste in music. We didn't have any heart to hearts, we weren't those types of people.

I so missed Kelly and was desperate to talk to her but knew I couldn't chance it. I knew that she had wanted to protect me and refused to help the police but still, that didn't mean anything. She might not want me back after what I did and who could blame her. I needed to try at least but couldn't whilst I had these stupid bail conditions against me.

Tommy brought back several black bin bags full of my stuff. Mostly it was my clothes but also some other stuff like shoes, toiletries, music and suchlike. It seemed Kel wanted me out and had packed all my stuff up. Then Tommy pulled out a letter folded up from his jean back pocket.

My fingers and thumbs had swollen and were in the way of each other. The paper seemed glued together and I rubbed at it to unfold. In my haste, the letter fell out of my hands. I grabbed it, held it for a minute, took a deep breath and opened it.

Kelly said that she loved me. She was confused about what had happened and did not know she could ever trust me again. She thought that I had broken everything but that she wanted to know if we could work things out.

A few tears fell onto the letter as I read those words. I would do anything to make things work and reunite our family.

Chapter Three

NAEED

Lisa, my team manager, and I went over to the McDowell's home. I drove there in my trusted little Ford Focus. I parked my car outside their home, though they had a driveway with space for a few cars.

There was a black BMW car parked on the drive. John McDowell was Andi's Dad and he lived with his parents, Mark and Cynthia McDowell. All we knew was that Mark was a full time Engineer, Cynthia helped at the local school and John was a factory worker. They had Andi over every other weekend and shared school holidays. These titbits were not going to cut it and we had to arm ourselves with a stockpile more. I waited until Lisa pulled up in front of me.

I jumped out of the car and Lisa met me halfway. 'Are you okay?' I asked.

'Yeah, good. Are you all prepped for this one?'

'As much as I can be for these things.'

'First visits are always tricky. If there is nothing you need to run past me, shall we get started?'

'Sure,' I replied, and we both then headed towards the McDowell's house.

I rang the doorbell, and a tall, stocky woman answered the door. I had phoned ahead and let them know we were on our way. I had given them the brief outline of the situation with Kelly and Matthew. I wanted them to understand a little about the concern we had for Andi. I hoped it would lend to a good working relationship for us.

The woman before us smiled warmly and introduced herself as Cynthia. We reciprocated and with the welcomes out of the way, Cynthia showed us into the living room.

Cynthia had a soft voice and her words rolled easily. Her azure blue eyes glistened with infectious enthusiasm. A pleated brown skirt flowed over her round hips which she had paired with a cream-coloured twinset. Her blonde hair was swept up in a loose bun low to her neck.

'This is my son, John, you know, Andi's dad,' she muttered out.

John sat on the sofa, and I joined him there. He wore a white creased shirt with black jeans. He kept flicking his floppy brown hair out of his eye line and tapped his fingers against each other on his lap. He shifted uncomfortably as I sat down next to him. It was natural for parents to feel nervous when they met us, it was the dynamics of a social work relationship.

Lisa placed herself in one of the armchairs to one side. Mark McDowell was still in work.

Their home was a large one with ample room for Andi to run around in. A large flat screen television hung above a roaring stove fireplace. The sofas snug around the television centrepiece of the room. The other side of the room seemed to be set up as a play area for Andi. They had a beautiful bay window overlooking the common at the front of the room.

It was clear to see that this was a world away from Kelly and Matthew's home. How did John and Kelly even get together in the first place? That was what I was here to start finding out.

We were completely at ease and settled in for preliminary enquiries. I smelt the cosiness of baking. Cynthia offered us some of the carrot cake she had made together with tea. Another marked contrast with the visit to Kelly's but of course, Kelly, hadn't had any pre-warning of our visit. We readily took up the cake.

Within minutes, we had a cup of tea in one hand and cake on dessert plates balancing on our legs. The cake was deliciously moist and just the right side of sweetness. I rested my tea down and cake on the tea table, grabbed my notepad and pen ready.

They provided their personal details for the DBS checks, basically criminal history checks. I banked quite the library of genealogy for Andi's family. I discovered their family backgrounds, siblings, nieces, nephews, and suchlike. John had two sisters and only one of them was partnered up with two boys aged seven and five.

As a family, they seemed picture perfect, but I well knew that you had to dig deeper to get behind the surface. They told me that they had never had any Social Services involvement. They also confirmed that they had no criminal histories.

'So, what is your relationship with Andi like?'

'It's great, she is my mini-me,' John replied. He spoke with a crisp, deep voice but there was an undercurrent there that I couldn't quite put my finger on.

'That is so true. She follows him around everywhere when she is over here and some of her mannerisms are exactly like John's.' Cynthia chimed in. I noticed her odd habit of rubbing down her skirt with her left hand over and over. There was an immovable stain, invisible to the rest of us but seemed very present in Cynthia's eyes.

'She is amazing and means everything to me,' John added.

'That's fab! And have you always been involved with her or was it a bit of a battle?' I queried.

John fidgeted by the side of me and kept his eyes lowered as he spoke, 'We've always had her as much as possible. You know, we all work full-time so weekends have always been the best.'

'So, you have a good relationship with Kelly too?'

'Well, it's okay. I mean we don't chit chat or anything, but I don't hate her either. My parents help with handover, though, because it's awkward. You know because she has Matt and all.' John trailed off.

I asked more questions about what they knew about Matthew. Cynthia took over this part of the conversation. She knew more about Kelly and Matthew. She said Matthew was reserved, and that Kelly seemed meeker around him. I got the sense that Cynthia found it a strained relationship but that she liked Kelly.

We arranged a further meeting in a couple of days' time, as I wanted to see Andi with them and headed off. We went back to the office, and it was about four in the afternoon when we arrived back there.

Lisa and I debriefed over the visits and agreed that Kelly needed time to work out where her priorities lay. We both liked the McDowells. I hoped that the further enquiries would prove us right on first impressions. They presented well and seemed committed to Andi.

When I was back at the office, I wanted to write up my notes from today and submit the DBS checks on everyone.

It always buzzed in the office. Social workers on phones, typing, copying, printing. Our admin people kept us all in order with barked instructions. It was a constant hive of activity. Over time, I had developed a tuning out skill, which let me focus on the notes scribing without disruption. In fact, when it was silent it was impossible to get any work done. This occurrence was few and far between.

Even though it is open plan, all the noise blended into the background. There were windows all on one of side of the office, letting the natural light in. The glare of the office light on the computers was sometimes sharp. By the time I finished what I needed to it was six in the evening. I should have finished an hour earlier but that was a rarity in this job.

By the time I reached home, my little girl was already fast asleep. My mum lived with me and took care of Alya, whilst I was at work. I don't know how I would have done it all without her.

Alya loved her nani-jan and Alya was my mum's princess. I'd often catch my mum standing in Alya's doorway, late at night, watching my sleeping beauty. It gave my heart such comfort knowing that my precious Alya was as much a jewel for my mum as she was for me. It was such a sweet and loving bond, something I missed with my own nani-jan.

My mum immediately fussed over me and warmed some food up for me. 'Sit, sit. It will be ready in no time. What do you want to drink, beta?'

'Mum, I'm fine. I can get it.'

'Don't be silly. I am here and I am your mum.'

'Yes, you are always taking care of me, mamma but who takes care of you. This is your time to relax.'

'I can only relax when I know you are okay.'

'Oh, mamma! I do love you.'

I ran upstairs and snuck a peek at my beautiful girl. She had her thick black hair plaited away. I breathed in the fresh clean soap. Alya slept on her front, and I could see her milk chocolate cheek. She was my perfect.

KELLY

It was already the end of January and things were still not much clearer or better.

It had snowed heavily. My baby bump and I waddled around in several layers and flat heeled boots to stamp through the snow. Even with my wardrobe full of clothes covering me, scarf, and gloves, I still had icicles on the ends of my hands and feet.

Everything was gloomy and depressing all around. It was such a lonely and hopeless start to the year, in the end. Just about everything had changed in that one night.

Before that fateful night, I had looked forward to having our little baby and firming up our family. The weight of my pregnancy wearing all these winter clothes were heavy on my neck and shoulders. The dull ache accompanied me everywhere. My eyes thirsty for sleep and my mind fogged over.

I didn't know what would happen with Matt and the court case. Would he end up in prison? Would he be around for our baby's birth? Would he be around at all, or would I have two children from two different fathers? Would I have to raise another child by myself?

Andi had begun back at school and was doing so well. After her first day, she couldn't stop gabbling. 'Mummy, Miss Graham said I had grown so tall that soon I would catch her up,' she glowed.

'I'll bet you will.'

'Mummy, she said I looked different but I'm the same aren't I, mummy?'

'You are always my baby girl.'

'But mummy, really what do you think?'

'You, my beautiful girl are growing way too fast. So slow down, okay?'

'No mummy, I want to be big, like you.'

Andi had been my hero around the house. She helped wherever she could. She put her toys away, got herself dressed and brushed her teeth without me watching over her or even asking her.

When I caught her doing these things, a swelling in my chest arose to match my baby bump. It lightened me a little and I was a little more agile than before. She was compliant at school and her teachers adored her. She had a good group of friends and rarely got into any kind of mischief.

Naeed visited us again a couple more times. I didn't like her at all; she judged me all the time and not in a positive way.

My hands were clammy before she came. They remained sweaty whilst she was there. They were sticky for some time after she left. My body tensed, and the pit of my stomach seemed endless. The nausea sat in my throat and high in my chest. My words edged out of me, but I still seemed to get everything wrong.

I worried that she had already made up her mind about me and that she saw me as weak. I was quiet but that did not make me weak.

She looked down on our home and on me. It had been a real struggle this past month. I just about managed to take care of the essentials for Andi and felt exhausted all the time. I still suffered with sickness with the little one and hadn't had the energy for anything.

Of course, the McDowells thrived off my predicament. I could see in the way that Cynthia looked at me that she was full of pity but also smugness. She had the nerve to ask me to let them take care of Andi for a while. She pretended it was to give me time to focus on the pregnancy and myself. 'It could be for a few weeks so that you can enjoy some of the pregnancy in peace,' Cynthia suggested.

'It's completely fine.'

'I mean, it might even give you time with that social worker,' she prodded.

'It's all good. I have it under control,' I forced out.

It took all my strength to keep locked away the simmering rage behind my gritted teeth.

'Well, the offer is there. You know we would take good care of her until you are ready to have her back.'

I was never going to be ready for Andi to go. That was never an option. 'I managed before and I will manage now,' I finally blurted out.

I missed Matt and needed to see him. I knew he was back in court today and waited to hear about the outcome. I had spoken to his mum a couple more times and she let me know how he was doing. I knew Matt, though, it was hard to read him.

My phone rang and 'Matt' flashed up on the screen. My hands were steady even if my heart fluttered like crazy. I trembled all over, my body engaged in involuntary gymnastics. 'Oh my God, Matt? How are you?' I managed to squeeze out.

'I've missed you, Kel...I'm so sorry....Can we meet?'

Matt's voice came through in a whisper. He sounded weary. I worried but felt the jitteriness of old when we first dated. My heart had picked up a pace as I squeaked out, 'I've missed you. Where?'

'I don't care, I need to see you and let you know how sorry I am. I'm so, so sorry.'

Matt was resolute but was also pained.

'It's okay, Matt. We can work it all out. Let's meet at the Village Café.'

'I'll be there in about an hour, is that okay?'

'Can't wait,' I replied.

I made my way straight there. It was a little café in the village, where we lived. I ordered peppermint tea and sat in one of the corner tables tucked away, with my hands curled around the cup.

I didn't notice when Matt walked in until he had

me in his arms in a warm bear hug. Oh, how I had missed his strong arms. I loved this man; I still loved this man, and I would always love this man.

Matt's words tumbled over themselves in a rush and repeated again and again how sorry he was. I held his hands across the table and stroked them to comfort him. 'I know I need to get help, Kel, and I'm going to get it. I am going to get it.'

'I know you will, and I know this won't ever happen again.'

'I promise. I won't come back until I know I have dealt with this.'

'What happened at court?'

'I've got a probation order and some community service. It's not enough.'

'Well, I'm glad that you have been sent back to me. I need you. I can't do this on my own.'

'You won't ever be on your own. I need to get myself sorted and hopefully this probation thing will do that for me.'

I got Matt up to speed with the Social Services' involvement in relation to Andi and that broke Matt. His eyes welled up with tears, but he quickly regained composure. He beat himself up about what he saw was the trouble that he had caused for me, for Andi, for the unborn, for Matt, for us all. He was inconsolably withdrawn.

He stood up and mumbled, 'You're better off without me. I'm so sorry.' With that, Matt walked out.

NAEED

Everything ran on autopilot, my slippers in perfect position by the side of my bed for my feet to slip into. My toothbrush with paste sat proudly on the basin ready to work its magic on my teeth.

Even in the height of winter, I slept in my glorious birthday suit so I could jump straight in the shower. Alya was up a little earlier today. I cuddled her up in my arms and smothered her with kisses.

I didn't get enough time with my little beauty and over compensated when we were together. I finished off my make up in between play with her.

We headed downstairs and I arranged some breakfast for Alya. I never managed breakfast myself and snatched a mug of hot, wake me up, coffee. That's all I needed.

I fed Alya and chattered away with her in two-year-old speak.

To coin the phrase John had used, Alya was my 'mini me'. We played stupid faces, stupid noises and stupid actions, everything stupid. All to hear that innocent, beautiful baby girl's laugh.

Oh, how I loved that sound...round and clucky. I loved how her dark chocolate eyes twinkled and scrunched up round the corners. Alya's baby giggle enchanted my ears and lifted the veil from my face. It's what I lived for.

My mum joined us at about ten minutes before I had to take off. We had a quick catch up, 'How are you, beta?'

'Refreshed and raring to go.'

'Always, go, go, go with you. You should slow down, beta.' Concern rung in her voice.

'Just like my mamma, hey?' I joked.

Before we knew it, it was kisses all round and I was out the door, in my car, headed to the office. The traffic washed away the glow from the love that ran through my mum, me and my daughter and back again.

Once at the office, I checked through my emails. The DBS checks had all come in now on the McDowell child.

I had had a couple more visits with both sides of the family. The perfect picture of plain sailing times that Cynthia and John had made out to us blurred. They had had to admit that they had not been involved with Andi at all in the early years and were very absent. It was Kelly's maintenance referral that then prompted John having contact with Andi.

Still, since then, he had formed a deep and fast bond with her.

I had also had the opportunity of meeting with Mark. He came across somewhat brusque but very much to the point. He was honest but at times that lended to challenge. I could see that he too loved Andi and enjoyed spending time with her. His whole demeanour changed when talking about Andi. He softened with pride.

The DBS checks for all the McDowells came back clear. Kelly's too but Matthew Barnett, he was another story. I had still not had the chance to meet with him. His DBS check had the recent assault conviction.

The enhanced check, which I had requested for

them all, showed up a drunk and disorderly offence. This Matthew had an issue with his behaviour. I had come across so many people like him.

Matthew had received a probation order and community service for the assault. This was as expected. The test was how he got on with that, especially the probation work. That involved understanding the impact of domestic abuse and perpetrator work. I needed to meet with him myself to assess matters fully.

Andi and the unborn child were my priority, and I would only place them somewhere that I knew they would be safe. At the moment, this Barnett guy was not safe, and no child was safe in his care.

I went to see Andi at Kelly's as planned. Kelly seemed cheerful, albeit worn down. The luggage under her eyes seemed ready for a holiday and her skin was pasty like thin dough.

I let Kelly know about the DBS checks and she was aware of Matthew's drunk and disorderly incident. She brushed it aside as if it wasn't relevant. It rang alarm bells for me. It was typical of someone willing to accept abusive behaviour.

Andi was reading a book when I went up to see her in her bedroom. She was a gorgeous little girl with blonde hair like her dad and curious blue eyes like both her parents. Her hair fell to below her shoulders. She was so engrossed in her book that she didn't even notice me entering her room until I called out her name.

'Hi Andi, how are you?'

'I'm okay. I'm reading about the Big Friendly

Giant. I've only just started but I love it already.'

'That sounds good, Andi and I will let you carry on reading but need to talk to you for a little bit, if that's okay?' I approached.

'Yeah, okay.'

I checked how Andi was doing and by all accounts, she was happy enough, had got back into school and normality.

I asked her about Matthew. She knew him as Matty and although she said she liked him, I sensed something else behind it. She seemed worried about Matty and protective of her mum. She let slip that mummy had met Matty the other day and that mummy seemed sad about it. She looked me straight in the eye and her brow furrowed. I put my arm around her and patted her shoulder in comfort.

I reassured Andi that she could always talk to me about anything that was on her mind. I let her know that I only cared about her and her happiness. I could see that Andi loved her mum very much. She had taken more responsibility for her mum than she should have for her age. She had been exposed to far too much.

I spoke to Kelly before I left and asked her about seeing Matthew. She admitted that she had met up with him on the day of his sentencing away from the home and away from Andi.

Andi had found out about the meeting because Andi had asked when they would see Matty again. Kelly had let her know then that she had met him but that it would take some time to work things out.

'Kelly, I need to be honest with you and let you

know that it would be a real concern for us if Matthew returned to live here.' I explained.

'But why? I mean if he works through what happened. He could show everyone that it won't ever happen again, why could we not be a family like we planned?'

'We are a long way off being certain that what happened before New Year's will not happen again. We can't put Andi or the unborn at risk like that. Does that make sense?'

'Yeah, I guess but what does that mean?'

'You have to choose between your children and your relationship.'

'You mean if Matt and I continue our relationship, I lose the kids. I can't have that. I won't let that happen. Should I get legal advice?' Kelly says.

'Listen, I am only saying that it will not work for you and Matthew to live together when he has a lot to work through. We need to see that you are putting Andi and your unborn child first.'

'Right.' Kelly replied.

I was not convinced that she got it or meant it.

KELLY

As soon as Naeed left, I called Matt and told him what she had said.

I told him that I didn't care what she said or even what he had said, I wanted our family the way we had planned it. I knew that what had happened that night was a one-off; it was not the Matt I knew and loved. Of course, we needed to work through that, but it was worth it.

I loved him, I loved our baby and I loved Andi.

I could hear Matt hold back the tears.

I was already in tears and talked through it. That seemed to make Matt stronger. 'I know that this is all my fault, and I am going to fix it, Kel. I'm going to do what I need to, to prove to you and to everyone that we can do this.'

'I don't know, Matt' I wept. 'I believe in you and trust you but, that Naeed seems to have it in for us. She's a complete cow.'

'We will show her and everyone, babe.'

'I hope so, Matt but I don't think that that Naeed is going to let us.'

'It's up to me and I will sort this.' Matt promised and I so wanted to believe him, but I sensed that he didn't get it at all.

I got dinner ready and called Andi down. She chatted away about the Big Friendly Giant and all that she had read so far. She loved reading and I often struggled to get her head out of some book or another. Other times, it helped. I could leave her lost in the world of her books whilst I got on with cooking, housework or some other chore.

Today, I wanted to spend a bit of time with Andi. As usual, Andi couldn't wait to get back to her book, so ate and gobbled up her food in a hurry. I slowed her down as best as I could. 'Andi, how has today been?'

'Yeah, okay mummy,' she replied.

'Go easy with the food, it's not going to run away

from you, sweetie,' I joked.

'Mummy, you're funny,' she giggled back.

'You're funny, baby girl. How was it chatting to Naeed?'

'Yeah, it's alright but I wanted to get on with reading my book.'

'It is okay not to talk to her if you don't want to, sweetheart.' I said.

'Aaaaw, it's alright. She's nice but sometimes I want to get on with what I'm doing. I like her.'

'That's good sweetie.'

Matt and I met up two or three times a week rebuilding our relationship. Our love had not changed but trust had been broken. I was unsure of myself around him in the first few weeks, unsure of him, I guess. The memory of that night still very raw. We usually met away from our homes and somewhere public.

I was careful and when we spoke about difficult issues, my right leg twitched. I didn't seem able to control it and had to tap my leg shut to close it off. I didn't want to think about it, but it didn't leave me.

After Matt's first session of Domestic Violence Perpetrators Programme, he was thoughtful. I worried about what he was thinking. 'I'm so sorry... not just for hitting you but the effect that that has had on us. I know that it has changed us forever, but I will find a way that it will change us for the better.'

'I know, Matt. You are already so different; I mean you were never good with words and telling me how you felt. Now I can't shut you up,' I joked to lighten the mood but remained apprehensive.

'I'm serious.'

'I know and I love you all the more for it,' I said.

'We have never talked about what happened that night. Maybe, we should?'

'We both know what happened. I don't know what good it will do raking over it all now.'

'It's important to be honest with each other.'

'And I am honest with you.'

'You have never told me how you felt or anything.'

'Please stop,' I said. My eyes brimmed over.

Matt reached over to my hand, I flinched and pulled away.

We apologised and the sink taps that were my eyes opened, and the tears flowed. 'I'm sorry, I need to go,' and I tore away. I saw the hurt flicker through Matt's eyes, but he blinked them back and I made good my escape.

I felt guilty for sending such mixed messages to Matt but couldn't help it. My heart desperately wanted things to be like they used to but somewhere deep within, I was unable to let go.

Naeed came back to see me a month or so later. My stomach was in knots and pulled in different directions. It was like this each time I knew Naeed was visiting. It was getting closer to the due date, only a few more weeks to go.

I knew she had met Matt by this time and given him a hard time. I wished she would give us a chance and got to know us, rather than judging us all the time.

It was increasingly difficult to keep meeting Naeed and talking to her about my life, my family, my world. I wanted to be able to live peacefully and enjoy these last few weeks of my pregnancy. These past few months had been so difficult that I so wanted some calm at this stage.

Naeed told me that Matt had had social services' involvement with his family. It had come up in checks on their systems and she had already spoken to Matt about it. Matt didn't know much of the details of why or how they had been involved but he knew he had spent time with an aunt of his.

Matt had not spoken to me about it before it came up with Naeed, which was what prompted him talking to me about it. He was young and couldn't remember the details but knew that his aunt had a lot to do with his upbringing. According to Social Services, he had spent some time in care. He then went and lived with his aunt. He stayed with his aunt until he was old enough to seek out his parents, which he did as soon as he hit the age of eighteen.

'The thing is, Kelly, we need to spend more time assessing the situation with Matthew much more. He is still only at the start of his domestic violence programme and probation.' Naeed started.

'Okay.'

'As you know, we do not want him to be around Andi until he has completed that work.'

'Yeah, and we are sticking to that.'

'So, the thing is that we also want to see how you would cope with baby and need both of you to be somewhere safe.'

I was confused where all this was going. My mind

was in overdrive and not able to focus on anything.

The whole family were being split off in different directions. This was not what family life was meant to look like. I had not done anything wrong and yet faced punishment with the loss of my family, my home, my world. I didn't understand what was happening.

'No. That's not happening.' I was in a blur of tears but still determined.

'I'm afraid, if you don't agree, we will go to court and get a Care Order to move Andi and place the newborn where we want, anyway. It'll be much better and easier if you agree,' Naeed replied. She was more forceful now.

Her words reverberated through me and there was nothing else I could hear.

Chapter Four

NAEED

I was at my office desk with the computer screen staring soullessly back at me. I checked all the family members details I had so far for the McDowell/Barnett(unborn) child. In particular, I searched our own systems. I typed each of their names through and waited a few seconds for the results to flash up at me. As they had all told me, there had been no prior Social Services' involvement before. This was somewhat surprising, given what I had learnt so far. They all seemed to have been swimming under the sea and had only now come to our attention.

The screen blinked at me the pattern of 'None,' for each name. I inputted Matthew Barnett's name and the pattern broke away; he was known to us. My stomach flipped a little as I edged a little closer to the computer. There was not much that the system could tell me.

I scribbled some notes to prompt me later. It affirmed for me what I had worried about from the start. Matthew was an issue. I had a sense about him.

We had arranged to meet at our office and Matthew arrived promptly. I'm not sure what I expected but he didn't quite match it. He was unassuming and thoughtful. I had anticipated a thuggish man; muscle bound with tattoos, and he was not that way at all. There was a lot to be said about preconceptions. Paper didn't match the multi dimension of people.

After exchanging pleasantries, I explained our concerns for Andi and the unborn child. I moved onto trying to understand this man, his relationship with Kelly and his part in that family unit. Matthew had two brothers and two sisters. Only his one brother was still at home with his parents. The other siblings either married or living with partners and with children themselves. Matthew was the last but one in line.

'Can you tell me what happened the night of the incident when you hit Kelly?' I asked.

'I'm not sure what I can tell you about that that you don't already know. We argued and I lost it. I lashed out.'

'But what was the trigger?' I probed.

'I don't know,' Matthew replied. His face squished into itself as he struggled, trying to reflect. His eyes narrowed in concentration.

'Has anything like that happened before?'

'No, I have never hit anyone before,' Matthew was resolute.

'You were cautioned before for drunk and disorderly behaviour,' I challenged.

'I never hit anyone before.' Matthew was more stoic now, his face and composure hardened, with an underlying calm.

Matthew's account of his relationship with Kelly accorded with what Kelly had told me. It was clear that Matthew loved Kelly. Theirs was a very traditional relationship. Matthew saw his role as the provider and Kelly's the home-maker. This was how they both saw their primary obligations in the home.

I went onto explore his childhood and what he was able to tell me about it. He grappled with this and shut off. Matthew recalled that he had stayed with an aunt for a large part of his childhood. He put his forehead to the tips of his two fingers and then stretched out his hand across his head. He rubbed one side of his forehead and then brought his hands together in a tightened clasp. I pushed the subject a little further.

I asked, 'Matthew, do you remember any Social Services' involvement?'

I dropped my pen onto the notepad, as Matt squawked 'What? What are you on about?' Matthew's reaction told me that he had very little memory of what had gone on in his childhood. He would not be able to fill any gaps for me and I would have to dig round some more elsewhere.

'What do you mean?' Matthew was agitated. This had come completely out of the blue for him. I was unsure on how best to manage the situation.

'So, as you will understand, I have been looking at everyone's histories with both the police and our own records.'

Matthew interrupted. 'Yeah, well, I know I have that caution but there is nothing with Social Services. Why are you making things up? I know I've done wrong, and you have a job to do, but why are you causing us grief for no reason?' Matthew was frantic.

'Please, let me try and explain. I'm not lying and trying to let you know what I have found through our records. It's not something that is an issue by itself, but it is something we need to investigate more,' I reassured.

'But I don't understand. Your records must have got mixed up with some other family.'

'Let me tell you what I have found. Our records show that we were involved with your family when you were all younger. It looks like you were all placed into care for a time. You ended up with your aunt.' I went onto explain that we needed to find out more about what went on to piece things together. I suggested he speak to his own family. It was unlikely that there had been any mistakes. I reminded him that he had also spoken about having lived with his aunt.

Matthew was completely dejected. He was quiet to start with but then lost his sense of speech. He withdrew into himself even more than when he first came in. There were always barriers with parents but usually you can work at bringing them down. Here the opposite had happened. What I had shared had aggravated those guards. I had assumed he knew. Whilst there would be a natural tension, I believed he had a grasp of his own background. As it turned out, Matt's history unravelled right here before me.

It was difficult to watch a man that had started nervous but as sure of himself as he could be, and now empty. His whole body shape mutated in front of me and the air around him seemed suffocating. He shrunk into himself. He did not understand or remember what had gone on in his own childhood.

There was no point keeping Matt any longer because I was not going to get anything from him now. I was not sure how he would come back from this, but my priority had to be to those two children.

MATTHEW

'Kel, I don't know what she was on about, but she said I was in care, all of us were – Sarah, Paul, and Tommy. I don't get it.'

'It's okay, Matt. You need to speak to your family and find out what happened,' Kelly said. 'It's not your fault. You didn't do anything wrong.'

'I'spose. I'm in shock. It's like I don't know who I am anymore.'

'You are still the same person, but you need to figure out what went on back then.'

'Yeah, but I thought my parents needed help and put me with my aunt. Now it sounds like something more serious went on with Social Services.'

'Matt, you are you and nothing changes that.'

'They have been lying to me, Kel. Why? What happened?'

I couldn't talk much more after that. My head felt like it had gone ten rounds with the heavyweight boxing champion. So many questions flew around that I was dizzy with it all. I steadied myself the only way I knew how, I took out my phone, scrolled to the candy sugar icon and clicked away.

I cycled home and mum was watching the television. Dad was still at work, and I assumed Tommy was upstairs in his room. I went into the living room and sat in the armchair.

The red flower embossed wallpaper hung depressingly. It matched the furry tapestry underfoot. The room breathed out heavy smoke, which competed against the boom of the television. 'Mum, I need to ask you something.'

'Course, son, what is it?' My mum looked over towards me, whilst reducing the volume of the television.

'Were we put into care?' There was no easy way of asking. I could have worked my way up to it, but the words blurted out before I had time to think.

Mum turned pale and quiet. Her neck tensed and I braced myself for whatever was to come. I needed to know, and I needed to know now. My mum took what seemed an excruciating long pause but might have only been a few seconds. She turned the television off. 'Matt, it's difficult to explain. Why has this come up... I mean how...,' Mum was dazed.

'You know social services are involved with Kel and Andi. They have told me. Mum, I need to know the truth.' I pleaded.

'A long time ago, dad had got himself into some trouble. It wasn't true but because of that, they took all you kids away.' Mum finally explained, her eyes glistened, her lips quivered and then she welled up with tears.

'What kind of trouble?'

My mum wiped at her eyes, turned her head away from me as she mumbled, 'Matt, I don't want to talk any more about this. None of it matters anymore.'

'It matters to me.'

'I'm sorry,' Mum cried and fled from the room.

I was even more confused now than I was before. There was a tiny part of me that had hoped my mum would explain it all away. I longed for the social worker to have got it wrong somehow or that it was nothing serious. Probably, mum and dad needed some help and that's how Social Services got involved.

That small internal prayer had been completely swept aside. I went up to see Tommo and told him what I had found out. He didn't remember anything, though he knew he had stayed with another family member. I wasn't sure what to do with what I now knew. I also didn't understand what it meant for me, Kel or our family.

After Kel called me about the Social Worker's visit, I immediately arranged for us to go and see Serena. 'Well, I wasn't expecting to see you again so soon, Matthew. What trouble have you got yourself into now?' Serena said. She smiled at Kel and me.

'Me neither.' Serena took us into her office, and we sat opposite her at her desk.

Serena took Kel's personal details. Kel then explained what had been going on with Social Services. She knew more about it than I did. Serena advised that Social Services could force the issue. They could begin proceedings immediately if we didn't do what they asked.

'I don't think that they will be able to take Andi or your unborn child into care.' Serena advised, 'They won't be able to show why Kelly couldn't look after both children. Kelly has been taking care of Andi all these years without any issue and the main issue is Matthew.' She expanded on this. If I stayed away until I addressed my issues, there was no reason why the children could not remain with mum.

Kel, though, could only see the risks, which Serena also had to explain. 'On a worst-case scenario, if social services got their orders, they would have the right to place the children as they think fit. For Andi, this would mean with her dad and his parents but for your unborn baby, it might end up being foster care.' Serena said, 'But as I said, I do not think that this is likely based on what you have both told me.'

This was not a risk that Kel was willing to take. As we talked it through, she conceded that we would do as Social Services wanted us to. We did not want to take any chances and have the children placed in foster care at all. We would do anything to avoid that.

That weekend, I went over to see Sarah to try and find out what she knew. Sarah did not get on with dad at all but would still join in on family get togethers for mum's sake. Paul was the same, though not to the same extent. We barely saw Sarah at the house other than when we all got together, whereas at least Paul would pop by.

I was closest to Tommy, but I always looked up to Sarah and had a lot of time and respect for her. I guess as my oldest sister, she always looked out for the rest of us. She took care of us in ways that our own parents didn't.

Sarah greeted me with a big bear hug. It felt so good to have that comfort. With everything that had happened, I had soldiered on. No one had reached out to me like Sarah did in that one move. I needed that.

Sarah's husband and kids were out. We sat in the

kitchen and Sarah made us tea. It was safe here. The wooden flooring gave a modern twist to the cosy kitchen, where the heart of the house was. The newly fitted cupboards set the rustic tiles off.

We sat at the one end of the long dining table and chatted over our hot mugs. 'The thing is, Matt, mum never wanted us to tell you young kids and we had to keep it to ourselves. I'm sorry,' Sarah started.

'I need to know, Sarah. I feel so lost, and I don't know anything any more.'

'I know.'

It all tumbled out. I did not know what to say or do. Sarah was in tears and could not get her words out. She and Paul went into foster care. They moved from one family to another but luckily were able to stay with that second family. I went to my mum's sister and Tommy went to her parents. This was hard to take. I tried to comfort Sarah as best as I could.

Dad had sexually abused them, and mum did not protect them from it.

NAEED

We were in a meeting with our legal department. Our lawyer, Sam, talked us through what we needed to get an interim care order. She had a husky voice but somehow her words carried authority.

Sam and I had worked together many a time, she was a straight shooter. We had had a few clashes and I would have preferred someone else from the team, but we never had a choice in it. This blond barbie was a shark underneath that deceptive veneer. The problem was that I was often at the brunt of it. It would be a tall order, but she was confident and right now, I had to work with her.

'I've got the template that you have sent me on that other case, Sam, so I'll work on that and get it to you.'

'Great, yeah, depending on when I get it, I'll check it through as soon as I can and get it back to you with any notes.'

'Cool and in the meantime, I will work on the family to see if we can sort something by agreement,' I replied.

I headed home after a long day, which had started with another child removed from her parents. That child had suffered all his life and was only five years of age, malnourished, mute, and beaten. It was heart breaking but he was finally safe.

I arrived home and sat in my car, tears streaming down my face, thick and fast. I did not want my mum or daughter to see me this way, though I was sure Alya was already tucked up in bed.

Both Kelly and Matthew wanted us to assess them together as well as apart. It made sense in ways but was not very effective. Separate assessments required an understanding of their commitment to parent separately. If they remained in a relationship, that undermined the reality of separate parenting. It also showed that neither could prove prioritising the children ahead of themselves. In that sense, they were bound to fail the separate assessments before even embarking on them.

The assessment was still in its infancy, and I had a way to go with this family. Conversely, the assessment of the McDowells was fantastic. I knew Andi would be both safe and happy there. She reminded me so much of, well it didn't matter. She deserved that happy, innocent, and healthy childhood that every child deserved.

I was sure that it would be difficult for Andi to leave her mum. I was also sure that she would settle in with her dad and grandparents in time. The short-term pain was worth the long-term gain. It would take a bit of time to see if the move could be negotiated and agreed between all the relevant parties. At least we had a back-up plan if we didn't get it done.

I had been to the McDowells and let them know the outcome of their assessment. I explained what aspects we had looked at and where the family were positive. I flagged up our concerns, lack of commitment in the early years, ongoing relationship with mum and the emotional burden for Andi. I wanted them to understand there would be a lot of pressures to cope with.

'We can manage anything,' John enthused.

'It's important that you go into this open eyed, John, it will not be as easy as you might think,' I cautioned.

'Yeah, yeah, I get that,' John said. His mother interjected, 'John, there will be tough times ahead. Naeed wants to know that we can cope and go to her as and when we need to.'

'Exactly that,' I said.

John might have been naïve, but he was fortunate to have the support of his mum, who I had a lot of trust in. We talked some more about Andi staying with them permanently, 'So, she will really live with us?' John asked.

'If you take good care of her, love and protect her, then yes. She will live with you guys.'

'I can't believe it. It's going to be perfect.' John enthused.

'She will not want for anything. We will do whatever it takes. Thank you, thank you. Thank you so much,' Cynthia echoed with pure delight in her voice.

Mark was at work, as usual, though he had participated fully in the assessment. He was not John's dad but his stepdad and so, Andi's step granddad. Andi looked up to Mark and he cared about her too. It was Mark's house that she would be staying in, and he had worked hard all his life. Mark enjoyed the simplicity of his life, and this was a major undertaking, but he loved Cynthia.

'I'm going to speak to Kelly in a few days and work out the best way of moving Andi.' I explained.

'What if Kelly refuses?' Cynthia asked.

'Well, we are starting Care proceedings anyway and so we will have to wait until it's in court. We will get an interim care Order. That would let us share parental responsibility for Andi with Kelly. Our parental responsibility would trump Kelly's. It would mean that we could move Andi here.'

'Okay, so it might take a bit of time to get it sorted if Kelly doesn't agree.' John interposed.

'Yes, and I would recommend that you get Solicitors to help you in the Care proceedings. Though we are on your side, you are entitled to legal representation, and it'll be free, so you should look into that.' I reassured.

Now here I was, at Kelly's home to talk about moving her daughter. I knew that this would be a difficult conversation. I had some empathy for Kelly, because she had raised Andi single-handedly all this time as I was with my own daughter.

My priority though was Andi. We had to meet her needs right now and ensure that she was safe. There was still so much we needed to scrutinize with Kelly and Matthew, that we couldn't leave things as they were.

Matthew was entitled to return to live with Kelly. Whilst there had been no mention of that happening, we needed to keep Andi away from that volatility. 'Kelly, I wanted to talk to you today about the McDowell's assessment.'

'Oh right. Okay.'

'It is positive, and you know that they dote on Andi and that Andi loves them too.'

'Of course,' Kelly replied. 'How's my assessment?'

'Well, that is still ongoing. We still have a fair bit to get through with Matthew and his ongoing work through Probation.'

'Right.'

'The thing is, we need to make arrangements for Andi so that you can focus on the pregnancy and the newborn.'

'Okay?'

'So, we think now would be a good time for Andi to move to her dad's,' I explained.

'Noooooooo!' Kelly screamed in anguish. 'This can't be happening.'

Kelly was in real distress now and I became concerned for the unborn baby. I did my best to calm the situation but, in the end, called for Matthew to come over.

Matthew raced into the house and immediately held Kelly.

I tried to tell Matthew what had been going on, but he was not having any of it. He ignored me and took Kelly upstairs, presumably to her bedroom. I waited downstairs and a short while later, Matthew returned.

'I think its best you leave now,' he said.

'I understand that this is difficult, but I do need to know what Kelly wants to do with Andi.'

'As I said, it's best for you to leave.' Matthew repeated.

'Fine, I'll go but it won't be left like this. We all need to think about what is best for these children as painful as that might be. We must do right by the children.' I said.

This would wait another day or so. Eventually we would need to take Andi, whether with Kelly's agreement or court order.

MATTHEW

I struggled with my father's history and what had happened to Sarah and the others. Tommy and I were saved from it all because we were taken away before anything happened.

Sarah and Paul both ended up in foster care, which I did not remember or realise. I had no idea what that was like for them. It did kind of make sense, why there had always been such a disconnect between those two and Tommy and me.

I could not look at my dad any more and it was difficult even with mum. I avoided them both. I tended to stay out most of the day and headed straight to my room at night. None of us spoke about any of it and I hadn't been able to tell Tommy. I couldn't get my head round it.

Kel felt low too with everything that had gone on. I tried to be strong for her, but she shut me out. The reality was that she crashed, which was difficult to see. She was quiet, stayed in her pyjamas all day and spent most of her time on the sofa. She seemed to go through the day-to-day rituals like a zombie. One time, she absentmindedly shook the salt pot into her tea and drank it all without blinking an eye.

All I could do was be there for her, but I felt so much guilt inside. After the Social Worker had told Kel about Andi moving to her dad's, Kel was distraught, and I tried to be there for her. I held her to try and comfort her but then when my mind ticked over about how all this started, I pulled away. Kel begged me to stay with her but with silly excuses I bolted. This was all down to me.

Kel agreed to Andi moving to John's and she went one of the weekends. It was easiest that way so that it was as natural as it could be. It was on John's contact weekend, though Kel had tried to explain what was happening to Andi.

She barely spoke to me or anyone else. The sparkle in her eyes had faded a while back leaving a hollowness that was difficult to reach. I couldn't remember the last time I had heard the tinkle of her laugh. Andi was an extension of Kel and the person that Kel was.

'We still haven't decided the long-term arrangements for Andi,' Naeed reassured.

'Fab,' Kel replied completely deadpan, all emotion battered out of her. There was only the shell of Kel left behind.

'I mean your assessment is still ongoing. We will work out what will be best for Andi after that assessment is complete.'

'Yup, fab.'

'When shall we meet again for the next assessment session?'

'Fab,' Kel said as she closed the door on the social worker. She was not with it.

There was nothing and no one that could bring her out of it… she would have to face this on her own.

I was there for her but that wasn't enough. I wasn't Andi.

Serena had already told us about mother and baby units. They were twenty-four-hour supervision places. They watched how mothers took care of their babies. After a period of assessment, if things went well, they returned home. It allowed an assessment without removal of the children. Serena had already told us that we had a good shot at challenging this, but Kel was not going to take any chances.

'It's happening,' Kel squeezed out on the phone to me.

'What do you mean, the baby? Oh my God. Okay, I'm coming.'

I raced on my bike to the local hospital. I got there in record time. Twenty minutes in what usually took thirty minutes on any regular day. This was anything but a regular day!

I gasped for air, that when I went into the hospital, the staff thought I needed help. They thought I had a medical emergency myself. I spluttered out that my missus was having our baby. I saw them looking quizzically around behind me.

I managed to get to Kel and was with her in the delivery room. It all happened in a blur. It was an out of body experience. The doctor was like a conductor, directing us all in what instruments to play and how. The midwife was our star performer. They were incredible and ran the show pitch perfect.

I was in a flap, scared and excited about everything but doing my best.

Kel was in pain, screaming out at us all and struggling with the enormity of it.

I had never seen Kel like it before. I mean I had seen her sad, angry, distressed, and happy but never this. Her shrieks were searing. I was completely helpless. Kel gripped my hand, her nails dug into my palms. I didn't even realise it until after when the indentations were still visible to my palms.

'Matthew, come down here. Your son is about to make his grand entrance,' the midwife encouraged.

'Oh wow! This is amazing!'

A few seconds later, he had arrived. Our beautiful baby boy. Out came the cry and it was the best sound in the world. Right there and then, I knew what love was.

Cutting the umbilical cord was a special, cautious moment for me. I filled up. I now understood what fatherhood was all about. We were his everything and he was most certainly mine. I knew that from the point on, my every step, my every breath, my everything would be about my boy.

Kel bonded with our boy immediately and she was so natural with him. I was a fumbling fool, all awkward and nervy but my love for him was limitless.

I knew that Kel was thinking about Andi. The old Kel was re-surfacing, or a different version, with Rodrigo in her arms. That was the name we decided on a while back and it seemed to fit. That was one of my happiest moments of my life and Andi not being there tainted it somewhat. It was almost perfect.

'Hi Matthew, Kelly,' Naeed said, followed with the obligatory 'Congratulations.'

'Thanks.' We said in unison.

'So, I understand that Rodrigo and you are being discharged today. I'm here to take you to the unit.' With that, we were brought straight back down to earth with a harrowing bump. We had been in the baby bubble since our arrival at the hospital and now rocketed crash bang back into reality.

'Okay,' Kel sighed.

'Can I come too?' I asked.

'It'll be better if we settle Rodrigo and Kelly first and you know, we will set up proper contact for you, Matthew. We need to make sure that Rodrigo and Kelly are okay, does that make sense.'

'Yeah, fine,' I said, looking at Kel with Rodrigo in her arms.

I hated this and all I could see was the innocence and utter dependence of my boy. Kel and I had looked forward to this moment for so long and I had ruined it all for us. We should have been putting our son in a taxi back to our little home. Instead, they ripped Kel and Roddy away from me.

I held Roddy for a few minutes and talked to him, telling him he was my brave little boy and to be a good baby for his mummy. He was beautiful, with dark chestnut brown hair and blue eyes. His little button nose was all from his mum and I knew I would never let anything hurt him.

I took him down with Kel and out of the hospital to Naeed's car. I couldn't bear to be apart from him or from Kel.

I strapped my boy into the car seat, kissed him on the forehead, kissed Kel, turned one hundred and eighty degrees round and walked away.

Chapter Five

KELLY

I watched as Matt walked away from us. He did not turn around at all, kept his head bent down as he strode away, his back bent over.

I had seen the tears well up in his eyes and as quick as that, he had snatched his head away and left us. This was not how it was meant to be. We were meant to go home as a family. We had made our home fit for our prince, now we had no idea where we were headed and what waited for us there. We had planned on using some of Andi's stuff but had bought a new moses basket and pram for Roddie.

Matt had so looked forward to being there with me to take care of our baby boy and now he was cut out. This was not what I had imagined through this pregnancy. My whole family splintered.

I buckled myself in at the back next to my gorgeous boy, who was fast asleep in the car seat. I stroked his soft hair more for self-comfort than anything else.

We went in Naeed's car, and her beady eyes glanced at us in the rear-view mirror. At least Roddie wore a baby grow tagged with 'daddy and me' on his stomach. We rolled along and Roddie slept all the way through the twists and turns.

Naeed spoke and I made cursory sounds to signal that I was listening even though I wasn't. I wanted her to shut the hell up but couldn't say that to her because then they would use that against me.

I focused on my beautiful baby boy. He had the bluest of blue eyes and mousy brown hair, like me. The eyes, though, they belonged to his dad. Crystal clear azure of a summer sky. Roddie's nose was a tiny turned up little button nose. I know I am biased, but he was the most wonderful baby boy ever.

We pulled up to this grey tower building with squares climbing up the front facing side. I got out of the car, unhooked Roddie and took him in my arms as we walked into the Crown building. It didn't just look grey from the outside but inside was dismal as well despite the magnolia walls.

Naeed introduced me to the manager, Jess Hardy, a beautiful, slim and young woman whose look belied her. When she spoke, her firmness shone through. She took us to a little room furnished with a single bed and cot. There was a small television in there and a fridge. There were also cameras in all the corners of the room. I felt something push into my chest. My nose hoovered up the hospitalised bleach of the room and twitched in irritation.

'I'll show you the other facilities,' Jess said and took me round to the toilets, kitchen and living area. There was also a contact room and a separate interview space. They had the same arrangements on each floor of the building. There were five rooms on each floor and two staff members to each floor. I was on the fifth floor and pretty much all the floors were booked out.

'Okay, Kelly. I'm heading off now and will let you settle in with Rodrigo. Jess and the others will look after you from here. I will be back in a week to see how you are getting on,' Naeed said.

'Fine. When can I see Matt?'

'Jess will explain all the rules of the unit and what happens with visitors and time out of the unit.'

'Okay and will she sort out Matt's contact with Roddie, too?'

'Well, yes but she will do that with me. We will work together to get that sorted and I will speak with Matthew to set it up. Jess will let you know when the first one is fixed.'

'Fine,' when everything was anything but fine!

Naeed headed out and Jess told me that she would let me get used to my room. We agreed that we would reunite in the interview room to talk a few things through in about an hour. Roddie was fast asleep and so I placed him in the cot.

I sat on my bed and cried. It all flooded out of me and was a huge release.

I picked myself up, touched up my make-up and brushed my hair back into a low ponytail. I lifted Roddie out of the cot and went to see Jess. 'Come on, in,' Jess waved me in. 'Take a seat.'

I sat down with Roddie in my lap. He was still sound asleep; I mean that's all those new-born babies do, sleep, feed and fill their nappies. So far Roddie had been golden. He was not a crier at all unless he wanted or needed something like sleep, feed, or nappy change. I wasn't used to him yet, so it took a few guesses each time to work out what he needed. It was only ever for one of those three things, so it wasn't difficult.

'So, you might have seen the cameras in your room. They are there for both you and your son. I guess they are also there for staff.'

'Mm-hmm.'

'In case of any issues, the camera will be on twenty-four, seven. If you or your son need any help, we will see it and can come to you.'

'That's fine.' I was quite the lab specimen.

Jess explained that there was also an alarm system in the room that I could press if I needed any help. There were always two women on the floor. That said, they looked to me to take care of Roddie as I would if I were at home with him.

'You are allowed visits from friends and family but must book this room or the living space for that visit. We allow two visitors at a time in the living room from ten in the morning to four in the afternoon.' Sam continued.

'Okay and am I allowed out to visit them?'

'Yes, of course, but only till eight in the evening and Rodrigo must be the priority. No overnight stays anywhere.'

'That's fine.'

'Social Services are concerned with your partner, Matthew. They do not want him to meet Rodrigo unless we are supervising it. That means that you cannot see him with Rodrigo. Does that sound okay?' Jess asked.

'Well, no but I understand and will agree to it for now.'

I became more and more aware of how much control I had lost to these people. My life was no longer my life. My family was no longer my family. These people owned us, and I didn't know whether I could take it. It was so intrusive and intense. I felt myself falling more and more into myself. There was no way out of this suffocating doom.

The artificiality of the scenario was not lost on me. Yet this was to be the basis of an assessment of my reality as a parent. It seemed a cruel twist of irony.

'You will have to provide a urine sample each time you go to the toilet.' Jess outlined, cementing the prison of this unit.

'What?'

'So, we can check it for alcohol/drug use,' Jess clarified.

'What the hell?'

What was this place and what had we let ourselves in for?

MATTHEW

'Your contact has been set up for Thursday at two in the afternoon. Is that okay, Matthew?' Naeed asked.

'Yup, okay.'

I didn't know what to expect. Kel had been in touch, and she sounded so despondent. I could hear in her thin, vacant voice; how much she struggled and there was nothing I could say or do to help her. It had only been a few days and I figured that she would get used to it with time and things would calm.

I needed to focus on what I needed to address. My domestic violence work was coming to an end and the probation order would continue for the rest of the year. I hoped when I completed the domestic violence work, our assessment would be positive.

Kel had told me what the unit was like; miserable and very bleak. I was tense and hesitant as I made my way there for contact. My internal organs competed in a gymnastics event at the Olympics or something. I was jittery and had a very restless night's sleep on the eve of my first contact. I felt scared that I would not hold him properly, maybe mess up his feed or not wind him fully. He was a baby and needed me.

I laid out freshly pressed trousers and white shirt on the bed whilst I showered. I pulled my trousers around my lampposts. I tried buttoning up my shirt with glued together fingers and thumbs. I took a last check in the mirror and pulled the fake costume off. Beneath there was a scared little boy that had stared back at me drowning in the sea of unfamiliar grown-up clothes.

I switched into my comfy grey trackies and blue t-shirt. I had unusually and hurriedly ironed them. I was much more at ease finally, but it would not do. The trackies and t-shirt were thrown on top of the trousers and shirt I had abandoned earlier. This little pile grew, and I settled back into the trousers and shirt I had first cloaked myself in. It was a bit more crumpled after everything I had put it through. Actually, the wrinkles sat more comfortably on me.

I had got a taxi this time, not taking any chances. My eyes were darting this way and that. I flicked my wrist, turned my watch, and glanced at its face in between phone clock checking.

I arrived at the high rise building that almost stamped all over me. I walked in through the heavy door. One of the women there showed me into the designated contact room. It was a nice sized room with boxes of toys and cuddly friends spilling out in one corner. There were some red worn sofas and a bookcase to one side with different fillings to suit all ages. The air was stifling and there was a concoction of baby smells, aftershave, and perfumes.

I sank into the old sofa, where the springs seemed to have waned. I was in the midst of settling myself when a middle-aged woman walked into the room. She introduced herself, 'Hi, my name is Laura, I am here to supervise the contact today.'

'Okay.'

Laura sat in the corner of the room. As well as the boxes of tricks, there was a little table for colouring and reading. The walls painted with a forest theme. It wasn't home but at least they had tried to make it nice for children.

Kel brought Roddie in and handed him to me with tears streaming down her face. I couldn't bear to see her like that and hugged her before turning away.

I concentrated the rest of my time and energies on Roddie. As soon as he was in my arms, my fears were overtaken by an overwhelming sense of love and warmth. I held Roddie close and tried to memorise every little nook and cranny on his face and body. He was the best thing I had ever made, and I was never going to let him down.'Hey baby, my sweet baby,' I cooed to Roddie. He slept in my arms, my beautiful baby boy. I continued chatting to him, 'Hope you've been a good boy for mummy. You need to help her mate because I'm not here right now. You are a good boy. Love you, baby.'

I chatted intermittently to Kel as well but only pleasantries. Neither of us wanted to say anything that the supervisor might report back. I wanted to savour my time with Roddie. He was so perfect; I could not believe that I had played a part in making him.

Half an hour into the session, Roddie stirred, and I gave him a bottle. Kel still breast fed and had expressed some for me.

I winded him, which took some time. I became anxious but Kel was patient and calm with me. 'Pat him slowly on his back but not too slowly. That's it. You are doing it.' She reassured.

'He has still not burped, though.'

'It's okay, it might take a bit of time, but he'll get there. Keep going as you are. You have got it now,' and then there it was, a clear bellow releasing wind.

Roddie fell back to sleep and shortly before my time was up, I changed his nappy. I was all fingers and thumbs with it but managed it. The old nappy was stuck to my arm whilst I tried to put the fresh one on. The fresh one got stuck into the old one and I had to pull them both away from me.

I became agitated with myself, my fingers, and thumbs clammy and in the way of each other. It felt like I had twenty fingers and thumbs rather than the ten. I snapped at myself and took a minute.

I looked down into my boy's blue eyes and I swear, he smiled back at me! That was it then, I grabbed a fresh nappy and took a piece at a time, put it altogether like a jigsaw puzzle and he was all done.

Contact was a couple of hours and as I finished off the nappy change, Laura let us know that the time was up. I kissed my boy on his forehead, kissed Kel and headed out.

I would be back again in a couple of days, Saturday. They had agreed that I could have contact three times a week – Monday, Thursday and Saturday.

I had my last domestic violence session the following week. It had been a tough process. In group sessions, I found it even more difficult than usual. It helped hearing the others though. At times, I pushed myself even further than I ever imagined I could. 'I have a lot bottled up from my childhood.'

'I was in care. My parents cared more about their drug fixes than they did about me,' Neil shared. Neil was one of the group members I got on well with.

'I was in care too.' I admitted.

'I was ten when I went into care, and then pushed from pillar to post with one home then another.'

It turned out that Neil had a lot of built-up anger and rage. Neil didn't make all the sessions, he found it too hard. He had beaten up his girlfriend, she had a fractured jaw from it. It was also not the first time he had hurt her, and they were still together. She felt for him because of his past but they had a kid together too. It sounded like his little girl was going to be put up for adoption unless his missus was willing to go it alone.

I wasn't sure how that would work out, but I felt for Neil and his little family. I determined not to let this happen to our family.

KELLY

As soon as Matt left, I headed back to my room with Roddie in my arms. Roddie's head nestled into my chin and after a short time, my chin felt wet from the top of Roddie's head. I stroked his hair, which was damp from the silent tears had travelled my cheeks onto his little crown.

I rushed back into the room and swiped the clothes away from the bed. I had thrown on one thing after another before the contact. Filled with the nervous excitement of teenage love earlier but now the cold reality hit me hard. I sank onto the bed and cried quietly, rocking Roddie backwards and forwards close to me.

It had been great seeing Matt and Roddie together, but I wanted that all the time. I hated this place, it was so oppressive, that there were days I could not breathe.

I had had a couple of panic attacks, which was something I had never experienced before. It scared me the first time, but the staff got me through it. My heart beat rapidly that I gasped for air. My head was lightheaded and dizzy. The staff saw me suffering on the cameras and came to my aid.

'Take a deep breath in, one, two, three and out, one, two, three,' Libby, one of the workers talked me through. She talked me down and my heart rate calmed, and my breathing became easier. I didn't know what had triggered neither it nor the others that I had had. I found it difficult to cope with everything.

A week later, Libby had agreed to take care of Roddie. I got myself ready, black trousers and cream blouse with cardi over it. I decided to wear my hair down with a clip pulling one side back. I never wore much make up but applied foundation and a bit of colour on my lips. I was set.

I met Matthew at the courthouse. It was a dark building with a maze of corridors. The waiting area felt brighter. There was more space but still miserable. People came in different shapes and sizes, some anxious and others pensive. We didn't talk much apart from me updating Matt on how Roddie was doing.

I could hear the clickety click of Serena's high length heels before we even saw her. She strode across to us in her smart black pinstripe dress suit. She looked the part and I hoped that she was the part.

Serena ushered us into a consultation room. We sat down in quite a small, stifling room which was darker than the waiting area. The bright, sharp light did little to help the atmosphere of the room.

'So, how are you both?' Serena asked.

'Okay,' we both replied. We looked at each other warmly.

'Well, I hope so. As you know, Social Services have applied for an interim care order...' And she outlined what it all meant. All I heard was that we were incapable of taking care of our children. I was not good enough and had put them at risk of harm. I'm not even sure now whether Serena ever even said these words but that is exactly what I heard and felt.

'As you have agreed the arrangements for the children, you should agree the Order today. It will be better to save that argument for a later date. We will have much more evidence then to support your case. Does that make sense?' Serena advised.

'Yeah,' we both replied. 'When can we get back to being a family?' Matt asked.

'It is going to take quite a while. Cases like this, should be resolved within twenty-six weeks. I know that sounds like a long time. There needs to be sufficient time for assessments and evidence. The court will then determine matters.'

'That's six and a half months,' Kelly sighed.

'The thing is, if things go well, the children can return to you sooner. A lot will depend on the current Crown assessment.'

'Okay,' Matt said.

As Serena had explained to us, the hearing itself went as expected. Social services now had care orders in relation to our children and could decide things for them.

Andi would remain where she was, with her dad and his parents, and Roddie would be with me at Crown. I had been there a couple of weeks now and it was still no easier. Andi was brought to me for contact twice a week. She was so good with Roddie, so gentle and careful.

I missed my family. I could not bear it. 'Matt, I don't think I can do this.'

'We can do this, Kel and we will do it.'

'I don't know.'

'Yes, we can. We must.'

'It's another ten weeks, Matt.'

Before we left court, one of the women that was in the court hearing came over to us. She introduced herself, 'Hi, my name is Barbara Cutler, and I am the children's guardian.'

Serena had told us about a Social Worker type person reporting to the court what was best for the children. Someone called the Guardian, which was confusing because I thought that that was someone that takes care of children who don't have their parents. Serena said that the Guardian was someone in care cases that took care of children's best interests but didn't take care of the children practically day to day. She explained that the Guardian was the most influential person in court. It was important for us to develop a good relationship with her. She was the woman with the power.

'Hi,' we both replied. She took our details.

'I will see you both again during the process. The most important thing is to work with Social Services and get through the assessments. We can then make informed decisions in the best interests of the children. That is what we all want, after all, the best for your children,' Barbara set out.

'Absolutely,' Matt said and 'Of course,' I echoed.

Matt and I grabbed a quick coffee together before we parted in different directions. I got a taxi back to the Crown.

As soon as I walked back, Libby said, 'Kelly, you

know I was only meant to watch Roddie whilst you were at court.'

'Yeah, thanks,' I replied confused.

'We got a call a couple of hours or so ago that court was done,' she continued.

'Okay.'

'It only takes ten minutes by taxi.'

'Right,' I replied. Nervous tension was building inside me.

'So, we need to know where you were and why you didn't think about Roddie?'

'I'm sorry. Our lawyer was talking to us and then the Guardian.'

'Kel, it doesn't take two hours. We need you to be honest with us in this process,' Libby pressed.

'Well, yeah, okay so Matt and I went and grabbed a quick coffee. I didn't think it would matter.'

'It matters. Everything you do now matters,' Libby chided.

This was exactly what I dreaded. I could feel myself tighten into myself and knew what was coming. This was habitual now as Libby counted me back down.

MATTHEW

After court, I headed home. I pounded towards the bus stop. Typically, of how things had been going for me, the bus I needed, sped past me as I ran for it. I waved my arms around like a crazy, malfunctioning windmill but the bus was long gone. The hurling wind swished around me, and I jigged from one foot to the other trying to keep warm. I blew into my rubbing palms.

I had moved back in when Kel went into the unit. I could smell Kel and Andi in the walls, furniture, and all around, I could hear and see them in my mind's memories. It was a vacant, soulless vessel. It didn't feel right, like I was wearing clothes glued to me that fit too tightly.

I struggled with sleep, a movie reel of Kel, Andi, Roddie, my parents and siblings all flashing around. None of it was in any order or were even real-life memories. Everyone merged into a horror show or something. I stayed up late into the night and stirred early.

As much as home no longer felt like home, it was still so good to have my own place back. It had become so painful at my parents. I still avoided them, and it was awkward with Tommo. I knew something about our parents that he didn't know, and he knew there was something up. The contagion locked inside of me and my desperate conflict to keep it quarantined!

For two brothers that had been the wheels of the one bicycle, we were now punctured. It messed everything. It messed everything up with the family. It messed everything up with the parents. It messed everything.

I hated being around my parents but at the same time hadn't been able to cut off from them.

When I saw Kel at the Crown, she had to have someone else keep an eye on Roddie. Quite a few times, he would get unsettled so Kel would go and see to him.

There was the odd occasion that I would be leaving as she went to see to Roddie. She would have him with her as we said our farewells. Jess had warned her about this but also her forgetting the dreaded urine samples. She was on her final warning, and we had spoken about it. We agreed that she had to stick to the rules from now on. There was no point taking any risks when we had so much to lose.

'Kel, what is Roddie doing here?'

'I had no choice. Eve couldn't do it because she had an emergency hearing come up, so I had to bring him.'

'You should have cancelled,' I replied, worried.

'Matt, my one time out of that place with you is what I live for each week. I would go crazy without it, I don't think you understand what it is like in there,' Kelly pleaded.

'I know, but if they find out, we are going to be in so much trouble.'

We only spent about half an hour that day. I was so stressed about Roddie being with us. Those thirty minutes were precious for us to be like any other normal family. Of course, Andi was missing but it was the next best thing. The reality is that it wasn't normal because we were on edge. We continuously watched over our shoulder, but it was the closest we could be to normal.

We had met at a café and usually would have something to eat together but this time, we only had a quick coffee each. It was a cosy café with a seaside feel to it. The tables and chairs in blue and the walls painted a sunshine yellow. It was worn, with the painting curling in the corners, but those quirks warmed the ambience of the place.

The staff and other patrons were kind, friendly and cheerful. The beautiful aroma of their harvest circled us. Roddie was six weeks and gurgled at us now; making tiny noises. He was a marvel. I could watch him for hours and got lost in him. I loved having them both with me for that short time but was very conscious that we broke the rules. I was a confused ball of contradiction.

I rushed Kel and Roddie away so that we could avoid getting caught out. As close to perfect as it was, I was tight with tension the whole time and needed to get them away. Though, there were snatches of bliss looking into Kel's and Roddie's eyes. We just about made it.

I had a meeting with Naeed as part of the ongoing assessment. I made my way to her office, again on my trusted bike. I was out of breath by the time I got there. Naeed, however, was stuck with another family and so was late herself.

I sat in the magnolia waiting area, the grey cushioned seats lined side by side against one wall. The brown carpet was grimy with stories of all the families before me and had tired now. The weight of those families seemed visible in the raggedness and dirt of the carpet. Chewing gum in the corner spat out by an angry Dad? The black butterfly by the security glass door perhaps a kid's Ribena?

'Hi, Matthew, come on through,' Naeed eventually waved me in.

'Hiya.'

'So, I wanted to talk through a bit more about your childhood, if that's okay,' she initiated.

'Yeah, that's fine but I don't remember much.'

'That's okay, we will work through what we can. Did you manage to speak to any of your family about it?'

'Well, yes. Sarah, my oldest sister told me what Dad had done to her, Paul, and Tommy. And mum didn't do anything to stop him,' I summarised.

'Okay, it is a real positive that she has been able to be honest and open with you like that. The thing is that there is much more.'

'What do you mean?'

'I'll give you this, which is all the stuff that he did. Matt, there were some things you talked about too when you were younger,' Naeed cautioned.

'I don't know what you're on about,' I replied.

'I'm sorry, Matt. As well as his previous convictions, I'll give you the chronology from your file. Take it home, go through it in your own time and come back to speak to me again if you need to. You could talk to your family as well.'

'I need to leave,' I rushed and got to my feet. I didn't wait but heard Naeed behind me, 'Of course.'

I couldn't bear it. I cycled, pumping the wheels round hard and fast. I didn't even realise that it was raining and didn't care. I pummelled in competition with the downpour. My trousers heavy with water, my jacket soaked through, my hair and face flooded. Drips of water fell from my hair into my eyes. This combined with the monsoon that thrashed into me, but I pedalled on.

I have no idea how long I had cycled for. It was only when I walked into the house shedding puddles that I realised I was wrung through.

The shrill of the phone broke me out of my head.

'Kel, what is going on?' I answered the phone but all I could hear was gasps of breathing and crying. 'Kel, calm down. I can't hear anything. Slow down.'

'They know. I'm so sorry. I'm so sorry,' she wheezed.

Chapter Six

KELLY

As it happened, they had found out. The Crown kicked Roddie and I out and they brought the assessment to an immediate end. Naeed came for Roddie. 'Get away from us!' I cried and shielded Roddie away.

'I need to take him,' Naeed said.

'Leave us the hell alone.' I raged through my tears. Roddie shrieked and I looked down at his reddened face, tears and snot all mashed on his face.

'Look at him, Kelly, please let me take him.'

'I love you baby boy. I'm so, so sorry.' I handed Roddie to Naeed keeping my eyes on him throughout. 'Shhhhh, shhh, it's okay, baby boy.'

Naeed turned and left, with Roddie still wailing.

I was hysterical. I screamed and threw things around the room after Roddie had gone.

They transported me home. My tears stung my eyes, and I had no voice left. The car bumped and twisted its way home. With each jolt, it hurt that bit more.

Matt waited for me, but I pushed past him, dragged myself to my bedroom and curled up in bed. Sharp pains flew through me, my arms tingled, and head pulsated. I couldn't lie down, sit up or stand. A darkness enveloped me. I seized some tablets from my bedside cabinet and washed them down, which sedated me for the night.

The following morning, it took me a while to understand what had gone on. Roddie. Gone. Roddie.

I didn't want to leave my bed, Matt was already up and somewhere in the house, I thought. I wanted to camp out in the comfort of my bed forever. Matt and I were children less, though between us, parents to two beautiful children. It was a cruel paradox in some alternative universe, but not, because it was our reality.

Matt came up and greeted me with a cup of tea. 'I've arranged for us to see Serena.'

'Okay.'

'We need to understand our position and what we can do.'

'Okay.'

'You need to be strong; we can do this. We can't give up,' Matt urged.

'Okay.'

'Snap out of it. I need you,' he yelled and then pleaded. The mix of sharpness and fear cut through me. I still carried an unbearable heaviness in my chest laced with sadness and fear. Matt's acidity had pressed some autopilot button for me.

'Give me a few minutes. I'll come down.'

I hauled myself out of bed and forced myself to reclaim some semblance of propriety. I joined Matt downstairs and we made our way to Serena's office. She called us straight in. She explained that the Local Authority had a Care Order. This meant that they could place Roddie wherever they wanted.

'They should return it to court because of the

change in plan but, there is little we can do, until it gets to court.' I didn't hear what she said.

'Can we apply for Roddie to come back to us?' Matt asked.

'Well, no but you can object to the interim care order. If successful, then Roddie would be returned but I don't like your chances, I'm afraid.'

'We have to do something,' Matt insisted.

'The thing is, Matt, Kelly didn't keep the rules and at an interim stage, they will not take any chances. We need to see what the assessment says. We would be better off challenging at the final hearing stage instead,' Serena advised.

'I don't get it,' Matt said.

'It's my fault, Matt. What don't you get? We've lost him because I messed up. That's it.' I blurted.

'No, Kelly, that is not true.' Serena said. She mustered as much comfort as she could. 'The fact is you may have made a mistake. It is not such a significant issue to justify that Roddie or indeed Andi remain away from you long term. There isn't enough evidence to show that you are able to care safely for the children. There is time still to get that evidence.'

Matt seemed to be in a whirr of confusion and shock. I could not see beyond what I had done wrong. We travelled back on the bus and sat side by side in painful silence.

As the bus reached our stop, the rain hurled itself at the bus like it was mad at us. I pulled my coat round me as we climbed out of the bus and Matt followed behind me. 'We should have got the taxi back,' I mentioned.

'We should have done a lot of things differently,' Matt replied.

'What is that supposed to mean?' I stopped midway and turned back round to face Matt.

'Doesn't matter,' Matt said and continued down the road.

'No, it does matter,' I shouted, 'You blame me!'

'I said WE, not you.'

'Get lost, Matt,' and I stormed off towards home.

Matt didn't say anything else and stayed a few steps behind me. Soaked by the time we got home, I made a quick change and I wiped dry the flooded hallway. Matt crouched down alongside me with towels and helped me. 'I'm sorry,' he whispered.

'I'm the one that should be sorry, and I am,' I replied.

After clearing the mess, we had made, I made us a pot of tea and we sat down at the kitchen table. Piece by piece, we worked things through. We spent all night hashing over what had happened, there were tears and a lot of snotty tissues around us. We were not quite there and were still a long way off, but we were still fighting.

Naeed came by a week or so later with the Crown assessment and it was damning. The report called me out as a bad mother. I was devastated all over again. Serena phoned us; she had the report as well. 'You're on loud speak, Serena,' Matt said.

'Okay, so I have had the report and it's not great.'

'We've had it too.'

'Oh right, that's good, saves me posting it out to you guys. I know it might seem bad, but it isn't completely terrible. I mean there are no criticisms of Kelly's parenting skills per se.'

'Yeah, but is that enough?' Matt asked.

'We need to push for another, fuller assessment that involves the both of you.'

My interest piqued at this, 'What do you mean?' I asked.

'Well, there is nothing so far about the both of you together. I know that there are issues with Matt's background. We will need to go through that too, but we need a proper assessment of you as a couple. That seems to have been lost in all this.' Serena outlined.

'That makes sense,' I realised. 'Naeed had talked about a joint and separate assessment. I don't know what has happened to the joint assessment or even Matt's separate assessment.'

'So, can I take it that you are happy for me to make that Application on your behalf?'

'Yes,' we replied. 'Absolutely,' I added.

We arrived at court for our application for an independent assessment. Social Services opposed the Application because Naeed had completed the assessment herself. It would be part of her final evidence. They said that the court did not need any more information. I knew that that assessment would be negative. Naeed hated us.

Serena told us that the Guardian's position would be the most important view. We needed her on our side. The Guardian was late getting to court, and we didn't get chance to speak to her before the hearing itself. Serena was strong on the reasons for the Application.

Naeed's Solicitor was flustered and all over the place in her arguments. She did not seem convinced by her own argument. I got the sense that she agreed that we should have the assessment but was bound by Naeed's view.

Finally, the Guardian's Solicitor stood up. She started, 'The Guardian opposes the Application...' I didn't hear the rest of the Solicitor's very lengthy and legalised speech. I already knew we had lost our only chance and ran out of the court room.

SERENA

As soon as the Magistrates confirmed their decision, I escorted Matt out of the court room. My heels struck the ground hard and stormed round looking for Kelly. I gestured to Matt to sit in the waiting area and pounded my way to the ladies. I let the doors bang shut behind me. I turned the hot water tap on, splashed my face with the still coolness of the water. My inside filled with angry blood pumping through my limbs, chest, and stomach.

This is what I hated about our so-called justice system. Kelly appeared behind me. She stood by the sink next to me, neither of us looked at each other or our reflections in the mirror ahead of us.

'We need to plan our next steps,' I opened.

'There is nothing left.'

'We will see, for now, let's go join Matt.'

I took them out for a coffee, and we found ourselves in a small, modern café. The gold swirls danced around the cream and black walls. The cushioned sofas stared at up us invitingly. We found an empty spot in one end of the café away from prying ears.

I wanted Matthew and Kelly to know that we were still going to challenge this, and it was not over. My rage would push me on and had to push Matt and Kelly on too, somehow. 'Listen, I know it's tough to keep getting knock backs, but we have to stay strong and drive on. You guys can do this.'

'I don't know,' Kelly said.

'We have to keep going, Kel,' Matt said.

'How?'

'We will be getting Naeed's evidence shortly. We can consider either appealing today's decision or making a fresh Application. It all depends on what Naeed says,' I advised.

'Okay,' Matt responded, and Kelly nodded.

'Go home, get some rest and we will fight another day. Let me worry about the case and I will talk to you again soon.'

We talked some more, what appealing might be like and what that would involve. I mean appeals were difficult. The court's powers were so wide and discretionary. This meant that the lower courts could decide whatever they wanted. Unless something was blatantly wrong, it was impossible to appeal.

Deflated, my heart, soul and body demanded that I went home. I took some of my own advice with some much-required rest.

Back at home, I fell into my wonderful dark chocolate brown leather sofa. I lay down and enjoyed a few minutes in the stillness of the evening. Leftovers from the night before made for dinner.

I had never married nor had children and that suited me. One long term relationship for most of my adult life had put paid to any more relationships for me. My whole world had become work. It was work that saved me and I would never betray that.

Naeed's assessment came in a week or so later and as expected it was negative to the parents. She was so petty and hadn't even completed all the sessions with them. They had no chance. I decided, there and then, we would appeal the refusal for independent assessment. A fresh application would be pointless. I needed to get this case in front of a proper judge rather than before the lay Magistrates. Only an appeal would do.

Everyone in the legal world knew that the Magistrates were not in the same league as Judges. Magistrates were great for volunteering their time. They undertook a public duty, a civic duty in fact but they were not trained or qualified in law. They were members of the public that had no legal background. I had a lot of respect for them serving justice. Care proceedings and the removal of children was a different matter. That should be left to qualified judges.

Within criminal law, Magistrates dealt with the lower end of criminal offences whilst more serious offences went to qualified Judges. Care proceedings involved the consideration of permanent removal of children from their parents. This was a life sentence for the parents but also for the children in some ways. If life sentences can only be issued by qualified judges in crime, why can they be issued by the Magistrates in care proceedings?

Qualified judges, having practised as lawyers, had years of legal knowledge and experience behind them. Being judged by your peers, as the Magistrates were, was an essential element of the system and it had its place. In my view it had no place when it came to separating children from their parents. That needed a legal expert. Justice and injustice were two sides of the double-edged sword. Justice broken down was just ice, cold, without feeling, just ice – justice. A strange word that we played at.

I dressed in my sharpest, best suit. I had my hair straightened and pulled back. My make-up was spotless, and I felt ready. I wanted to look and feel the part today. It was an important day.

'Your Honour, this is a case where the Assessment of these parents will be the ultimate factor. Without which, these parents will not be afforded access to justice,' I began. I continued to outline where and how the Magistrates had erred. I developed the themes of the written grounds of appeal. 'The Magistrates were plainly wrong. Refusing this application was the promise of a miscarriage of justice,' I ended.

The Local Authority mounted their opposition.

I remained confident until the Guardian's Solicitor stood up. She supported the Local Authority position. I felt sucker punched out of the ring. She made some valid points and I shrunk back into my seat.

Following her strong submissions, I somehow managed to stand back up in rebuttal. I delivered a reply to each of the most impressive points from the Guardian as best as I could.

Then we had wait for His Honour Judge Carter's decision, which wasn't a long wait. Sometimes, Judges disappeared off to their lairs hidden away. Other times, they stayed on their regal thrones. They took a few minutes and composed themselves. Then they reeled off their judgments from their silver tongues.

His Honour Judge Carter was renowned for his sharp, swift delivery of justice. His Honour announced, 'And so, I grant the Appeal. I direct an independent joint assessment of the parents forthwith.'

There were gasps of relief from behind me and Kelly had tears streaming down her face. Dumbfounded, Matthew didn't seem able to bring any words or emotion out.

'Having made this decision, I remit the case back to the Magistrates.'

KELLY
I couldn't quite believe it and flopped listlessly back into my seat. We had been handed a lifeline. We would not let this one slip out of our hands. We would grip onto it, tightly and never let it go until we got our kids back.

I flung my arms around Matt and held him close. I don't think it sunk in for Matt. Matt was stiff and nailed to his spot.

Serena again took us to the same coffee place we went to last time like our lucky charm.

The Judge seemed more willing to give us a chance than the Magistrates. The Magistrates were more authoritative. First because there was usually three of them. Then there was the fact that they never said much during the hearings. When they made their decision, they all agreed it, as far as we could tell. They took copious notes of everything, it seemed. Then they always disappeared into some secret chambers for hours at a time.

When there is only one Judge, it didn't feel as powerful. They were all Judges, but when there was a panel of them, it was more serious. The fact that we would be back before the Magistrates again, worried me because they had been against us, so far.

'So, the Judge has given you another chance. You need to show through this assessment that you can take care of Roddie.'

'What about Andi, everyone has forgotten about her in all this?' I asked concerned.

'For right now, you need to focus on showing that Roddie will be safe in your care. Andi is with family anyway and she will stay there until we can show that she can return to you. The situation is much more precarious, sorry, dodgy with Roddie. If he can't come back to you, he can't go anywhere other than adoption and he will be lost forever.'

'Mmmm, right,' I replied.

I asked Serena about the Magistrates. She explained that they were below the Judge we had just had. The Magistrates were ordinary volunteers from the public rather than qualified judges.

Completely thrown, I was unsure how I felt about this. It didn't seem right that an anybody could decide our children's lives. I had always believed that they had had years of study and experience behind them. It turned out that they were everyday men and women off the street.

'That's so wrong.'

'It is the system we have. We have to work with it.'

'But how can Joe Bloggs have the right to take kids away from their parents,' I ranted.

'We can't go back to them,' Matt interjected. He was still dazed.

'We've got no choice,' Serena replied.

'We never have,' Matt said.

Serena went through Matt's Dad's convictions and the chronology she had for him. We had never read it ourselves, there was too much, and Matt had struggled with everything. Matt didn't want to think about it or face it.

I wrestled with it too and it was easier for us both to keep it hidden away under the manhole. Matt's family had not spoken much about it either. We were aware that Naeed had rung round the family. She had told them all to make sure that the children were always supervised around Matt's Dad. They did that anyway.

'Mr Barnett senior was convicted of over one hundred sexual abuse assaults. Almost one hundred and fifty, actually.'

'Whooooo!' I let out. Matt sat there numbly, it

seemed.

'The thing is that he undertook an assessment a while back. That showed that he could not say that he would not stop himself again,' Serena shared.

'Wow! What is he on? I don't understand how anyone can be like that,' I responded. I glanced sideways trying to read Matt's expression free face.

'Matt, are you okay?' Serena asked.

'Yeah, fine.'

'The thing is,' Serena slowed. 'There were disclosures you made when you were younger. He did things with you as well as your older siblings.'

'I don't want to talk about this, but I will say, I don't remember any of it,' Matt replied. His face hardened and washed out.

'Well, that's okay but it is something you will need to show you are dealing with or have dealt with. It will also be important for you both to show how you will protect Roddie from him. Does that make sense?'

'Yeah,' Matt replied.

We continued seeing Roddie three times a week in a contact centre. Once the assessment started, this would remain the case. It would then build up. Towards the end we would have time at home if everything went well. I couldn't wait to get to that point.

Matt still had shared very little about what we had found out about his dad. Serena said she needed to speak to him about it again for the purposes of his Statement but that it would keep for now. She seemed to want him to take time to process it all and speak to someone professional about it too. I tried to talk to him about this, but he was reluctant. I sensed that it was the burning monster that Matt wanted locked away.

Roddie was about three months by the time of the assessment. He developed so much, and time whizzed past. We were in the bubble of a racing time machine.

Our lives were within the strict routine and remit of the assessment. We had time with the assessor for a couple of hours before Roddie arrived. Then a couple of hours after our sessions with Roddie. They gave us a diary to make notes in each day and they would look at them weekly and talk to us about anything of concern.

The centre was deceptive set in a street of residential homes. There was a park opposite and locals went about their day to day lives.

Inside was more business-like, the lounge had a letterbox cloth sofa that was worn but clean. The odd spring poked into us if we were perched in the wrong spot. There was no television but a box of toys, a dark wooden oval shaped table and chairs. A small bookcase with children's books, scrap paper and pens stood shyly in one side. The rainbow rug was aglow on the floor.

The assessors, Sue and Jill were great, and we worked well with them. We were able to get through to Matt about some counselling with his childhood issues.

Whilst, he did have a handle on his anger. What had happened that night was long behind us, I got the sense that it came from blocking out his childhood. Matt had learnt strategies to cope with any frustrations. We hoped that some counselling would help him work through what was underneath it all.

Naeed came to see us at the house, she had phoned

ahead.

I did not like her, and I was sure that the feeling was very much mutual. I offered her tea, which she took up and we all sat in the kitchen. 'I'm not quite sure how to say this,' she said.

'Okay,' I replied whilst Matt waited for her to continue.

'I'm afraid, Andi has made a disclosure. She has said that Matt touched her inappropriately when she was in the bath,' Naeed divulged.

'I don't believe it,' I said.

'It's completely twisted,' Matt interjected. His eyes enlarged, his nose flared as his lips tightened. 'What exactly has she said?'

'Yeah, I mean, when was it supposed to have happened and why is it only coming out now?' I added.

'She says that Matt touched her down below and she first came out with it to Cynthia. I have also spoken with her, and she has repeated it again.'

'They have made her say this,' I said knowing that it wasn't possible. 'We will discuss it with Serena. I think it would be best if you leave now.' I said.

'No problem, but I should let you know that the police have been called.'

SERENA

I was finally able to focus on some of my other cases, which I had neglected. I was in the midst of preparing a witness statement for one of my other clients. These usually took at least an hour or so. My fingers tapped away, pausing often to rifle through some of the case papers. The perfect statement could turn a case and do all the work the best cross examination could not undo.

I had some idiosyncrasies that I tried to follow; some might call them superstitions. My statements had to finish either in an even numbered paragraph or a multiple of five. I don't know where this came from or why, but it worked for me.

I had my head in this statement when Janet called with Kelly on the line. I readily took the call; I always took client calls if I was in the office and not in a client appointment. Clients were my bread and butter. Kelly was panic stricken, 'Serena, they are saying that Matt's sexually abused Andi now. How is that going to affect things?' she asked.

'Slow down, slow down, Kelly. Start again from the beginning and let me grab some paper and a pen. Okay, what has happened?'

'Naeed has been here, and she reckons that Andi has said something about Matt touching her.'

I let out an alarmed sigh and hoped that Kelly hadn't caught it. 'Do you know who Andi has said this to and when?' I asked.

'Andi told her nan first, but she has repeated it to Naeed.'

'Kelly, I'm going to have to make a few phone calls and get to the bottom of this. Once we know exactly what we are dealing with, I can discuss things in more detail with you and Matt. Does that sound okay?' I had now got a handle on my instinctive emotions and was in business mode.

'Yeah, okay.'

I was already sitting but needed to sit down. I couldn't quite digest what Kelly had told me and needed some time to process it.

It was unnerving because sexual abuse of any child was unforgivable. To conspire with someone responsible for that is unthinkable. I had a job to do, and I would do it. It was not for me to judge but to make sure that my clients had the best representation I could give them. It would be for the Judge to test everything and make a judgment, mine was to present my clients' case. I can only do that if I have all the information and worked through the list of emails that needed to go out.

I needed to let off steam whilst waiting for the replies, so I joined Tara in the reception area with Janet. I updated them about what Kelly had told me and they were as aghast as I had been.

'They are being stitched up,' Janet immediately and instinctively exclaimed.

'But are they, or could there be something in it?' I pondered out loud.

'Yeah, but why has it only come out now when this has been going on for months now,' Janet reasoned.

'Maybe, that little girl has only now felt comfortable,' Tara interjected.

'Exactly, I mean a child of her age can't be making something like this up, can she?' I continued.

'I can't believe that poor man would do something like that,' Janet empathised. I heard some doubt creeping in there. 'I mean they do say there's no smoke without fire.'

'It's a tricky one. We still don't know for certain what has happened,' I said. I struggled to articulate the confusing thoughts spiralling around in my head.

Janet made us all tea and we each returned to our work.

Sam, the Local Authority Solicitor emailed through, 'We are still gathering the information. Andi has disclosed to her grandmother that Mr Barnett got into baths with her. This was further expanded on in an initial discussion with the Social Work team. Andi alleged that Mr Barnett touched her genital area and forced her to touch him in his intimate parts. The Assessment is now on hold. Contact with Rodrigo will remain supervised in the contact centre.'

I fell back into my chair, completely winded. It felt so cold in black and white. The words jarred and sneered out at me. I needed some time away from all this. I knew I had to get back to Kelly and Matt so couldn't go too far.

I grabbed my keys, strode out of the office, and jumped into my car. Sometimes I needed to drive. I had the radio on full blast. I drove and drove and drove. The tension in my body made me press hard on the accelerator and with time eased from my head.

I focused on the greenness as I took the scenic country route. I breathed in the leathers and rode the music of the airwaves. An hour later, calmer, and ready to fight again. I tapped my office address into my phone to direct me back – google maps was one of the best creations of all time.

I had a clarity of mind that had been severely lacking a couple of hours earlier. My thoughts were more lucid, and I got straight onto the phone to Kelly to explain what I had learnt so far. I read out the email exactly as it was.

'Oh my God! That's disgusting,' Kelly replied.

'I will need to take yours and Matt's instructions. We can work out the best way to proceed,' I replied. I had a composure that had been entirely absent only a little while earlier.

'It's not true, Serena, it can't be true,' Kelly said in disbelief.

I wasn't sure whether she was trying to convince me, herself or the both of us.

'Well, one step at a time. I will get proper notes of discussions that have taken place with Andi. Then we can go through all that together.

'Naeed said something about the police being involved too,' Kelly filled in.

'I guess that's inevitable, and we will find out a lot more through the police anyway.'

'I suppose so.'

'Kelly, don't say anything to the police until I get there.'

'Mmm, okay.' Kelly replied distantly.

'Kelly, you need to listen to me,' I urged. 'Do you hear me? Do not say anything to the police until I am there, nothing at all, do you understand?' I directed.

'Yup, Yeah, I get it, Serena,' Kelly replied seeming to return from wherever her mind had trailed off to.

'That's both of you. Keep schtum until I am with

you. Okay, well let's keep in touch,' I said as we ended the call.

This was becoming difficult now if it wasn't already.

Chapter Seven

KELLY

I relayed what Serena had told me to Matt and we went over it between us. Matt was adamant that he had not done anything to Andi. Before Matt, it had been just Andi and me.

There had been hard times until Andi's dad finally decided to show himself in our lives. My life revolved around Andi that I didn't have time for anything else. I had no time to dress most days leave alone have time for dating.

There was a part of me that worried that no one would be able to treat Andi as their own. I did not want a man coming into our lives that might mistreat Andi. I wanted Andi to know and feel number one and in my world she always was.

When my dad first introduced Matt to me, I was very sceptical of him. I humoured him as my dad's work colleague and mate. The first time we met, dad had brought him home to lend him some tools. 'Matt, here, is staying for dinner with us tonight,' dad said.

'Okay, that's cool. Hiya!'
'Hey!'
'You and dad work together then?'
'Yup.'
'I'll go and get an extra plate and serve up.'
Matt was quiet, thoughtful, and hungry!

Matt was in blue oil-stained jeans, black t-shirt and checked shirt. He had dark, heavy workman boots on his feet and a baseball cap on his head. Scuffs and mud gripped the corners of his boots.

Matt tapped the crown of his cap. He lowered his face, using the peak to shield himself and peered from underneath.

He was more at ease with Andi, talking animatedly to her about fairies and angels. He came alive, his eyes glistened and a crow's nest of smile lines around them. Andi was in her element, her whole face shone.

Matt chatted effortlessly with my dad. They exchanged factory stories and their gripes with the bosses. I was the odd one out.

Matt became a bit of a regular visitor to the house and conversation became easier between us. I became attracted to him but did not want to introduce a man into Andi's life until he was a stayer. The problem was that she had already become attached to him. Matt finally plucked up the courage to ask me out on a proper date and I agreed.

He took me for a drink at a nice little pub. I found out that he had spoken with my dad about it, which I thought was sweet and made me fall that bit more for him.

Matt paid for all our drinks that night, not that he was much of a drinker, but he would not let me pay for anything. I felt like he wanted to take care of me, and I wanted, maybe even needed, to be taken care of.

I told Matt about my somewhat rebellious younger days until Andi came along. 'I was wild, before Andi!'

Really, how so?'

'Yeah, for sure. You know, out late, drinking, out late and more drinking,' I laughed.

'Mmm... I suppose that is normal for all teenagers.'

'I drove my dad crazy with worry. Gave him attitude all the time.'

'I can't see it.'

'Well, that's because that is not me anymore, not since Andi.'

'I like you now.' Matt looked away.

He was easy to talk to and made me feel safe. I opened up in a way that I couldn't remember I ever had before.

I told him about Andi's dad, John and how we got caught up in this very young and crazy love. 'He was my first boyfriend and I believed him when he said that he loved me. I believed him when he said that sleeping together would make our love stronger. I believed him that having sex with each other showed our love for each other. I believed him that I wouldn't get pregnant the first time. I believed him.'

'That's okay.'

'No, you don't get it. I believed it all, but it wasn't true... I learnt in the cruellest of ways that he didn't love me. I learnt that our love was a lie when he dropped me straight after we slept together. I learnt that having sex was having sex. I learnt that you could get pregnant even after the first time. I learnt that I could not believe him.'

Our relationship went from strength to strength after that. I moved out of dad's a year into our relationship. Matt helped us move and I remained near to my dad. My dad had been with me through thick and thin. I wanted to make sure that Andi and my dad would continue the incredible bond that they shared.

Matt only moved in with us when I knew that he was a stable fixture. He had spent more and more time at the house anyway that it made sense for him to move in. We felt like family and when Matt wasn't around, it felt wrong. There seemed to be a jigsaw piece missing and Andi felt it too. There were times when Andi would cry out for Matt and of course, Matt wouldn't be there.

What finally convinced me was when he spent hours fixing the toilet, with his hands in the grime of it. I had mentioned it in passing to him when he came over one time, because I asked him to use the upstairs toilet instead. I had told him that I was going to call a handyman to have a look at it. Before I had had a chance, the next time, Matt came over, he arrived with tools in tow. He then took it upon himself to get to playing with the toilet without any prompting from me.

It was funny because there were so many times that he seemed to be getting nowhere fast. To make matters worse, he kept banging his head against the little wall cabinet. He kept on going and hours later, the toilet was fixed right as new. I knew, right there and then, that he was the man for us.

Jolted out of my reverie, my dad, who was visiting, broke my reminiscing, 'What's going on love? Matt?'

I was queasy and light-headed. My arms were cold and my mouth dry. I was not sure how to have this conversation. It was in this moment that I wished I had the power of invisibility.

I explained what Naeed and Serena had told us. My dad was shell shocked and lost for words for a minute or two. 'Where has all this come from,' my dad finally questioned, looking first at me, then at Matt and back at me.

'We don't know, dad.'

My dad tentatively asked, 'I mean, Matt, it's not true right?'

MATTHEW
'I'm sorry, Kel, I need to get some air,' I stuttered as I rushed out, disappointment flashed across Kel's face.

I had to get away. Everything mounted and I wanted out. This was where it was always going to wind up. I knew this was their endgame and it had finally come. It would be my word against Andi's. I couldn't put her through that, but I couldn't have my family torn apart the way it was. I marched into town and found myself at my parents' home.

When my mum let me in, I pushed straight past her and into their living room, 'How could you do this to me?' I raged at my dad.

'Son, we haven't done anything.' My mum had followed very quickly behind me, tried to soothe and pulled me back. I was in my dad's face and he didn't even flinch.

'You did this, you!'

'What's happened, Matt?' My mum had me by the

shoulders.

'I hate you!' I screamed.

'You need to calm down lad,' my dad said without missing a step and looked straight through me.

'You are sick. What have you done to me?'

'I'm going to sit right here. Let me know if you want to talk,' my dad said evenly.

'I'm going to kill you,' I shouted and lunged at him. My mum got between us and suffocated me in her arms.

'I hate him, I hate him, I hate him.'

'Shhhh... I've got you, Matty. Tell me what has happened,' my mum tried to coax out of me as she rocked me in her arms.

'You're as bad as he is,' I snapped back and pulled away from her grip.

'You can say what you need to if it helps,' my mum responded.

'They think I'm the same as him,' I gasped through sobs.

I pointed angrily at my dad, as I broke down right there and then. My mum hugged me as I shook in tears. I hated myself and what I had done to my family. I struggled to be free of my mum, but she held on as we tussled together.

'Sorry, Matt,' my dad mumbled. He patted me on my right shoulder before he walked calmly out of the room.

I pushed my mum away and stormed out of the house. A dam had been broken and there was nothing I could do to quell the rapids inside me. I couldn't head back home in that state.

I pounded the streets, leaving embers of my fire behind me with every step. With every stride, I felt the blustery wind smacking me harder and sharper around the face. I pushed on, battling away at the cold harshness of nature, and ended up at Serena's office. I didn't have an appointment, but I also had nowhere else I could go.

Janet, the receptionist told me that she didn't know whether Serena could see me but that she would do her best. Serena did see me, and she told me what she had already told Kel.

Andi had told her paternal grandmother that I'd touched her. It was in her genitalia area whilst bathing her. Paternal grandmother reported it to Social Services the day after disclosure. Supposedly, this was then repeated when the Social Worker saw Andi at the house. It has been reported to the police and there would now be a joint investigation.

'What am I meant to do?'

'Look, we will fight this,' Serena tried to assure me.

'Everyone will always think I did something,' I squeezed out.

'Well, it's up to you to prove that you didn't.'

'They say, you're innocent until proven guilty. The truth is that society works in the opposite way, you are guilty until you can prove your innocence.'

'We have to wait to see the proper disclosure and Local Authority statements.'

'None of that matters. I am guilty in the eyes of everyone that matters, Kel's family, my family and Kel and the law will see it the same way.'

'You can't give up, you have to push on.'

'Are you telling me that I'm wrong? That somehow justice is pure and simple? That justice is fair and righteous? That injustice doesn't have a place in justice?'

Serena couldn't answer me that one but instead instructed me to head home to talk things through with Kel. She said to leave all the legal wrangling to her, but I wasn't sure how. As I left Serena's office that day, I wondered, why she had never asked me if any of it were true.

I had no choice but to return home. There was nowhere else I could sleep unless I wanted to take up one of the fancy new metal benches they had put up. In the freezing cold temperatures with the wind still howling, that was a non-starter.

As I walked in, Kel threw a hundred and one questions and statements at me. I put my hands up in the air and asked for some space.

'We need to work out what we are saying,' Kel insisted.

'I'm going up to shower.'

'Yeah, but we need to make sure that we are saying the same thing,' Kel explained.

'Later, Kel.'

'This is important.'

'What do you want from me?' I yelled.

I regretted it almost immediately, as I saw the fear whizz by Kel's almond eyes. 'I need to shower.'

'You never bathed Andi, so that is what we will say,' Kel persisted. She said it as if it wasn't quite the truth or there was something else on her mind. It left me uneasy. I couldn't make sense of it but was too exhausted to think too much about it.

The police came to the house and told me that they needed to speak to me about Andi's allegations. They took Serena's details and agreed to arrange with her the best time for me to go in for an interview.

Kelly told me that they had already spoken with her, and she had stuck to what we had said, I never bathed Andi. Andi had also said that I had jumped into the bath with her, which was not true. The lies worsened.

A few days later, I met Serena at the police station. I was more scared this time than the last time I was here. The last time, I knew I had done wrong and deserved punishment. I had come to the police station voluntarily. This time was very different, and it felt it. The cold harshness of the police station hit me full in the face much more than before.

Serena was as poised as always. That should have made me more comfortable, but I couldn't shake the fear. This was the most heinous of crimes. I couldn't even be in my own skin with these allegations. I was damaged, angry, and shell shocked all at the same time.

I waited in the interview room, whilst Serena got the details of the evidence. The walls were murky and pressed into me. As it turned out there was nothing new in the evidence.

The police officer was thick set and older than the one that dealt with me for the assault matter. His paunch hung a little over his black trousers as he sat down and turned the tape on.

'Your partner's daughter, Andi has said you touched her private parts. Have you ever touched her private parts?' PC Smith asked.

'No, never.'

'Maybe accidentally?'

'No,' I replied resolutely.

'Let's take this one step at a time. Andi says that you bathed her on occasions. Is that true?'

'No.'

During the interview, we went through the relationship with Kel. I went through the routines for Andi. I confirmed that Kel was responsible for most things round the house. She was in charge in relation to Andi. Before we started living together, I hardly did anything for Andi.

This changed only a little when we all began sharing a home together. I wanted to help Kel with Andi as well as around the house. I wanted to pull my weight. I hoovered and put the bins out. I played with Andi and got her breakfast in the morning, but Kel tended to her bathing routines.

I didn't say this to the police or Serena, but I was always worried about getting accused of something like this.

'Are you sure there wasn't an occasion when Kelly was busy with something else. Maybe you helped with bath time routines?' PC Smith questioned.

'No, that never happened.'

'Maybe she had a toileting accident and you had to clean her up?'

'No.'

'She is saying that you rubbed her in the front and touched her in the back as well?'

'No,' my voice, louder.

'Matt, are you saying that Andi is lying?'

'Not deliberately but what I know is that I didn't do the things you are saying she has said,' I said.

'Matt let's get straight here. If what Andi is saying is not true, why do you think she is saying it?'

'I think that someone has got into her head and put these thoughts there.'

SERENA

The police did not charge Matt but put him on bail to return to the police station a couple of months later. This case took its toll on me. I was desperate to get to the truth. I wanted justice for my clients but that might mean their life as a family was obliterated.

'So, we will need to meet to go through everything in more detail.'

'Sure.'

'I will need to see you both.'

'Yeah, okay. But I'm free to go, right?'

'Yes, but this is not the end. You understand that don't you?'

'Yeah, yeah. I know.'

I worried about there being any truth to the allegation. Sexual abuse of a child was unconscionable. I always said that it was not my job to judge. I was there to represent my client and the judge was there to judge the case. I was, however, a truth seeker as well as my client's truth speaker. All that being said, I could not deny my own value system. Any form of child abuse went against everything I was.

It was a Friday evening, and I was cosily wrapped up on the sofa in front of my sparkling fire. The dancing, raging autumn flames roared at me. I smothered the hissing fire out before snatching my keys.

I hurried to my car as the rain pelted against my back. I turned the engine on and blasted up the heat as I headed off for my volunteering counselling shift.

I had volunteered for about five years and loved that feeling of helping a child or young person. Tonight, I got a call from a young girl disclosing sexual abuse by her stepfather. I felt the pain of her anguish. My mind's eye had to blank out the reality of the horror. I tapped away into the computer, the notes of the interaction, as it happened, to ground myself. My fingers moved purposefully.

I held onto the headset to listen as intently as I could so as not to miss a sound. She was fourteen and at times she struggled to breathe through her tears. I was the first person she had disclosed to, and she was scared her mum would not believe her. The self-hate and loathing were palpable. I listened, let her know I believed her, and she had not done anything wrong, that the abuser was at fault.

It was both heart breaking and uplifting. This young girl took her first tentative steps towards change. The undercurrent of her intense spirit interwoven with despair. That I could be there for her, empowered her to share her truth in the most precious way was humbling. It seemed so perverse but doing these shifts was the best start to weekends. Witnessing that the indomitable human spirit can battle and succeed against most anything.

The following Monday was a fresh week, and the disclosure came through thick and fast. My head felt hot and full. I was irritable and even my skin was scratchy.

I typed furiously into my laptop, 'Please send all the records about this disclosure. We need them from the paternal grandmother, social worker, and the police.' I later reflected how instinctively I positioned myself into disbelieving this allegation. This was so far removed from how I responded as a volunteer counsellor. The irony.

My mind whirred like crazy, plotting how to play this. I would not allow these parents to be sabotaged by scared family members that did not want to lose what they now had. At the same time, could I allow children to be placed in the care of an abuser?

The office arranged for the parents to come in to see me. I saw each of them separately this time before seeing them together. I saw Matthew first.

I finally asked him outright, 'Matt, I must ask you this, but have you ever touched Andi on or around her private parts?' I was more interested in the reaction to the question rather than the answer itself. It's what we lawyers did. We watched out for any giveaway signs in body language, tone, silences than the words themselves. We became pros at reading between the lines and it was those skills I tuned into then.

'No, never, I swear,' he replied decisively.

'Is there any possibility that you may have touched her by accident?'

'No, never. I don't know where this has come from. I'm gutted'

'Okay, fine.' I remained unsure.

There was a certainty in Matt's tone and no momentary pause of hesitation, but he had not been able to look me in the eye. Matt's left foot tapped quietly into the wooden flooring like a nervous twitch. It left me like a twisted ball of knots.

I took further instructions from Matthew about bathing Andi before he moved in. Matt confirmed that he only gave Andi a bath a couple of times as he preferred to leave this to Kel. He always left the bathroom door open and would sit by Andi instructing her to wash herself. If she struggled, he would call Kelly for help and then leave them to it. Matt accepted that this was different from what we had presented to the police. This was a problem. We discussed this at length.

Once Matthew had moved in, Andi was more independent. He would sit by the bathroom door whilst she bathed. Again, this only happened a handful of times. There may have been a couple of occasions when he helped Andi dry off. He was adamant and consistent. He had also been adamant and consistent in his police station interview. He can't have told the truth both times.

Kelly was next up, whilst Matthew waited outside. Kelly confirmed everything that Matt had said. I mean she didn't remember the times when they had not been living as a family. It all seemed to merge as one period for her. 'Kelly, it's okay if you have doubts and are worried that what Andi is saying is true,' I enticed.

'No, I know Matt. He would never do that, and I've always been around, if anything like that had happened, I would know about it.'

'Yes, but by your own admission, there were times when Matt was alone with Andi in the bathroom,' I tested.

'No, it's not possible,' Kelly shook her head. Her hands clasped together, 'I don't even believe that Andi has said it. They are putting things into her head.'

'She is your daughter. Perhaps you should take the position that you believe her. Otherwise, you are putting your relationship above your own daughter,' I suggested.

'No, I am putting my daughter first because she doesn't know better, and I have to stand up for her. It's not her fault that they are messing with her head like this. I'm her mum and will be there for her.'

'Perfect,' I replied. I was impressed and knew if she performed like this in the witness box, we had a fighting chance.

I spoke to both Matthew and Kelly together. I recommended that they have separate representation. They were both determined to continue instructing me together.

Both Kelly and Matthew understood what I was getting at and Matthew waivered. He encouraged Kelly to seek her own separate lawyer. 'We are going to show everyone. It's like you have always said, Matt, we can do this; we need to prove it to them all. Serena, you tell us what we need to do next,' and with that, we talked strategy for the rest of the meeting.

I had to admire Kelly's steeliness and Matthew's perseverance. Together they made a great team, I hoped a winning team! What though was a winning team?

NAEED

I always had a sense that this case would unravel to become something much more alarming than what we were seeing. This was my deepest fear. I knew there was something dark underneath it all. I could never put my finger on it before, there was no evidence of anything damaging as there was now. Here it was, Matt had sexually abused Andi. We surely had him now.

When I got the call from Cynthia, I knew what she was going to say before she even uttered a word. She told me that Andi had disclosed to her at bedtime last night that Matt would jump into the bath when she was in there. Matt would then get out of the bath and Kelly would then get in.

'It started when we were out shopping. I was with Andi, and we were going around the aisles with the trolley. I had put some sanitary towels in the shopping trolley. Andi shouted out that you put them in your pants,' Cynthia explained.

'What do you mean?' I asked.

'Well, at the time I didn't think much of it. Andi was more worried that I was mad at her. I wasn't, I was taken aback that she knew about sanitary towels.'

'Right.'

'But then later that night, she said about the bath thing. Now I am thinking that she was exposed to a lot more than she should have been when she was with Kelly and Matt. I mean it can't be right that he would get in the bath with her, can it?' Cynthia asked concerned.

'We will need to look into it a lot more,' I reassured.

'Yes, yes, I understand that and there was that time when she first came to us when she was kissing boys in her class. You remember?'

'I do, Cynthia. Leave it with me, I will need to come out to see Andi but will have to come back to you about when.' We agreed to keep in touch and Cynthia would keep a diary of any further disclosures.

There had been warning signs before but nothing definitive. I knew that we still didn't have enough. The problem was that Andi was only four when all this happened, and she hadn't lived with Matt and Kelly for a while now. It might be very difficult for her to remember all the details to the extent that I knew a court would need.

I discussed matters with my Team Manager, Lisa and explained the latest development. Lisa was easy to approach and always took quite a collaborative approach. She asked my view on how we should manage the situation.

We talked it through so that we could weigh up the issue and come to an agreed conclusion. It always felt like a joint effort. Even when I initially disagreed with the final decision, I could see that it was the right one by the end. Lisa was able to take me with her and I could see for myself why we did things the way we did.

'Andi has told granny that Matt used to get in the bath with her,' I summarised.

'Right, well you need to find out more. It could be very innocent.'

'I doubt it, I mean, remember her sexualised behaviour when she first moved.'

'Yes, but we should keep an open mind. Take the family support worker with you. We must be very, very careful with how we manage this.'

'Of course.'

'We cannot make one false move, with this one. This could be a detonator, but it could also be nothing at all.'

'I'll set it up and let you know how it goes.'

I felt for Andi, she had tried to tell us for a while now and we had dismissed her. I refused to let her down. I arranged to see her with the family support worker that had worked with Andi for the last six months, Rita. After making all the arrangements, I made sure that I left work on time and was home by half past five.

Alya was in the living room, on our rug watching cartoons on the television. She was approaching the age that Andi would have been when Matt first came into her life. I curled myself around Alya on the rug and kept her safe.

Rahul, Alya's Dad and I had separated when she was only a year old. I had hounded him into maintaining some contact with her. He saw her one night every other weekend and even that had been a strain. Rahul had met someone else and, Alya and I did not fit with his other life.

We had had an arranged marriage. He never stopped his relationship with his girlfriend, Kate. Even as we prepared for marriage. The marriage itself made no difference either. They had a little boy, Charlie, a few months younger than my Alya. I did everything I could to make sure that Rahul and Kate treated Alya and Charlie the same when they had Alya.

I always worried what his girlfriend would be like with Alya. My listening skills were always in overdrive whenever Alya mentioned Kate. Luckily, Alya seemed to get on well with Kate and Charlie but that did not curb my paranoia.

Rita and I drove separately to the McDowell's house. I got there a few minutes before Rita pulled up and I waited until she arrived. We approached the house and Cynthia let us in. It was not the same warm welcome I had had the very first time, apprehension filled the room. Andi drew pictures at the coffee table. Cynthia slipped out of the room whilst Rita and I made ourselves comfortable.

Rita and I were seated on the sofa and glanced at each other, unsure of quite how to start. I decided to take the lead and so crouched down next to Andi. Andi was oblivious and scribbled her masterpiece away. I gently asked about the drawing. Andi pointed out her gran, granddad, and dad in the kaleidoscope of squiggles and lines.

I then asked Andi about baths and whether she had already had one today. She said she hadn't bathed yet and then told us about how much water she usually has in the bath. Andi showed us with her hands that the water was often up to her chest area and sometimes up to her neck.

At times, Andi seemed shy and reticent to talk to us but at other times she was bold and lively.

'I have something upstairs for you,' Andi squealed and bounced up the stairs.

I followed her and we went to her bedroom.

I had been in Andi's room a few times before. It was very much a girly girl room, with pink wallpaper and a princess bed. It was quite small but plenty of space for her toys and a little play area in one corner. There was a fresh, cotton candy flavour smell in the room. The carpet underfoot was soft and melted to the touch.

Andi showed me a teddy bear that she said her dad had bought for her. He was brown with blue eyes, one of his ears had been chewed a little. I used this in role play about bathing and Andi showed me how Matt bathed her using the teddy bear. She gestured that Matt scrubbed her face.

'Can you tell me what happened when Matt was in the bath with you, Andi?' I asked.

Andi looked down and said, 'he scrubbed me.'

'Where did he scrub you, sweetie?'

Andi didn't say anything but instead pointed to her genital area. She still looked down and avoided any eye contact with me. Andi went onto say 'I scrubbed him' and pointed to my private area at the front and back.

Chapter Eight

MATTHEW

We were back in court again to agree how to deal with Andi's disclosure. I kept my head down, because each time I glanced up or around me, I felt the burning eyes shooting arrows in my direction.

I saw Naeed march up the stairs and into the waiting area. She was stony faced and kept her eyes focused straight ahead. There wasn't even the cursory pretence of politeness towards us. I tilted my head down instinctively. The heel of my foot tapped away to an unheard rhythm, and I pressed down on my knee in a full stop.

Serena talked to us about some fact finding hearing or other. She went off to grab a coffee from the vending machine downstairs.

I'm not sure I understood everything. My mind was foggy with the accusations on a repeating film reel. All around me were whispers and pointing.

Naeed's lawyer had arrived and breezed right past us without a second glance. They colluded and occasionally Naeed nodded in our direction. They disappeared off into a separate room together.

'It's cold in here, isn't it?' Kel asked.

'Is it?'

'I, think so... Have you seen the Guardian or even her solicitor?'

My foot was at it again, I wasn't sure how long it had gone on for before I squeezed on my knee to squash down on it.

Kel and I were seated in the hard, unmoving, screwed down chairs. I knew it was a court and all but apparently securing their worldly goods was top of their priorities. Kel placed her hand on my juddering knee that I only then realised had been knocking up and down. I wanted this to all be over.

The justice system though didn't quite see it my way. It rolled much more slowly. The court wasn't going to decide whether I did it or not that day. The court put matters off for another day so that everyone could gather their evidence. The only people that knew anything were Andi, Kelly, and I but somehow it wasn't going to quite work like that. Serena said that Andi was too young to give evidence.

This seemed grossly unfair to me because how was I or the court to know what she said if we didn't hear it from her. Andi's nan, social worker, lawyers would tell us Andi's story; none of whom had ever even been there. I didn't want to put her through it but wanted to know if she had genuinely said these things.

'It will be both of you, the Social Worker, grandmother, and the guardian. Actually, I doubt the guardian will give evidence. The guardian is only looking after Rodrigo so she won't be speaking to Andi about any of this.' Serena explained.

'Right, so the guardian won't be giving any evidence on this issue?' Kelly clarified.

'That's right but she will be there to listen to all the

evidence and the court's findings. That will impact her analysis of what should happen long term for Rodrigo and Amelia.'

'It's all so wrong,' I said in a daze.

Our contact remained supervised with Roddie at the centre twice a week. We made the best of things. Serena said to leave the case to her and to concentrate on making the most of our time together. He was growing so fast and loved playing on the floor with the cars they had. He was playful and cheeky. He was settling into a personality of his own.

It felt cold in the centre. It was an unnatural environment. They tried to make it homelike by having a little kitchenette as well as a living area. The kitchenette was in a separate room that looked into the living area with a hole in the wall. The lounge area had a sofa, comfy chairs, beanbags, and a dining table with chairs.

There were all sorts of different toys in storage boxes around the room organised in age groups. There was also a garden with goalposts in the lawn and a basketball hoop. Roddie was too young for football or basketball. It would be good to play ball with him in the summer if we still came here, which I hoped we wouldn't be. Despite all this, it still felt alien to real life.

The good thing was that we got on well with the contact supervisors. Generally, it was the same woman that supervised our contact, a young plump girl called Mel. She was great with us and tried to keep in the background as much as she could. Occasionally we would have someone different, but they were all good with us.

The parenting assessment was on hold. The court wanted the findings about Andi's allegations factored into that assessment.

I never wanted to speak to that Naeed again. It was obvious that she hated me. Naeed believed that I was a paedophile long before Andi made this alleged disclosure.

Serena sent us the statements of Andi's disclosure. My insides were topsy turvy; my internal organs had had an almighty combustion. I went to my safe place, which was withdrawing into myself. I went off for days at a time on my own, I didn't have anywhere else I could sleep and so would come home late at night. I spent the daytime hours in various local pubs to keep warm and have time to myself. I didn't drink very much but wanted to be alone. I didn't mean to push Kel away, but it was how I coped.

I pulled away from everything. I wasn't seeing or speaking to my parents, brothers and sisters. I wasn't going for footie anymore I wasn't doing much of anything. I couldn't bear even looking at myself let alone anyone else.

'Matt, please talk to me,' Kel urged.

'We should go shopping soon for some new outfits for Roddie,' I replied.

'We are still a team, I'm here for you,' Kel persisted.

'Kel, let's work out when we can go shopping. What do you think about tomorrow?'

'Yeah, sure.'

These kinds of conversations went on between Kel

and I a few times. Eventually, Kel tired of it and gave up. We played happy families and got on with our day-to-day routines. I cycled in the mornings for about ten miles, which took about an hour and helped me release all my pent-up emotion.

In the evenings, I spent some time reading over the documents Serena had sent us through. Often times, as well as reading over anything new that had been sent through, I read back over all the other stuff too. I pored over every word, line, and statement. I don't know what I hoped to find but it became some sort of comfort blanket for me.

KELLY

Matt pulled away from me and I didn't know how to reach him. I had tried to talk to him a few times, but he had shut me down. It hurt that he couldn't turn to me. I stopped asking him after a while. I felt completely alone. I was scared. I was angry. I was sad. I was alone.

We carried on as normal as we could. There was a distance that had crept between Matt and me, that made everything less than normal. Serena kept us up to date with the documents that came through. I wanted to look through them with Matt. This was the battle of our lives and we fell apart. I alone rowed a two-person boat with an invisible peephole.

Whatever was going on for Matt, I needed him. We needed him. On the days that Matt disappeared off on his own, it was hard in the beginning.

After a while I had a new routine for those days. I

walked to my favourite café. I took a short cut through a nearby park. At that time of year, the trees that lined the paths were naked with their bare branches reaching out. The lake was still and clear. The bridge over the lake stood strong and majestic. The stroll gave me time to breathe and appreciate everything around me.

I had made friends with a woman I met at the café, Sanita. She had come a few times before we got chatting, well before she got chatting to me. Sanita was an older woman, in her fifties, I'd say and a retired teacher. She had a warm face, came over to my table and said 'You look like you have the whole world on your shoulders, dear. You are far too young to be so weighed down.'

'I'm okay,' I laughed back.

'Do you mind if I sit for a moment? It can be lonely at times sat over there on my tod.'

'Of course,' I replied.

'It seems like you could do with a friend too,' Sanita replied.

There was something about Sanita that made me share with her what had happened. I didn't tell her all the ins and outs, but I told her about Andi, Roddie and Matt. I told her about the recent allegation and Matt disappearing from me. Sanita listened without judgment and let me get it all out there.

Sanita made me realise that I needed to talk to Matt and force the issue on him. I remembered things that might have made us look like we had hidden something before. I needed to make sure that Matt and I were on the same page. I needed to make sure.

I hated any confrontation and that had put me off when I had tried before. I backed off when Matt locked me down. Sanita made me see that an honest argument can clear out all the cobwebs. We had to be candid with each other if we were going to get through this as a team, as a family. Though, for now, I was still putting it off.

'Have you two had it out with each other, then?'

'Erm... no, not really,' I said.

'How come? I thought when we last met, you had said you were going to sort this out once and for all.'

'It's difficult.'

'It's not going to get any easier as time goes on.'

'I suppose.'

'I mean, how are you ever meant to know whether he hurt your daughter unless you ask him. Every child is innocent and pure. It is the adults around them that either make or break them. Are you making or breaking your daughter?' Sanita asked.

It had become a regular thing that on the days Matt vanished, I'd meet Sanita at the café. It was so good to be able to talk to someone.

Sanita had been married for thirty years to her childhood sweetheart. He had died after a short bout of cancer a few months ago. Sanita had retired when her husband became ill. She had spent all her time caring for him so there had developed a real void when he passed away. They had a daughter, but she had died in a car accident a few years back. Sanita had suffered a lot but was still cheerful.

I still maintained contact with Andi. It was in a contact centre once a fortnight for a couple of hours.

Matt didn't come to those contacts, but I was able to have Roddie there too so that they were both able to see each other.

I juggled between the two children. For instance, I played on the floor with both children but then Roddie would need a feed. If I fed Roddie, I could see Andi visibly become frustrated but trying to contain herself. Sometimes she managed it but other times, she threw things around. I tried to remain calm but firm.

There were times that I couldn't manage the calmness. My head full, my body battered, my neck tensed, cheeks flushed. In those times, I tasted the bitterness of my harsh words before they even left my lips. Fortunately, my harshness was always in the tone and delivery rather than the words or volume. The contact supervisors seemed to understand.

Andi played nicely with Roddie, and I joined in. Most of the time, Andi was able to play on her own if I needed to tend to Roddie's nappy change, a feed or something else. Andi was such a good big sister to her little brother, she revelled in it and took pride of role in it.

There was a time that this would have been almost perfect but now the allegation hung over us, I felt more on edge. I shoved it with all my might to the side and focused on enjoying these precious times together as a family.

Andi and I didn't often have time just the two of us. In this session, Roddie tired himself out scuttling around and needed a little nap. For a change, Andi and I had some one-to-one time. 'You're growing so much, beautiful girl,' I praised.

'Mummy, I miss you. I miss Matty. Can't I come home now?'

MATHEW

Some weeks passed and I decided to go over and see Tommo. I rode my bike over like usual but this time, I knocked on the door rather than bounding straight in.

My mum answered the door and went to hug me, but I brushed straight past her and took the stairs two at a time to Tommo's room. We exchanged grunts at each other by way of greeting and I sat in the armchair next to Tommo's bed. Tommo was on his bed playing a game on the PlayStation. I took the other controls and joined in.

'What's going on with the case, then?' Tommo asked.

'Rubbish, actually,' I replied.

'I thought you'd won the appeal or something.'

'Yeah, but now Andi is saying I touched her, you know..., down there.'

'Oh shit!'

'They think I'm the same as that sick bastard,' I raged.

'Which sick bastard?'

'Ah shit,' I mumbled. 'I meant that they think I'm a peado, you know, that I'm a sick bastard like the peados out there.'

'Ah, right. Well, you gotta show them that you ain't.' Tommo said very matter of factly.

'You don't want to know if I, did it?'

'I know you, Matt, I know you didn't do anything to that kid.'

'I don't know that Kel thinks like that.'

'Nah, Kel knows you too. You need to talk to her, you have talked to her, right?'

We chilled together for a couple of hours side by side, gaming and talking. It was good to spend time with Tommo and feel like I had someone on my side. He was right, I needed to speak to Kel. I needed to know she was on my side and not have any doubts about that. I went back down ready to head home and mum called out to me from the kitchen.

'I've got to get going,' I said and backed away.

'Wait, Matt, please.'

'What is it, mum?' I asked. It was sharper than I had intended and could see the pain flicker across my mum's face.

'I just wanted to see how you were getting on.'

'Not great to be honest, mum. I don't think I will be able to see you and especially not Dad for a while.'

'I understand and I am sorry. I love you, Matt.'

'I've got to go, see you mum,' I replied and rushed out.

I had struggled to sleep since this whole Andi thing blew up but after seeing Tommy, I had the best night's sleep. It was still disturbed but better than it had been. I woke up with a renewed spirit. I needed to clear things up with Kel and would try and do that today.

The post was delivered after breakfast and the other social worker's notes came through. That hit me in the stomach. She wasn't saying anything new and pretty much repeated everything that that Naeed had said. It threw me off kilter again.

All the good intentions I had woken up with seemed to float out of me. Kel's dad had come over. He had become a frequent visitor anyway but a little more so now because of everything that was going on. To support Kel, probably, as I had been missing in action.

Kel's dad and I were genial with each other, and I had a lot of respect for him. He had worked hard for his family and had taken care of Kel and her sisters on his own. Even now, he still took care of Kel.

'Matt, I know that things are tough on you right now, but you need to work with Kel to get through it,' Kevin said to me.

'Erm…, yeah, I know,' I said. I was a little shocked because Kev usually stayed out of everything.

'No, I don't think you do. You can't leave Kel to deal with this on her own. She needs you.'

'Yeah.'

'If you can't step up, then step out,' Kev said.

'No, no. I am there, all in.'

'Well start showing it.' With that, Kevin put the television on and talked to me about whatever it was that was on at the time.

Kevin stayed for a while when he visited and often had a meal with us. After a while, Kevin said he wanted to get the newspaper. He was a fan of crosswords and often spent time working through them.

Kel, as always, tried to get me to communicate with her about how I felt but I was still not ready. We repeated the same pattern as all the other times but this time, Kel seemed different. I couldn't quite put my finger on it because she hadn't said anything, but it felt different. Kel prepared lunch and I tidied up but heard Kel screech out. I ran to her, and she was running her bleeding finger under the tap.

'What's happened?' I asked alarmed and went to Kel to help her.

Kel pushed me away, 'Stop pretending you care,' she replied.

I stepped back, taken aback, and stinging from the rebuff. I retreated into the living room and after a couple of minutes, I went back into the kitchen to check on Kel.

Kel was flushed red, her body stiff and seemed volcanic with hot molten and lava pouring out. 'You know, I am trying to understand and be there for you, but you make it so damn hard. You keep pushing me away. What am I supposed to think?'

'You are supposed to know that that is my way of dealing with things,' I retorted.

'That is all great but how long am I meant to put up with that? It hurts. Have you ever thought that my way of dealing with things is to talk it out?'

'I don't know what you want from me,' I said.

'Andi is my daughter, Matt. I need to know what happened.'

'So you do think I did it! I knew it!' I shouted and stormed out.

KELLY

'What the hell is going on here,' my dad asked as Matt pushed past him on the way out, as my dad headed back in. I fell into the sofa, tears streaming down my face and sobbed out loud. My dad rushed over to me, hugging me as he tried quietening me down.

'I've lost him, dad.' I cried.

'Breathe and tell me what happened.'

I let my words tumble out. I told dad the whole sorry story, how I had struggled with Matt pulling away from me. How I desperately wanted to reconnect with him so we could put on a united front in the case. How I somehow accused him of molesting my daughter.

Dad held me and listened. I curled into his chest and felt his warm body around me. He was resolute. He had been my rock for so long and here he was still guiding me. Then my dad stood up and very simply said 'Well you need to tidy yourself up and fix it.'

With my dad's words ringing in my head, I cleaned myself up and got ready to get the bus over to Matt's parents' home. I wasn't sure what I wanted but I wanted to be sure of what I wanted. A clear out with Matt, I thought would put me on a path towards more certain sureness. I had tried calling him with no answer and I hoped he would be there. Our earlier conversation recycled over and over in my head. I knew I had to make Matt see that I didn't mean what I had said in the way he thought.

As I was ready to leave the house, Matt had arrived back home.

'Hey, I was about to come over,' I said.

'I'm sorry, Kel. I shouldn't have stormed out.'

'I'm sorry, everything I said came out wrong.' I responded.

Matt stepped aside and I gestured him in. We settled in our living room. It was a little worse for wear, but still had that sense of comfortable familiarity. So many memories engulfed us here, the good, the bad and the ugly. Our lives steeped into these walls, and this was where our family was first created. I loved this place. Matt made us tea and we talked more steadily than we had earlier.

I explained that I was worried about the allegations Andi had made because Matt wasn't talking to me about any of it. I wondered whether there were things we had overlooked. Andi might have mentioned things that had been misconstrued by her dad and his parents. I wanted to know what Matt thought and where Andi's allegations might have come from.

'I thought you believed I had done something to Andi,' Matt mumbled.

'I had to know from you.'

'I couldn't bare it, if you believed it.'

'I knew you hadn't done anything wrong but needed to hear it from you too.'

'I don't know. What if I did something without knowing it?'

'There is no way.'

'But, you know, what my dad did, that is in me.'

'You are not your dad, Matt.'

'He is in me.'

'No. You are not him.'

'I don't know. I don't know anything anymore.'

Matt had lost sight of what was true and what wasn't. He hated himself and beat himself up for what his dad had done to him. I hated seeing him like that. We both revealed our darkest fears, we were closer than ever before. He promised over and over that he hadn't touched Andi. I believed Andi but I believed Matt too. We cried together and held each other.

Matt reached over and stroked my hair away from my face. I turned my face and felt his sincerity. I leaned into him and kissed him gently. It grew more ferocious as Matt's hands travelled along the side of my body, around my back and pulled me into him.

My body ached for him and soon I was beneath him, my insides shivered with anticipation. He circled my breasts, first with his hands and then with his tongue that melted me. I wanted him and kissed every part of him I could reach as he entered me. We fell into each other, and it felt so good.

We lay on the floor coiled into each other and the embers of our body heat still burned. We made our way to the bedroom, collapsed into our bed for another course. I was still insatiable.

I rubbed my nakedness next to him with my right hand caressing his waist downwards and all around. That was all the spark Matt needed and the fire flamed away inside and around us. We were ravenous after these weeks of separation. We were as one at last and soon enough fell into a peaceful, deep sleep. It was one of the best night's sleeps I'd had in a while since this whole Andi thing had flared up.

The next day things were so much better between Matt and I; we were connected. We took the chance to talk through what had happened again.

'Matt, I've been remembering stuff that we hadn't thought about before.' I broached.

'What do you mean?' Matt asked.

'Well, do you remember how there were times when you were in the bath and Andi would jump in there with you?'

'Erm... Yeah, I guess... I hadn't even thought about that. Andi has been saying that she was in the bath, and I would jump in with her. That's all I've been thinking about.' Matt replied in deep thought.

'I know, I know.'

'But you're right, she did sometimes jump in. I called out for you, though, honest, always. I never let her stay in.'

'I know, Matt, I know. I think that the poor mite got things mixed up from that.'

I went onto tell Matt about the last time I had seen Andi and that she had said she missed us. It helped Matt to hear that.

'I never touched her the way they say. I swear, I never ever did,' Matt pledged.

Chapter Nine

MATTHEW

We were at Serena's office, in her reception, waiting for her to call us in. 'Hi guys, do you want to come through?' Serena burst through.

'Sure,' I replied and both Kel and I walked to her office.

'So, you have seen the stuff we have had come through. We still have the formal statements that need to come in.'

'Yeah,' I said.

'The thing is, Matt and I have been talking things through. We have realised that there were times when Andi was in the bath with Matt,' Kel interrupted in a rush.

'What? Oh man, what are you saying?' Serena asked. Her tone betrayed the alarm she felt.

'I didn't touch her,' I urged.

We explained how there had been times that Andi jumped in the bath with me. I always covered myself with a hand towel when this happened. Serena asked why we had not explained this earlier. She was particularly worried about our police interviews.

'Honestly, I didn't think about it,' I admitted.

'We were so shocked with the allegations that we focused on that,' Kel explained.

'I'm not sure that that is going to wash,' Serena warned. 'Everyone will think that you were hiding it because you knew it was wrong and that something more went on.'

'Well, if that were true, we wouldn't be admitting to it now, would we,' I challenged.

'I don't know how this is going to work out now,' Serena advised.

'Well, that's your job,' I said.

'I'm sorry. I know we should have thought about things more carefully. It's taken us some time to get our heads round everything. We have been thinking about it all more and more as we got the evidence through.' Kel explained.

'Well, I get that. My job is to advise you based on the information I have and present things you tell me. If I don't have all the information, I can't give the best advice,' Serena said.

'I know... sorry, I didn't mean it,' I said.

'Fine. We will need to explain all this in your statements so that we can get ahead of the game.'

When we left Serena's office, we knew we had made things more difficult. At least now we were all working from the same page. We had to tell her the truth, despite it making things worse for us.

Serena told us that it was lucky that this was not going in front of the Magistrates. She reckoned the Magistrates would have made findings against us without any hesitation. I knew Serena would do her utmost to get the result we wanted.

We never made things easy for her. I had been difficult, not listening to her advice and doing my own thing from the start. Now, not thinking things through about what went on with Andi. It made it appear that we had changed our story. I wouldn't have blamed her for giving up on us, but she was still doing the best she could for us.

A few days later, Kel and I made our way for our contact with Roddie. It was still at the contact centre and Roddie changed every time we saw him. We packed some food and drink as well as nappies. We took the bus and about half an hour later arrived at the centre and waited for Roddie.

They brought Roddie about thirty minutes late, which was quite routine these days. They always made it up to us at the end of contact instead and we got used to it. When Roddie arrived, he was always a little shy at first. We gave him some love and he soon played with the cars on the floor. It was still too cold for us to play in the little garden area they had outside.

Kel and I both got down on our knees and played races with the cars with Roddie. I made funny noises and Roddie lapped it up. I loved Roddie's cheeky laugh and ramped up the funny faces and noises to hear the gurgling of his laugh. Suddenly during this play, I was sure that I caught Roddie as he said 'Dadda'.

'Kel, Kel!' I squealed, 'Did you hear that?'

'What do you mean?' Kel replied.

'He said 'Dadda'.

Kel missed it but I held onto those precious words like jewels. My first child calling me 'Dadda' and not baby babble. Kel dismissed it as baby noise, but I knew it was my boy's call. This is what would keep me going through the darkest of hours to get through this case.

Roddie transformed before our eyes and yet behind our eyes.

Roddie was a lively teddy bear. His head full of earth brown waves with tonal shades through the tufts. The sea blue eyes shone like ripples hit by the sparkling sun. His personality peeked through, and it was exciting to be around that.

The couple of hours a session we had each week were paltry sips of water in the desert. At the same time, they were nuggets of pure gold.

There had been so many firsts that we have already missed. His first sitting up, his first roll over, his first night sleep through. How many more firsts would we miss? We had to make a stand.

A few days later, I wanted to talk to Kel about what we would need to do if the court decided I had done something to Andi. After we had lunch, Kel and I had some time to chat.

'Kel, we need to talk about what we will do if things don't go our way with Andi's allegations.' I started.

'No, we don't because that's not going to happen.'

'I know it's hard, but we do need to think about the worst-case scenario.' I pressed on.

'I'm not doing it,' Kel muttered.

'I get that you don't want to think about it. So, I'm telling you that if the worst happens, you will need to go for the kids on your own and I'll back you.'

'You mean you're breaking up with me,' Kel asked. Her eyes brimmed over.

'You know that's not what I want but that's what we will have to do.'

SERENA

The Local Authority statements rolled in. First up was the social worker who went with Naeed to see Andi, Sonia Collins. Sonia had worked with Andi for a while as a family support worker. She co-worked the meeting with Andi after the paternal grandmother's referral. This Sonia woman had engaged in various activities to build rapport with Andi. They had a good relationship. There had been no mention of anything untoward throughout this time.

Sonia repeated what both the paternal grandmother and Naeed reported. What was odd was the timing of her notes and even Naeed's. They were dated much later than the date of the meeting with Andi. Not by a couple of days later but about two and a half weeks later.

'What else did you notice?'

'There is something interesting about Sonia Collins,' Tara responded.

'Definitely, what is it, do you think?' I questioned.

'I'm not sure, she doesn't say much about the disclosure.'

'Yes, why do you think that might be?'

'I don't know.'

'Think, Tara. Think. Why would she not talk more about it?'

'Erm... because she didn't hear it?'

'Good girl, well done. You are getting there.'

'She doesn't know whether to believe it?'

'Exactly! She seems to want to distance herself

from the so-called disclosure. There is nothing specific, but I get the sense that she doesn't want to be involved in all this, don't you?'

'Oh wow! Do you think?'

'I need something more solid. There is bound to be something that is not consistent with the rest of the evidence.' I couldn't put my finger on it right this minute, but I would keep looking.

'You are so good.'

'I haven't got there yet but I will. Its late, you should head off home. I'll see you tomorrow.'

'You should go home too.'

'I will in a bit.'

I jotted a few pointers and a couple of hours later, my eyes strained, they stung and watered over. I could feel hunger aches deep in my stomach and my head hurt. Time had floated silently by.

I was meeting a friend for dinner. I had planned on going home to make a quick change before dinner but went straight from the office instead. Jag was never good with time keeping but I hoped this time might be different. To my pleasant surprise, he was already at the restaurant waiting for me, which made a nice change.

I had met Jag through a mutual friend and at first, he was not my cup of tea at all. Jag was a wheeler, dealer type. He didn't always play it straight but at the same time he was charming and funny. He ground me down and we were soon fast friends.

'So, what time do you call this?' Jag joked.

'I make it time for dinner,' I replied.

'You're so cheeky!'
'Takes one to know one!'
'And here I am, early as always!'
'You joker! I need food!'

Our starters arrived and we dived right in. 'This case is doing my head in.'

'What's it about?'

'We are representing parents whose children have been taken from them. We are trying to get them back.'

'Why are the children in care?'

'It started off because the guy hit the mother.'

'She probably deserved it,' Jag joked.

'It's so frustrating. It has spun into this whole other story now and there is no stopping it,' I vented. Jag couldn't understand the ins and outs, but he gave a different perspective on things. He made me realise that I needed to dig deeper but also trust my instincts.

A few days later, paternal grandmother's statement dropped. I couldn't read it straight away. My stomach was queasy at the thought of it. The twisted knots pulled in different directions within me. It became more and more tangled. I knew it would be difficult reading.

I left it a day but eventually went through Cynthia MacDowell's statement. She came across as a formidable woman. Devoted to Andi and doted on her granddaughter, maybe a little too much.

Mrs McDowell was clear about what Andi had said. She talked about Andi pointing out the sanitary towels in the shopping trolley. Andi had shouted out that you put them in your pants. Then as they walked to the car,

Andi said that Matt got in the bath with her.

Mrs MacDowell also described how Andi kissed people inappropriately. This had included adults and she described this as sexualised behaviour. The statement finished with what happened when Naeed and Sonia spoke with Andi. This mirrored the Social Workers' statements.

Mrs McDowell's diary left out entirely the sanitary towels situation. It seemed a glaring omission considering she made so much of it in her statement. Still, granny would prove quite difficult to shake down.

A week later, Naeed's statement landed. Naeed did not veer from the script. Andi had displayed sexualised behaviour when initially placed with paternal family. She now disclosed bathing with Matt and that he scrubbed her in her private areas. Naeed's notes were like Sonia's completed much later than the date of the visit to Andi but also contrasting.

Sonia's notes suggested that Naeed had heavily prompted Andi when they were all present. Naeed's statement made it seem like it was a more open conversation. This could be an important distinction.

Strangely, Naeed's statement made it sound like she led when she had one to one time with Andi upstairs. Yet her notes did not reflect the same. What were we meant to believe? Why would the star witness for the Local Authority, gift such a leading statement? My brain ticked over, and my fingers twitched as I scribbled some notes.

I knew I needed to set some time apart to look at all three statements. I'd have to cross-reference their respective notes to analyse the best forms of attack. I needed to allocate time preparing the parents' own statements.

Before that, I shot off an email requesting all other notes. These notes had been typed on their systems. All through the evidence, references to handwritten notes had been littered everywhere. I wanted them and I was going to get them.

This smelt a lot like collusion and stitching evidence together. That was not okay, and I was determined to get to the root of the truth. The truth, though, was what you made of it. There was the Local Authority version of the truth. Then there was the parents'. Somewhere in between those competing truths lay the Judge's truth.

MATTHEW
Kel and I went to see Serena to do our statements and she again saw us separately. Kel went in before I did and seemed relaxed when she came out.

When it was my turn, my heart pounded, and fists clenched. I marched into Serena's office and my heart rate seemed to gather at pace. I don't know why because I knew both Serena and Kel were on my side. I suspected that Serena would be asking me thorny questions. I worried that I would be squirming, well squirming more than I already was.

I was right to be concerned because Serena gave me a right grilling. It started off easy enough. Serena asked me outright whether I had ever sexually abused

Andi. 'No, of course not.' I replied.

'Have you ever sexually abused any child?' Serena asked.

'That's ridiculous,' I responded.

'Should I take that as a yes, no, or maybe?' Serena persisted.

'No! Obviously no!' I said. My voice raised.

'Have you ever sexually abused anyone?'

'No,' I muttered.

It was only then that I noticed how I gripped the sides of the grey cushioned seat. My arms were tight, the tension dissipating only slightly, as I released my hands. They were now placed in a viceroy lock on my lap instead.

I had not seen this side of Serena before. Her face was taut. Her jet-black eyes seeming to x-ray my mind behind thin rimmed glasses. Her long, slim fingers with bloody red manicured nails danced along her laptop.

The meeting went downhill from there. Somehow or other, Serena got the statement she wanted from me. In the process, she presented me with good practice for the interrogation I would face.

Dealing with the sanitary towels issue, I explained that we often went shopping together. On those occasions, Kel would pick up sanitary towels. Andi never asked about them, nor did Kel ever explain what they were to Andi in my presence. I could not say what might have been discussed between Kel and Andi, when I wasn't around.

I repeated what we had told Serena the last time we met about Andi jumping into the bath when I was already in there. The paternal grandmother mentioned that Andi had told her that Kel and I used to be in the bath together. I accepted that this was true to save on water and gas. Andi was always put in bed or at least in her bedroom before we did this. I remembered that Andi also jumped into the bath when Kel was in there; she didn't do it only with me.

'Did you ever scrub Andi when she was having a bath?' Serena asked.

'Only her face. There was the odd occasion when I had to scrub her stomach and legs because she couldn't scrub hard enough. The one time I did that was because she had got nail polish all over,' I explained.

'Were you in the bath with her?'

'No, no! I was kneeling on the floor outside the bath.'

'Why did you not tell the police about this when you were first interviewed?'

'Because I'm stupid,' I said.

'Matt, I know I'm being tough, but you've been doing well, you can't lose it now.'

'I am stupid. I didn't think about it. It only happened once or twice, and I forgot.'

Serena picked out certain things from the evidence that I agreed. We added those things in my statement. For instance, the fact that Andi's manner changed when talking about living with Kel and me. In my statement, I said that that could have been a result of all manner of things. It might have been because someone had coached her to say things, she knew were untrue. It could be because she missed us, and it made her feel sad to think about us. It could have been because of the pressure for her to say what they wanted her to say, and she couldn't work out what that was. Only Andi knew.

Serena did well picking out holes in the Local Authority evidence. We had the police statements and police DVD interview with Andi too. Andi had not made any disclosures in that interview. The interview revealed other odd things that helped us. So, whilst I felt beaten during the meeting, I saw up close what Serena would do to the Local Authority witnesses. I hoped that on balance they would come off worse.

A few days later, I went to see my dad. There were things that needed to be said and I had finally got the guts to face him. I had thought it over for ages but did not think I could face him. I mean he was still my dad.

I did not want to be the one to cause trouble in the family. I also did not want to cause trouble for my family – Kel, Andi and Roddie. It was no longer an equal balance between my family with Kel and my family with my parents and siblings. My family with Kel came first and that was that.

I took longer than usual riding my bike over and felt queasy by the time I arrived. My breathing was measured. My mouth was dry and my tongue too big to be housed in my mouth. My arms and palms were itchy, and I drummed away on my bike's handlebar. The cold air swept around me.

I knocked on the door and mum let me in. I went through to the kitchen and mum made me a cup of tea, accompanied with her tin of biscuits. I sat at the square wooden table, whilst mum busied herself in the kitchen and chatted away aimlessly. 'Mum, where's dad?'

'Oh, he has gone to get the papers, you know what he's like with his dailies.'

We heard the door go and mum called him to the kitchen.

'Oh, hi lad!' Dad greeted me.

'Dad.' I nodded back in acknowledgement.

Dad moved off and I called him back, 'Dad, I need to have a word.'

'Oh okay, what is it, lad?'

'The thing is, I won't let what you did to us demolish what I have. You destroyed our childhoods, damaged our adulthoods and lives but I won't let you take my future.' I said, having practiced this so many times in my head and yet still shaking as I spoke.

'Right, what does that mean?' Dad asked.

'You won't be seeing our kids.'

'Okay, you have to do what you have to do.' Dad replied, shrugged his shoulders, and then left the room.

Mum had stopped whatever she had been doing and was standing still at the sink with her back to me.

'Mum,' I called over.

'Sorry, Matt, I have to get some washing sorted,' she choked out and ran off upstairs.

I sat there for a few minutes, grabbed my keys, and headed out on my bike to home.

SERENA
Eventually the Local Authority relented and sent

us the handwritten notes. Sonia's notes did not record the conversation that Naeed had with her about Andi's disclosure. A stark absence. Her notes helped us show that Naeed pushed Andi for a disclosure. There seemed to be a lot of prompting and leading. Andi seemed oblivious and had no disclosure to make. This looked like a dangerous cover up. Dark forces seemed to be at work in this conspiracy against the Barnett/McInleys. How did it go from Andi's innocent mutterings to the murky allegations?

Some time away from this was essential and so I headed home early. I went to see my parents and had dinner with them. They knew I was involved in a heavy case and that sexual abuse was a running theme.

My mum was as small as me, in height, but a little rounder. My safe haven shared my midnight black eyes. My mamma's eyes had an expanse of love as infinite as the night's sky with stars sparkling with fun. Her voice was as warm and smooth as frothy hot chocolate.

'How are you kunchu?' My mum asked. My whole being immediately aglow.

'I'm okay, how are you and Doug?' I asked.

Doug was my mum's partner, my birth father having left my mum and me, when I was three years of age. My parents had had an arranged marriage. My father abandoned us when I was, no doubt, a demanding little toddler. He disappeared for twenty years, deserting his parents and siblings too.

By the time he reappeared, I was grown. I had no use for a father, my mum had been both a mother and father to me during my childhood. Doug came along when I was sixteen and there was only one Doug. Doug stuck with us through thick and thin. Everyone else might have had a dad but I was the only one with a Doug!

I would not allow this man, who was my father only by virtue of biology, into my life. He had provided no support at all to my mum in raising me. This was a man of means.

In contrast, my mum had married young without any formal qualification or experience. My mum who had had to carve out a life for herself and her young daughter in a foreign country. She had none of her immediate family around her. All so that we would not suffer the stigma of being a 'broken' family. We were anything but broken; we were strong and whole.

'Well, you know, we are old, and my legs and back are achy. Doug always says he is okay, but you know, we are still going every week for his treatment,' my mum replied.

'It is amazing how positive he is with everything that he has been through,' I said.

'Yeah, he is much better than I am like that. You look tired darling, is it that case, you are working too hard.'

'I'm okay. You know me, I love my work.'

'Mmm, that's what worries me. You need to look after yourself too.'

My mum's food was always delicious and hit the spot. The heady mix of flavours and spices enlivened my senses. The green chillies from my mum's own garden stung my tongue, which I curled inward. I breathed in widely but then blew out through pursed lips in my vain attempts to calm the burning fire. My high tolerance for spicy heat enjoyed these challenges.

The coriander chutney was tantalisingly good. It was one of my favourite dishes, the smell alone was intoxicating. I devoured the food in front of me. There was nothing else quite like my mamma's homemade curries. Feeling rejuvenated, I bid my parents goodnight and headed home. I soaked in a hot bath filled with bubbles before heading to bed.

We had a couple of days before the fact-finding hearing. I took some time to look at the DVD interview the police had with Andi. I compared that to the transcript of the interview. She looked so small and young on the DVD. I felt for this little girl that was being pulled in all different directions. She played with some dolls desperately wanting to be anywhere other than where she was. Naeed Kaur, the social worker sat on the sofa with Andi. There was a table in front of them and PC Adams was opposite them.

'Andi, can you tell me what you know about being here today?' The policewoman asked.

'Erm... not sure.' Andi replied. She kept looking down at the doll she twiddled around in her hands. Occasionally, she looked up through her fringe, shyly and unsure of herself.

'That is okay. I want to ask you some questions about your life at home with grandma and what it was like with your mummy and Matt. Is that okay?'

'Yes,' Andi said looking up.

'I need to make sure you know about telling the

truth.'

'Of course, telling lies is naughty.'

'That's right, Andi. If I said to you that I have green hair, would that be true?' WPC Adams asked.

'Hehehehehe. That's funny. That's a lie,' Andi replied with her face twinkling.

The rest of the interview was uncontroversial in that there were no disclosures. When PC Adams asked Andi how she felt about baths with Matt, Andi tried to draw a mouth to show her feelings. PC Adams asked whether the picture meant Andi had felt 'sad?' The typed transcript read that Andi said 'sad' rather than a description of what I had seen her do: drawing a mouth. Again, more leading! Andi herself never said that this was how she felt. This part of the transcript needed changing.

The DVD provided a completely different texture to the supposed transcript of it. In these essential parts, the transcript was way off base. My paranoia about a Local Authority set up was becoming difficult to shake off.

Naeed, later in the interview asked Andi about the sad face she had drawn earlier. Andi was very clear in saying that she drew faces like that to show that she was happy. Naeed refused to accept this. She drove Andi to say that she had felt sad, which put more and more unfair pressure on Andi. Was it any wonder that the poor girl became more subdued during this interrogation? And what on earth was Naeed doing interfering in this police interview? I must have missed the moment she acquired her professional police credentials!

Exhausted, I poured over the evidence, dug deeper, analysed, and prepared. I barely ate or slept and lived, breathed this case. We were finally on the eve of the fact-finding hearing. I was ready to collapse but the thought of only three more days nourished me. I had spent the best part of the day preparing my cross examination.

By chance, I thought I would take a quick look through the earlier statements. I ran a cursory look through the Sexual Offenders Expert Report in relation to Matt's dad. Suddenly it sent shivers down my spine. He had touched Matt and the other kids. I already knew that, but the blind spot, here it was, open and in broad daylight.

It all happened whilst in the bath with them! Damn, this was what it was all about. Here was the lynchpin to their whole case, Matt repeated his dad's abuse!

Chapter Ten

KELLY

Matt and I headed to court for the first day of the fact-finding hearing. Matt wore a suit he borrowed from his brother, Paul. It drowned him but still he looked handsomely serious.

I put on an old plain brown dress, tied around the waist with a belt. It was one of the smartest outfits I had. I left my hair loose, falling behind my shoulders. I didn't wear much make up and today was no different.

Matt and I walked side by side towards the court after the hour, two buses journey. My full stride was a third of Matt's, but he matched my steps. We didn't say very much, and Matt held his head down as we neared the court building.

The early Spring morning whirled around us. The cool blue sky entertaining the sole black bird that circled around. Cars, lorries, and vans hurtled past us with their own journeys for the day ahead. The motor vehicles, the flying bird, Matt, and I, we all had a story and ours would be played out over the next few days.

This family court was not like the Magistrates one, it was larger and more stately but also more imposing. We climbed up the stairs in silence. We joined the queue of ruffians, concerned mothers, bravado fathers. There were a few suits dotted here and there.

We moved a person or two at a time forward and finally it was our turn for security. It was a familiar routine now. I placed my unzipped handbag on the side table for the security to check through. I walked through the sensory arch, and it beeped as always. The court's bouncer swiped me before waving me through. Matt was not far behind and as we went through, Serena found us.

'Hi guys. How are you both doing?' Serena asked.

'We are okay, I guess,' I replied. 'Nervous, but okay.'

'That is completely natural, but we are ready.'

Serena swung round and gestured for us to follow. We all headed into the court room. This arena was different from those at the Magistrates. First it was loftier, with what seemed like a public gallery to either side of the room. They gallery was a few rows of light brown wooden seats linked together and fixed to the floor.

We all moved like a train; each person held the stable-like door from the gallery to the main stage. We were immediately behind Serena. She headed to the front row of seats like the gallery, directing Matt and I to sit in the row behind her. All the lawyers sat in that same line and ahead of them was a long mahogany bench that seemed elevated somehow. On the wall behind that majestic bench was the legal logo of two lions glaring down at us. This was where our lives would be decided.

We were in front of His Honour Judge Carter once again. Before the Judge entered the courtroom, the clerk instructed us all to stand. We were all in position and the Judge took his place, indicating that we could return to our seats. We were all set.

Someone somewhere must have shouted 'Action,' because Sam got to her feet. She outlined the case for the Local Authority. She explained, 'Your honour, I refer you to A3 – A6 of the Bundle. The facts sought are set out there. We say that is what establishes the significant risk of harm to the children.'

We all turned to the relevant pages as Sam highlighted, paragraphs 6(a) to (c) of A4 and 6(d) to (f) of A6,

'The children are both at risk of sexual harm because of the following:

1. Their half sibling, Andi has disclosed to her carer, social worker, and support worker that Mr Barnett used to get in the bath with her.
2. Andi disclosed to the social worker that Mr Barnett scrubbed her whilst in the bath and pointed to her genital area.
3. Andi also disclosed to the social worker that she scrubbed Mr Barnett in the bath and pointed to the social worker's genital area and said, 'and behind.'
4. Mother has failed to protect Andi from the sexual harm from Mr Barnett.'

Sam went on to outline issues around the transcript of Andi's DVD interview. Certain amendments had already been agreed but that there remained some outstanding discrepancies. His Honour Judge Carter confirmed that he would view the DVD himself and retired to do that.

The DVD was about an hour in duration and so

we all went off in different directions. Serena told us that she wanted to go over Cynthia McDowell's evidence as she would be the first witness. Matt and I headed to the cafeteria for a coffee and to quell our anxieties.

'I'm so scared, Matt.'

'I know, it will be okay.' Matt mumbled. He was never able to look me in the eye when he was being untruthful. He would never win at poker, and I could sense that behind his confident words was the fear of the unknown. Matt was wringing his hands in a tight clasp and his eyes glossed over blankly.

'How do you know?'

'I don't,' Matt admitted as he sipped on his coffee. I could see the worry etched in his face too. This had been the biggest test we had had to face so far, and it could still break us. Matt's words about us splitting if things went wrong still rung in my ears. The coffee was insipid, but I barely noticed, my thoughts too a blur with our case. We didn't say very much else.

When we returned, the Judge confirmed the amendments he had made to the transcript. They were pretty much in line with what Serena had requested, from what I could understand. Hopefully she would explain everything when we next had a break.

Cynthia was called into the witness box. As she walked through the court room, she avoided looking at me. She kept her head turned away until she was in the witness box. She wore a long green skirt and cream puffy jumper. Elaine was sworn in, confirmed her details and statement.

Sam kicked off asking Elaine to explain her diary notes.

'Well, I was the only one to use it and I used it solely for appointments and recording anything that needs to be addressed.'

Q: I see. I need to clarify some things. By the time Andi said what she did about the sanitary towels, she had been staying with you and your family for a while. Had Andi seen any sanitary towels during that time?'

A: Not as far as I am aware. She shouted it out that day about them going in your pants. I told her that I wasn't angry.

Q: Can I ask you to look at page D254, 3 lines down in the second paragraph for the entry on 30th November?

A: Yes, I've got it.

Q: Were these Andi's own words or how you have described it?

A: No, Andi's words, she came out with it when we were in the car park and had quite a serious expression on her face. She said 'Matty used to get in the bath with me at bath-time... Matty would get out mummy would come in'. I was shocked but tried to stay calm and did the best I could to reassure Andi and said OK that's OK.

Q: Did you note it the same day it happened?

A: Oh yes, because I was concerned about it and so wanted to make sure that I made a note of Andi's exact words.

Cynthia still refused to look over in my direction. She came across strong and loving. It was hard to keep quiet and sit there. I had so many questions that I wanted to ask, like how the hell Andi remembered any of this after all this time now? Like where had they been when Andi was first born? What did they ever do to try and help me? I burned inside.

We listened as Cynthia explained that Sonia Collins had worked with Andi for a while. Andi had inappropriately kissed others, including adults. Sonia and Cynthia had both gone into Andi's school to talk about these concerns. It had not occurred recently.

Sam continued with the questioning: -

Q: Naeed came to the house on December, fifth?

A: Yes that's right, Miss Collins and Naeed came to see Andi. I was in the house but doing work upstairs to keep away.

Q: Did you know that Andi and Naeed went upstairs?

A: I heard Andi come upstairs during this time and heard Naeed too. I wasn't sure if it was only Naeed or whether Miss Collins came up too.

Q: What did you hear between Andi and Naeed?

A: I couldn't hear anything between them when they were upstairs, even though I was upstairs too. I was in my own room, which is down the hallway.

Cynthia's main evidence finished with her saying that Andi had also come out saying one night that Matt had kissed her. Again, this came from nowhere and was when she was in bed getting ready to sleep for the night. The most innocent of things twisted into something evil.

SERENA

It seemed to me that this grandmother had come across as sincere. Here was the thing, this grandmother had already reared her own children. She was now supporting her son to take care of this little girl, his daughter, her granddaughter.

The court always places family members in these positions in the highest of esteem. With that in mind, there was little to gain in attacking this witness. Doing so, would anger this Judge as well as not provide any helpful ammunition to my clients.

The gentleness of grandmother hardened as I stood up to begin my cross examination. I saw her body stiffen, and her face was marked with wariness. Her soothing voice from a few minutes ago was now icy cold. An internal switch had been triggered to the defence.

I started off softly with Mrs McDowell. I got her to explain the reasons that Andi was placed with her.

Mrs McDowell confirmed that there had been domestic violence between my clients. She said there might have been neglect issues. It seemed that she was informed of Matt's father's history some time later. She had had training around sexual abuse when Andi had displayed 'sexualised behaviour'. Oddly, no training or guidance had been given around how to respond to any 'disclosures'.

My main aim with Mrs McDowell was to show that the reality was that what Andi had told her was not sexual abuse of any kind. I needed to show that it was not something she was that worried about. That was the strategy anyway.

She was one of the strongest witnesses, in that there wasn't much by way of contradiction with her diary notes. In some ways she was the least damaging to our case because of the content. She had not said that there was any inappropriate touching. Inappropriate behaviour, perhaps, by sharing a bath the way Matt had. That by itself, though, was not sexual abuse or harm.

If Matt had looked for some sexual gratification, then that would be harmful. This witness could not evidence that. Only Matt knew his intent in behaving in this way.

In a strange way, this Local Authority witness was the most helpful to our case. She reported questionable behaviour. However, she was not able to say why such behaviour was harmful. To that extent, even better reason to befriend this witness. Grandma, though, wore a coat of barbed wire. I had my work cut out to chip away at her instinctive barriers.

So, I continued my gentle approach to draw Mrs McDowell into a false sense of security.

Q: Your diary notes say that Andi was anxious that 'granny may be cross coz of comments made about sanitary towels'?

A: Yes, that's right. Then Andi says this about Matty getting in the bath and she would come out and mummy would get in.

Q: What time of the day did that happen, would you say?

A: It happened at about three in the afternoon.

Q: And what time would you have noted it in the diary?

A: I think I made the entry that same day at about half past seven or eight in the evening.

Q: Did you ask Andi anything about it?

A: No.

Q: Didn't ask Andi anything else even at bedtime?

A: No, I wanted some advice first.

Q: Given what Andi had said, why was it so concerning?

A: Well, I wasn't sure.

Q: But from what you have told this court, Andi had just said that she was in the bath with Matt. She said it out of thin air, and I'm trying to understand why it was so concerning to you?

A: I was unsure that's why wanted advice.

Q: Andi didn't seem upset when she said it; not anxious nor distressed?

A: No, that's correct.

Q: What was going through your mind to record it?

A: The way it came out as opposed to what she said...behaviour strange...

Q: What do you mean about strange behaviour? Your notes don't say anything about Andi behaving strangely?

A: Well, erm, I suppose it was because she wasn't having a bath at the time. She was in bed and that was strange.

Q: Anything else that was strange?

A: No, I guess not.

Q: Andi didn't act out in any way?

A: No.

Q: So, no strange behaviour but maybe strange

setting? If it had been said during bath time - wouldn't have thought, it strange?

A: Erm... I don't know.

Q: You spoke to the social worker, Naeed, on December second but said nothing about what Andi had said, why not?

A: I wanted to run it past school.

Q: But you said a few minutes ago that you wanted advice, why did you delay?

A: I thought I could get advice from school.

Q: So not concerned enough to get Social Work advice?

A: I have more regular contact with school.

Q: Did you get the advice from school then?

A: Well, no, Andi's usual teacher wasn't in.

Q: And you still didn't contact Naeed for another couple of days. If you were really concerned, you would have mentioned it to Naeed the very first opportunity you had.

A: But I knew Andi was in my care and safe.

It was then the turn of the guardian's Solicitor, Margaret. Margaret's cross examination did not add anything useful to Mrs McDowell's evidence. It was short and to the point.

Margaret's role was to fill in any gaps or uncertainties in the evidence. The guardian tried to keep as neutral a position as she could. Of course, she represented the child's best interests, Rodrigo that was. She couldn't possibly know what had happened between Andi and Matt. Her Solicitor's job was to try and get to the truth. To be fair, that was exactly how

Mrs McDowell came across – truthful.

The Judge interjected with questions of his own. 'Can I just check a few things, Mrs McDowell?' His Honour Judge Carter nudged his glassed higher up his nose. He then summarised, 'You were upstairs, Andi downstairs with Naeed and Miss Collins?'

'That's right,' Mrs McDowell confirmed.

'So, there came a point when you heard footsteps. You understood Andi was coming upstairs and became aware later that there were adults upstairs later too. You leave them to get on with it?'

'Yes, your Honour.'

'Naeed then tapped your bedroom door?' His Honour Judge Carter queried.

'Yes, Naeed said Andi had made a disclosure. Andi had told her Matty had been in the bath with her. They touched each other's parts Matt had rubbed her there and pointing to area.'

'Then you all moved downstairs?' His Honour Judge finished.

'Yes,' Mrs McDowell replied.

Mrs McDowell was released from the witness box. Relief stretched across her whole face and body. She walked out of the court room without a second glance.

We had got as much as we probably could from her. She had remained steadfast with what she recounted but did get a little shaken at times. It was tricky because she came across as genuine in reporting what Andi had supposedly told her. She was a loving grandmother, worried for her granddaughter.

Had it not been for Matt's history, I doubt this

grandmother would ever have reported this 'disclosure' if it could even be called that. I guess that was what I was getting at with my questions around her not being alarmed. Mrs McDowell was careful not to say she had made assumptions because of Matt's history. She had been well prepped for that.

Next up was Miss Collins. Before that, His Honour Judge Carter called for a lunch break. We all breathed a heavy sigh and just like that, dispersed in different directions.

KELLY

We went into one of the conference rooms with Serena.

I was on edge, maybe even more so than earlier in the day. I was unsure whether the situation now was the same, worse, or better than it had been in the morning. It was hard to tell. My blunt, chewed nails rattled the table. Matt's suited knee bounced up and down as he patted away to his own rhythm. Serena's face was tightly pulled, and the veins of her neck protruded more than usual, I was sure.

'How do you think we are doing?' Matt and I asked, almost in unison.

'It's hard to tell. We made some good points with grandma, but she stood firm on the whole bath sharing thing,' Serena replied.

'She is a lying witch,' I snapped. 'I'm sorry, I don't know where that came from.'

'She wasn't that bad. I mean she is not the one

saying Matt touched Andi in her private parts. She is saying what we kind of accept anyway and that is that Matt was in the bath with Andi.'

'Yeah, I s'pose. It's all the frustration from years ago when they didn't care and now, here, she is playing the doting grandmother.' Kelly explained.

'Yes, I can see that that would have been a tough time for you but hang in there. We are doing okay at the moment.' Serena calmed.

Serena asked us to keep the room. She wanted to grab a sandwich and drink to work through lunch from the conference room. 'Do you think she's right?' I asked.

Matt shrugged his shoulders and replied, 'I guess. What else can we do?'

'I mean, why would he believe us against all of them.'

'Maybe.'

I heard the staccato beat echoing in the corridor before the door pushed open. Serena strode back in, resumed her spot at the table. She let Matt and I go off and asked us to return before two in the afternoon, which was when the Judge wanted us back in.

Matt and I took a walk into the town, which was quaint with shops lining the pedestrian crossroads layout. There were a few known shops, some independent stores but also quite a few charity shops. Different shapes and sizes bustled in and around.

The fresh air heightened the warm rays as we looked out for somewhere to have a drink. We found a cosy little café with quirky sofas and chairs. It was small, but the smell of coffee and cake was large and comforting. Neither of us was hungry but we ordered mugs of hot tea that steamed away on the table between us.

'I guess we need to keep going, right?' I said.

'Yeah, but it doesn't look good, does it, Kel?' Matt replied looking down into his mug of tea.

'You heard what Serena said,' I tried to reassure.

'Yeah, but she has to say that. We must face up to things, Kel. No matter what the truth is, they will believe what they want to believe, because of my bastard dad.'

'Matt, we have to take one step at a time and stick to what we know.'

We sat quietly for a while sipping on our tea.

The café became busy. An older man looked around for a seat, he had a hot drink in his one hand and an order place in the other. Matt gestured at me that we let the man join us at our table and so I called him over. He cheerfully joined us.

'Thank you, you good people,' the man said in a kind, friendly voice. His sparkling blue eyes framed by crow's feet and set in a time chiselled, weather-beaten face.

'No problem.' Matt replied.

'What are you two up to?'

'It's a long story,' I replied.

'I have time and it looks like you lovebirds do too!' The man chuckled.

We only had another half hour or so and there were so many other eyes and ears about. The man understood and told us a little about himself instead. He was in his fifties. Happily married, with two adult children and a couple of grandchildren from the one child. The man's wife was with the grandkids today and he had come out for a breather. He was a retired social worker and told us some horror stories of children that he had tried to save.

It became progressively tough with more and more children to help. More and more paperwork and less and less time and pay. This gentle soul realised that he also lost his effectiveness. He tarred families with the same brush of others, unfairly so. It came to the point that he wasn't giving parents a chance. He had stopped supporting them the way he could have. This ultimately led him to early retirement.

He opened our minds to another perspective but still this was our family. It frightened me to see this man's war worn wounds in Naeed.

I glanced down at my watch and there was only fifteen minutes left of our break. 'Matt, we need to get back.'

'Oh right. It was real nice meeting you, sir,' Matt said.

'And a pleasure meeting two such kind young people,' the man replied. Matt shook the man's hand, and I gave him a light hug as we left.

We hurried back to the court building. I was an insignificant insect going through the poor imitation airport security checks again. Matt was ahead of me as we raced back to the room, we had left Serena in.

We panted hard as Serena rushed us into court. We

took up the seats that had cooled off in that break. I had no hopes at all for this Miss Collins. She was part of the machine of the State, and they all had it in for us. I knew she would back up Naeed and do what she needed to against us. Whether any of what they said was true or not, they all stuck together.

I had never met Miss Collins. She was a stocky woman with short blonde hair and blue piercing eyes. I would estimate that she was in her thirties. As she walked into the court room and towards the witness box, she had an air of confidence and authority about her.

I got the impression that she was well used to giving evidence. This was, most likely, her bread and butter. It was hard sitting there and listening to all these lies. None of these people knew Matt and me but made judgments about us and our lives. They were making decisions for the rest of our lives.

The Local Authority Solicitor didn't have anything to ask Miss Collins. It was straight over to Serena. Serena stood tall, even if she was quite short in real life even with her five-inch heels. She wore a grey skirt suit; her skirt fell below her knees in a fishtail shape. The jacket fell nicely about the waistline and fitted. Serena always seemed to dress with style and composure. Her hair was tied back in a low bun.

I could tell she was ready for business and prayed that she was.

SERENA

Miss Collins looked warily towards me from the witness box. This was a difficult situation; I wasn't sure whether she was a friend in disguise or an all-out enemy. She wore her sleek bob framed close to her face, her eyes glistened, and her disposition unnerving. The few words she had spoken were clear and solid.

The playbook was a double bluff.

I decided on the attacking angle so that at least she could preserve her role as a Local Authority witness. That way, it would look like she had crumbled under the pressure rather than because she wanted to help us. What the reality was, I would never know.

Of course, there was always the danger that it would be a flop and I would be the big bad bully. Trials were a strange affair. Intended as an explosion of truth. Often that explosion sprayed multiple truths. The one that splattered the judge was the one that counted.

I started my cross examination.

Q: Can you tell us about your involvement with Andi?

A: Well, I did crafts and activities with Andi. It was about six months. I have a positive relationship with her, Andi.

Q: Had she ever said anything about baths with Matt or Matt doing anything inappropriate to her?

A: Andi never made comments about Matt and the bath with me.

Miss Collins voice was confident. She maintained steady eye contact with the Judge and me. She switched easily from listening to my question and directing her replies to the Judge.

Miss Collins explained that the decision for her to co-work the discussion with Andi. She had developed a good relationship with Andi. It was felt that it would help Andi to have someone she trusted and liked.

Remarkably, the two social workers had not agreed how to conduct the discussion. There seemed to be a complete lack of preparation in advance of this meeting. Miss Collins was told that it was a follow up meeting with Andi.

No guidance had been given about the notes of that meeting. In fact, note taking had not even been planned, it happened spontaneously. There was a definite change in her tone and manner when discussing note taking. A quiver belied her replies.

Miss Collins said, 'Naeed gave me her notepad and told me there you go. She told me to take notes when we were there.'

'You are sure that you took the notes during the visit?'

'Yes.'

'Maybe, you made a mistake, and it was Naeed?'

'No, it was me.'

'Maybe, you have forgotten? It was a long time ago, after all.'

'It was me,' Miss Collins was firm with a creeping tetchiness in her voice.

'How can you be so sure?'

'The handwriting is mine and it's my initials at the bottom.'

'So, you are certain?'

'Yes.'

'There can be no doubt at all?'

'Miss Sharma, this witness has answered the question five times now. Please move on,' the judge interjected.

'Of course, Sir.' I asked, 'What were you told was the purpose of the visit?'

A: Nothing.

Q: What were you told about what detail was needed in the notes?

A: There had been no guidance on how detailed the notes had to be.

Q: So, what were you told about the purpose of the notes?

A: I took notes as things were happening, I did not have it confirmed by anyone. I recorded it as it was happening.

Q: Did you usually take notes in your role as family support worker during your sessions with Andi?

A: Not normal that I had to write notes, I usually did them after the session.

Q: Do you know the purpose of those notes?

A: Well, yes, to record Andi's progress and give me something to assess later.

Q: There is always a purpose to notes, right?

A: I guess...

Q: And actually, that purpose helps you with the note taking, what content is needed, the detail and so on.

A: Yes.

Q: So not knowing the purpose of note taking on

this visit, meant that you did not know what content was needed, the detail and so on.

A: I suppose so.

Miss Collins spoke with a fruity voice. She had a quiet confidence but, on the note taking, she seemed jarred. I was able to tease out of Miss Collins quite easily that her notes were not necessarily word for word. Some of it was Miss Collins' summarising what had been said. They stayed together downstairs for about ten to fifteen minutes.

When Naeed had gone up with Andi to Andi's bedroom, the notepad stayed downstairs with Miss Collins. Strangely, Naeed took the notepad away with her after the visit. Apparently, Naeed also made notes, but it is not known when those notes were written up.

Q: Did you make notes of what Andi had told Naeed upstairs?

A: Yes, but that was in the case notes, which were prepared after... I had to request my handwritten notes first from the day to prepare my case notes.

Q: The handwritten notes don't include that do they?

A: No, my case notes include what happened when Andi went up with Naeed. This was added weeks after I got my handwritten notes.

Q: That doesn't seem good practice.

A: No.

Considering how clear Miss Collins had been, her last answer was so faint, it was like hearing a falling feather. Yet, given the oppressing silence that echoed around the room, her honesty could not be missed.

Rather than hitting the ground, the feather fell into a river sending ripples all around.

I asked a few more questions about the note taking and asked Miss Collins to look at a particular page of the Bundle. Her bamboo fingers flicked the corners of the pages. Somehow, her fingers seemed covered in toffee as she fought the pages away. 'I'm sorry, my fingers seem to be getting in the way.'

'Take your time, if you move to the divider section D first of all.'

Flustered, 'It's okay, I've got it now.'

It was a handwritten note. It described Andi looking blankly at them and Naeed prompting her. I questioned why Miss Collins' later case notes made no reference to this, nor indeed, her statement. Miss Collins confirmed that her recollection was that Naeed had recorded that note.

I let Miss Collins continue down this line, even to the point of justifying why she had not included it in her notes. 'I only included in my notes, what I had seen and heard,' she argued. Then the punch line question. 'But as you made very clear earlier, five times, in fact, Naeed was not taking the notes at this point, you were!'

There was a deafening hush that descended round the court room.

'Let's move on from that,' I continued after sufficient dramatic pause for the last point to take effect. Miss Collins confirmed that only Naeed went upstairs with Andi.

Q: Why did you not take it upon yourself to go up, you were given the notebook?

A: I wasn't asked to go up.

Q: It was a joint visit?

A: Which is not the norm for me.

Q: This was an important visit. Andi was being asked questions about having a bath with Matt. You would have known any response she gave would have been important. I'm struggling to understand why you didn't ask to go upstairs or take it upon yourself?

A: Naeed made no comment about it, and I never asked her.

The cross examination ended uneventfully after that. Miss Collins confirming that Naeed was upstairs for about ten minutes with Andi. Then a few minutes with the paternal grandmother.

Naeed told Miss Collins what Andi had said to her when she came downstairs. Andi had initially come downstairs with Mrs McDowell but then had been sent back up. It was unclear whether Andi overheard what Naeed told Miss Collins or not.

Miss Collins had helped us during her evidence. Whether deliberately or accidentally, I didn't care. It was still early in the game though and it was Naeed's turn next. I knew she would do what it took to address any of Miss Collins' shortfalls. Her aim was to tie everything up with a nice red bow, but I had other plans.

Chapter Eleven

KELLY

In our huddle, Serena again, gave very little away. As in the morning, she felt that we had got what we could from Miss Collins echoing her words about Elaine.

It was difficult to read how the Judge felt about these witnesses. He had remained stony faced throughout. Hardly a facial muscle movement, involuntary or otherwise. He was statuesque apart from the occasional blinking of his eyes. There was also the movement of his head as he kept pace with his note taking. I wished we could have seen him when he watched the DVD interview with Andi. It might have given us some clue, but he guarded his judgments meticulously.

We had decided to stay at my dad's during the trial. That evening, when we got back to dad's, he pulled me in for the warmest of hugs enveloping me in love and comfort. I breathed in his Old Spice and his greying beard scratched at my cheeks. It took me back to my childhood days, comforted after a fall, or after some friendship issue or other.

Matt watched us intently. I wasn't sure what whirred away in his mind, his family were not affectionate in this way at all. We had another couple of days of this and that would determine what our lives would most likely look like. We would either be a family reunited or pulled apart in separate ways. As much as I had not wanted to hear or talk to Matt about this, I had heard him and inside, knew he was right.

We all had dinner together, dad had made us microwave steak pie and chips. We sat around the table and talked about what dad had been up to that day. It sounded like he had his usual, regular workday, though they missed Matt there. Matt and I were quiet this evening, neither of us knowing what to say about the day we had had or about the days to come. We needed to ride it out as best as we could.

After dinner, I sat with Matt and my dad either side of me on the sofa, my dad's arm reached over my shoulders and held me close. I felt secure with dad, though it hadn't always been that way. When I was younger, I was difficult and out of control. My dad and I clashed constantly. Eventually I got myself pregnant and was back under control. Dad was there for me through it all and became my safety net.

Then there was Matt. He had a strength I never fully appreciated or understood. As isolated as he could be at times when he became introvert, if it weren't for him, I would have given up by now.

Matt, with his short but strong way, steered our course when I couldn't, and I took up the baton when he couldn't. I knew that this killed him piece by piece, but I hoped that I could put him back together if things went our way. The unknown was where we would be if it went against us. I could barely bring it to my mind, though somehow it sometimes snuck in, and I shoved it away again.

Sanita messaged me asking how we were. I hadn't had chance to see her in a few weeks at our café. She was a dear friend, with words of comfort and advice.

'It's hard to tell,' I typed to Sanita.

'It will work out exactly as it is meant to,' Sanita replied.

'Yeah, I guess so. There isn't much we can do for now but sit back and let our solicitor do her thing.'

'Being powerless is frustrating but you said Serena is top drawer. So, trust in that,' Sanita reassured.

'She is and you're right. You're pretty top drawer too, Sanita!'

'Bless you.'

'Thank you, Sanita.'

'Don't be silly, it's what friends are for. Try and get some sleep. Speak soon.'

I signed off with kisses and felt at peace for a minute or two there. Matt and I left dad with the television for company as we went up to try and sleep. I wanted to be fresh in the morning but knew that some of the day's events would keep me up for a little bit. Snippets of evidence from the day replayed like an old broken DVD disc that jumped around and froze. My eyes strained and my mind tired itself out with the torch of memories flashing away.

I stirred at around five in the morning. I dreamt of Roddie cradled in my arms, breathing in his baby smells and soft skin. I held him close to me whilst he fed. He was precious and so perfectly innocent. I looked into my baby boy's deep eyes, lost in thought.

All I could see were my children, both Roddie and

Andi. I woke up with a jolt, tears rolled down my cheeks with the realisation of the stark reality I still lived. Somehow in my mind's eye, I could see both children together, probably a year from now. Roddie was saying the odd word here and there and Andi bossed him about. The thing was, I couldn't see Matt or myself anywhere.

I shook the image out of my head and focused on the here and now. After some time adjusting to the morning, I got myself ready for another day at court. It was early but there was no point going back to sleep.

I put on some black trousers and a cream jumper. I would add a printed scarf when heading off but for now, went downstairs to have some cereal and tea. My dad came and joined me a little while later. He was still in his pyjamas and walked around me to squeeze my shoulders with affection.

'Hey, love. How are you doing?'

'I'm okay, dad,' I mumbled.

'Remember, you haven't done anything wrong, and the truth will come out.'

'Yeah, I hope so,' I said.

'Don't worry about anything else, concentrate on what you need to, today,' my dad reassured.

An hour or so later, Matt came down and gulped down a cup of tea. He had the suit of yesterday and pulled at his collar. He didn't have any suits of his own. He was twitchy and yanked at his shirt. It was either his collar, the bottom of his sleeves or tucking and re-tucking it into his trousers. Then he brushed his hair to one side before resuming his shirt tugging.

'Shall we head out, then?' I asked to jolt Matt and

we headed off.

We arrived at the bus stop as our bus moved away. We ran for it, but it was no good, that bus was not waiting around for anything. It was bitterly cold but there was nothing for it but to wait. Matt tried to keep warm by blowing into his palms and moving on the spot.

'We are still early, so we should be okay,' Matt said.

'Yeah, I know... Matt, how do you think it's going so far?'

'I don't know,' Matt said looking down.

'I mean, they haven't got anything other than what Naeed is saying, have they?'

'Yeah, I guess.'

'It's going to be okay, Matt,' and reached up to hug him. We stayed like that until the bus arrived.

NAEED

Alya had started nursery part-time having turned three and was doing mornings. She had begun there in the New Year and struggled to settle. She was always tearful and held me tight that it took every sinew of my body to drag myself away to leave her there. I hated seeing her eyes well with tears, her lips quivering. Then the pained screeching as tears flowed down her puffed out cheeks. On some of the days I worked from home, I took her back home with me than leave her at nursery when she was crying like that. Today, there was no such choice.

I was up at six as usual. It was peaceful at that time of the day, fresh and new. At that time of year, the bleak sky hung sadly. That morning, the rain pelted against the windows interspersed with the shrieking winds. The boiler whirred away in the background as the kitchen warmed and my limbs defrosted.

My hands curled around a warm mug of coffee, sparking all the endorphins. I liked this time to myself before the realities of the day hit. I didn't know what the day would bring but I knew that for the case, it was a turning point.

Sam had gone through the main issues that she was going to cover in her questions and what I needed to think about. The noise in my head battled the pummelling gusts outside, eventually giving way. Sam had asked me to meet her at court at nine, to go over the potential cross examination from the parents.

I sat at the kitchen table looking out into the garden, the season choking everything there.

My little girl was my everything and I would stop at nothing to keep her safe. I felt that same sense of duty for Andi. Sexual abuse was vicious and a near impossible cycle to break. I would not fail Andi or Rodrigo. I knew what she had been through and would not let another child suffer at the hands of this man. I would do everything I could to break that cycle for those children. During these difficult thoughts, Alya's waking sound brought me back.

My mum was already busily getting Alya dressed and ready. I got breakfast ready for them both and waited downstairs. We were a well-oiled team, mum, Alya and I. Alya was in a denim skirt, with pink tights and a sparkly white long-sleeved top. She bounced into the kitchen. She was the best part of me and could never look anything other than perfect in my eyes. My mum had put Alya's hair in two little pigtails and she showed them off to me.

'Mummy, mummy, look at my hair,' Alya squealed.

'Oh wow! Don't you look gorgeous, my little button,' and gave her nose a little pinch. I grabbed her up in my arms and gave her a cuddle. Her skin was so smooth, and I breathed in her sweetness. I put her in her highchair and fed her.

'She is the cutest isn't she, with her little plaits?' My mum exclaimed as she joined us.

'Not that we are at all biased, right mum?' I chuckled.

'Yeah, but still, she is cute, ena, beta?' My mum said as she stroked Alya's chin and kissed her gently on the cheek.

My mum sat with us and had her tea and toast. We chatted aimlessly over breakfast. Mum was taking Alya to nursery today so that I could get to court on time. We still had time for some play before I had to get going.

I put on my favourite grey trouser suit today. I liked how well it fitted me, how it felt and how I felt in it. It was my most expensive suit and was an armour of power that acted as my shield. The jacket sat snugly on my waist. My crisp white shirt underneath tucked into my straight slim legged trousers. It hugged me in comfort and safety. I felt as ready as I ever would be. I kissed my mum and my baby girl before leaving the house to go and fight for some other babies.

Sam had already parked herself in one of the

interview rooms at court and I joined her. My team manager, Lisa hadn't arrived yet, but Sam talked me through my statement.

'So, one of the main things that you will face today is the fact that you were leading Andi to make the disclosures she did. You know that that falls foul of all good practice,' Sam outlined.

'Mmm, right,' I replied.

'So how will you respond to that?' Sam asked.

'Andi was struggling and needed help with explaining it.'

'Yes, but you will need to acknowledge that it was in breach of good practice. That there was a better way to conduct that discussion,' Sam tried.

'But there wasn't any other way,' I said resolutely.

'Naeed, you need to show some regret or humility over the way things happened. I mean you can still say that you were helping Andi disclose but you must accept that it was very clumsy. That it was not the best way. You can say that that does not make the things she said untrue.' Sam asserted.

'She did not know how else to explain it. I had to help her so that we could get to the truth.'

'But it was wrong and worse than that, looks like it was your truth, not Andi's!'

'I don't think you understand,' I started.

Sam interjected, before I could continue, 'No, actually, you don't understand.' Sam stood up, turned her back to me and walked out of the room, as Lisa entered. 'I'll be back, we could do with a breather.'

I pushed back in my chair, stood up and paced the

room. Lisa was bewildered and I quickly filled her in. I had been in the game long enough and had had regular training throughout. I was familiar with good practice guidance of interviewing children. We were to use only open questions and not lead them. Leading children contaminated what they told us. I was well versed in all this, but Sam needed to get well versed in real practice.

When Sam returned, she repeated what she had discussed with me, and Lisa supported what I had said. Sam needed to work with that and find a way of justifying things to the court. Unfortunately, real life was not a textbook and doesn't follow a nice little set of rules. I had to do what I had to so that we could get to the truth from Andi. I didn't regret that. Of course, I wished Andi had come out with it herself, but she was a scared little girl. She needed someone to believe in her.

As much as I could sympathise with Matt a tiny bit, Kelly had no excuse. As a mother I could not understand how she had chosen Matt over her own daughter. If anyone was meant to be on a child's side, it was meant to be their mother. If Kelly wasn't going to believe in Andi and protect her, I had to make sure that I did. That is what I took with me into the hearing that day.

KELLY

Serena had told us to get to court for half past nine and we met her in the cafeteria. We arrived after nine.

The waiting area buzzed with even more people today. The suits were lawyers, and the rest of the herd were the ones facing the guillotine, so to speak. There was a wave of conversations all around, some furrowed faces, some stony, and others blank. We were an eclectic bunch.

Serena hadn't been able to get us an interview room today and so we had a quick catch up in the cafeteria. She looked as polished as ever, her bright pointed, red nails stood out ready, I hoped, for attack. There wasn't much that she needed to talk to us about luckily. Serena summarised that she expected that the Local Authority evidence would end today.

We were all marshalled back into court and took up our seats, all of us in the same ones as yesterday. It is funny how quickly people form territorial habits. Here we were again. Naeed, looked professional and knowledgeable. Even I was not sure that I could disregard what she had to say. How could I possibly expect the Judge not to take what she had to say as gospel? Naeed was sworn in, confirmed her name, professional address, and statements.

Naeed's solicitor kicked off letting Naeed provide her narrative. The solicitor wore a pinstripe skirt suit. All these professionals looked intelligent, calm, and authoritarian. The solicitor always wore her blonde hair tied back in a low bun with some wisps of hair floating around her face. She was beautiful as well as smart.

In the main evidence, Naeed provided the back story for her involvement in the case. She confirmed that she had been Andi's social worker for about a year and a half. Naeed had had about ten visits with Andi in that time and the visits usually lasted for about an hour.

Andi was happy when she saw Naeed. Naeed said, 'She runs to me and enjoys one to one interaction. There have been times when she has become upset when it's time for me to leave and she asks when she will see me again.'

Naeed's lawyer then asks questions about the joint visit Naeed made with Miss Collins to speak to Andi.

Q: Can you tell the court what preparations you made for note taking?

A: I had a notebook on that day. We agreed that Sonia would take the notes.

Q: What happened to the notebook after the visit?

A: At the conclusion of the visit, I made some notes in my car in the same notebook.

Q: What was the purpose of the meeting?

A: Purpose of visit was about the comment Andi had made to her grandmother.

Q: How did you decide who would talk to Andi?

A: Nothing was said about who would talk to Andi.

Naeed went onto explain that they had asked Andi about having baths and what it was like at our home. Andi had told them how much water was in the bath by demonstrating with her hand and her hand was by chest and neck. Naeed had used role play to recreate bathing. They used a box for a bath and a flower for a person having the bath. It sounded like Andi was not saying very much or at least not anything noteworthy about bathing.

It seemed to me that Naeed was confident. She looked intently at the Judge as she gave her evidence.

Her taut face held her wide eyes that dilated as she responded to the questions. There were times that a ghost of a frown appeared and almost a whistle from her pursed lips. Her hands beat to the drum of her words too and it was a strong performance.

Q: What happened next?

A: Andi asked if we could go upstairs. She had bought a teddy bear for me and then for me and Miss Collins... Andi asked if we could go upstairs.

Q: So, you both went upstairs?

A: Andi went up and I was a few steps behind.

Q: What did you ask Miss Collins to do?

A: Nothing was said to Miss Collins about what she was to do.

The evidence continued and Naeed said that they went to Andi's bedroom. Naeed suggested playing a shopping game, which they did for about ten minutes at the most.

Then Naeed took the conversation back to bathing. 'I made a comment about going home, having a bath and I indicated that I was going to scrub my hair and face. I was gesturing,' Naeed said.

Sam asked, 'Did Andi say anything?'

'Andi then gestured that she scrubs her belly.'

I glanced over and saw the grey wool atop the Judge's bowed head as he jotted furiously. Occasionally, the Judge prodded his spectacles back up his nose, but his pen did not seem to take a pause. His head seemed to nod in agreement with what Naeed testified. Serena was bent over in front of us too, scribbling away in between brief peeks up.

The questioning continued:

Q: What happened then?

A: At that point I asked her what happened that time when she was in the bath with Matty. I said something like, 'Can you tell me what happened at the time when you were in the bath with Matty. I used a gentle tone because I knew Andi was apprehensive with questions.

Q: What did Andi say?

A: Swift response by Andi. She looked down, then said, 'Matty scrubbed me.' I then asked where Matty scrubbed you. She pointed to her genital area.

Q: What did Andi say?

A: There were no words. No eye contact, she continued to look down.

Q: Was anything else said?

A: I asked what she was doing, and she said, 'I scrubbed Matty.' I asked where.

She pointed to my genital area and said, 'and behind.'

Q: Any other words?

A: No and still no eye contact.

Oddly, Naeed went onto recollect that having said all that, Andi jumped up and wanted Naeed to put a CD on. Naeed claimed that she didn't react to what Andi had said and carried on as if everything was normal. Andi then said she wanted to tell Miss Collins something so both she and Naeed went back downstairs. That was when Naeed managed to let Miss Collins know what Andi had said.

Throughout, Naeed remained sincere and

unwavering. It was unnerving and with each part of her evidence, I had an internal sinking. I fell into myself more and more.

I glanced over at Matt several times and saw the veins prod from his neck, his facial muscles tensed. I reached out to him, but he jerked his knee away and his whole body stiffened next to me.

'What exactly did you say to Miss Collins?' Sam asked.

'I told Sonia that Andi had shared that Matt had touched her inappropriately in the genital areas.'

'Where was Andi?'

'She was underneath the stairs playing. I made sure Andi couldn't hear.'

That was pretty much Naeed's evidence. She had stuck to her statement and expanded on certain points. It was hard to listen to and some of the time I blocked it all out. I felt sick inside. Naeed seemed to bear into me at times in her evidence and her eyes filled with contempt.

My head burnt hotly and a rising shame in the pit of my stomach. I kept my eyes down.

NAEED

I had seen Serena in action before, so I knew this would be gruelling. As soon as Serena stood up, I felt myself tense, my body rigid and muscles constricted. I was on edge and determined not to get caught out like I had a few times before when I have gone head-to-head with Serena.

She was one feisty lawyer, and I knew that the slightest lapse in concentration, she would exploit. I needed to be on my A game. Andi needed me to bring the best, Rodrigo needed me to be the best.

Serena eyed me with disdain. Her stare, Antarctic and glassed jaw jutted beneath. She opened with some of the historical background information, going through the chronology. She continued with questions around my involvement with the family.

Next up was Andi being placed with the paternal family and before that, living with Kelly and Matt. She then moved onto the initial incidents of sexualised behaviour. It had happened a month after I had been allocated to the case. Andi was only four or thereabouts at the time. My heart rate quickened as my nails dug into my hands, they were so tightly clasped together.

'Can you turn to page D two hundred and sixty-six. You will see that the sexualised behaviour was Andi peeing on toys.'

'I can see that,' I agreed.

'Can you explain how that is sexualised?' Serena asked.

'Well... erm... it's a culmination of things.'

'So, you agree that peeing on toys is not of itself sexualised?'

'Yeah, I suppose not,' I conceded. I kicked myself for having tripped through this trapdoor so easily and so early.

I explained during cross examination that Andi had been referred to a psychologist. The reason for the referral was Andi's episodes of screaming and defiant behaviour. The work was in a safe environment and over a period of time.

'There was then, an opportunity that Andi could explore her feelings etc of what was going on at home?' Serena questioned.

'Yes.'

'But she made none of these disclosures that time.'

'No.'

The cross examination was relentless and prolonged. I was under constant attack; the gunshots were fired non-stop. Most times they hit but occasionally I dodged a bullet or two. My insides rattled as my nerves were ever increasing circles.

I tried to keep Andi and Rodridgo at the forefront of my evidence to steady me and keep me on track, but it wasn't always easy.

This Serena didn't get real life at all. There was no let up. She had no idea what it was like to be a child, suffering abuse and keeping it a shameful secret. Unless you have been through it, how could you know?

Q: What was your reaction to what grandma told you?

A: It was new information. I was surprised.

Q: At that point Andi had not made any disclosure about anything of a sexual nature, had she?

A: At that stage we didn't think there was anything inappropriate. We wanted to investigate.

I tried to explain that I had looked at the risk assessment of Matt and he had been assessed as low risk. I had followed that and had not thought he was an abuser. When Andi made a disclosure about being in the bath and knowing Matt's history, we had to investigate.

Even though, there was nothing untoward from what Andi had said, it was important. Important enough, that it had to be explored.

I had to accept that Miss Collins did not undertake any real preparation in advance of the visit to Andi. I admitted that there was 'no discussion about how the topic would be addressed.'

There was no stopping the onslaught, a ravaging fire took hold.

I was more and more flustered. Pockets of sweat formed under my arms and stuck to what had been my freshly cleaned shirt. I became aware that I kept tugging at my hair, pulling it behind my ears.

Serena's lips curled, her nostrils flared, and eyes glared down at me. Serena asked me about what discussion there had been about taking notes. Whether any guidance had been given to Miss Collins? I had sunk into myself. I said, 'I assumed she would take adequate notes.' The fleeting frown and pressed lips let me, and no doubt, the Judge, know exactly what Serena thought.

From that point, I tried to stop looking over at Serena and instead maintained my eyes on the Judge. He was side on to me as he kept his notes in sync with my evidence. Occasionally, he turned towards me and looked curiously at me. I felt sure the Judge empathised and was on our side.

When we moved onto the actual discussion with Andi, I tried to regroup and responded shortly. I accepted that I had approached the topic pretty much straightaway. We told Andi that we had come to talk to her about what she had told nan.

I was forced to accept that in hindsight I could have approached it in a different way. This concession set the ball rolling yet again with my rising apprehension. At every turn, Serena boxed me out of the ring. Somehow, Serena got me to see, that the way I had questioned Andi, could be perceived as misleading.

Despite all Sam's efforts, I had never conceded the point. Somehow with disarming skill, Serena had cornered me. On the very point that my lawyer had strived to prepare me on.

I felt my face gradually flush; my palms were sticky and shaky that I had to sit on them to keep grounded. Even my voice felt squeaky, but I gulped down some water to even myself out.

At this juncture, the Judge intervened. He said, 'Your method was deeply flawed. Your approach ensured that Andi would have said the same thing she would have told nan. That is not the way of getting Andi to open up to the truth of what happened.'

'Yes, your Honour,' I replied.

There was then analysis of the notes by Miss Collins and my case recordings. Serena highlighted, 'the word 'nothing' was missing from your statement and case recordings. Miss Collins stated it in her notes. You had those notes in front of you, both when you did your statement, and when you did the case recordings.'

'I don't know why,' I said. 'Andi said 'I can't remember' she didn't say 'nothing'.

'So, Miss Collins, who was making notes at the

time, is mistaken. We are to accept your memory a couple of weeks after the event,' Serena said rhetorically.

I faced more criticism for again introducing another topic. This time it was my asking about the scrubbing.

Serena read out part of my case notes, 'You say that 'she eventually volunteered...'. So how hard did you have to try for Andi to say that her 'mummy scrubbed her'?'

'I talked about washing my hair and the gestures,' I stumbled.

I knew I was coming across as having something to hide or worse, deliberately misleading. It looked like I had pushed my agenda onto Andi and forced her to say what I wanted to hear.

As much as this was nonsensical, it lent itself to the picture Serena was painting. Her story was that I was some zealous social worker on a misguided mission.

Sam was right. I should have got a head start and owned up to the mistakes in my main evidence rather than let Serena prove me wrong. I peeped over at Sam, and she definitely avoided me.

The cross examination moved onto what Andi told me in her bedroom:

Q: How did you continue the conversation with Andi upstairs?

A: I said, 'Can you describe to me what happened when you were in the bath with Matty?'

Q: When Andi said that Matty scrubbed her down there, what words did she use?

A: No words were used. I asked her what Matty did, and she said he scrubbed her. I asked her where and she pointed to the genital area. There were no words, she pointed. Then I asked her what she did, and she said she scrubbed Matty. I asked her where and this time she pointed to my genital area and said, 'and behind'.

My evidence closed with discussion of the police station DVD interview with Andi. I had described there having been no disclosure during that interview. The Judge's ear pricked up. His face paled and he grew as his back straightened like a tightrope.

His Honour Judge Carter said, 'I have been hearing time and again reference to 'disclosures'. The lessons of the Cleveland Report have surely been learnt. Terms such as disclosure and victim put everything on the wrong footing. It starts the premise of any investigation from a belief basis of the allegation. For any investigation to be seen as independent as well as being independent, we must all be very careful to avoid such language,' he admonished.

Finally, this torturous interrogation came to an end. I was spent but pushed myself out of the witness chair and walked quickly back to the safety of my seat behind Sam. I kept my head down and avoided eye contact with all in the court room.

I was completely and utterly shredded to pieces.

Chapter Twelve

KELLY

Naeed's evidence took us to the lunch break, and we managed to get into an interview room with Serena. We had no time to talk about Naeed's evidence because after lunch I would have to face the inquisition. Serena released both Matt and I but asked me to be back in twenty minutes to go over my evidence.

We went to the cafeteria in the court building and I could only manage a cup of coffee. Matt had a sandwich with his cup of tea. I should have had tea too, as I was already full of nervous energy that the coffee made me feel queasy. Nonetheless, I gulped it down burning my tongue en route in my rush to return to Serena.

Serena explained that she would start by asking me to confirm my name and address. She would then take me to my statement, which I would confirm.

My insides were jittery, and my mind raced. My ears were full of wax that I could barely make out what Serena said. I got bits and bobs. She said something about her questions to me being open, rather than leading ones. I was completely lost in this world of legal jargon.

My heart throbbed that I had pains in my chest. I clutched my chest as Serena talked. 'Kelly, did you hear me? Kelly?'

The sharpness of Serena's voice cut through me

and brought me back. 'Yes, yes, I'm sorry what was that?' I asked, pressing down the pains.

Serena explained again that the only issue she had for me was the bathing routines for Andi. I'd have to address what happened when Andi jumped into Matt's baths. We had gone over it so many times and yet I was completely a blank.

My nerves were shot, as the minutes ticked away, I felt a heaviness in my heart. I struggled to focus and felt nauseous. I tried to steady myself. I read and re-read my statement over and over to ground myself but all I saw were black squiggles and blurred lines.

'Do you know what the others will ask me?' I asked.

'The main thing will be why you didn't tell the police about Andi jumping into the bath when Matt was in there. They will try and make it look like that is because you know that that was inappropriate.'

'What do I say to that?'

'The truth. What you told me, that you overlooked it.'

'Okay, you think that's okay?'

'Keep to the truth and you will be okay. You have got this,' Serena said with a confidence I was certainly not feeling myself.

We were all called back into court and with every step, I felt more and more tense. I was the ant crawling into the lion's den. Serena called me into the witness box, and I took the oath on the Bible. That was the only part of this experience that was scripted out for me, readymade. Everything else would have to come from within me. There was no more auto cue from here on out.

Serena asked me to explain Andi's bathing routines when she was at home with us. 'She had a bath every day. I had a bath with her too as it made it easier to have the bath together. So that Andi wasn't on her own,' I summarised. I had calmed a little.

'What was Andi like in the bath?' Serena asked.

'Andi loved water. She enjoyed the bath.' I replied shortly.

Serena's questioning continued. It was something I had practised in my head so much that it came naturally. As nervous as I still was, I felt as comfortable as I probably could in a situation like this. I hoped that I came across as sincere and honest because my replies, as practised as they were, were also my truth.

Q: Can you tell us about Andi being in the bath with Matt?

A: Andi did jump in the bath with Matt around five times.

Q: What do you say about the suggestion that Matt got in bath with Andi?

A: I never saw Andi in the bath and then Matt getting in after her.

I explained that it was my responsibility for washing Andi. Often, I got Andi to wash herself so that she would learn to do that independently as she got older. She was still young and so I had to lend her a helping hand but tried to encourage her to do as much as possible for herself.

'Kelly, did you ever have any concerns about Andi

jumping into the bath when Matt was in there?' Serena asked.

'I didn't think it was inappropriate at the time that they had a bath together. My view has changed now because of the work we have carried out. My views have changed on a lot of things.' I acknowledged.

'What do you think about the role model that was set for Andi back then?' Serena probed.

'It's not a good role model. Andi shouldn't be in a bath on her own with a man and shouldn't see things that are not necessary, I mean a naked person.'

'So why did you let that happen?'

'He used to cover himself with a hand towel or flannel; I used to see him do it. Like I said, I have learnt a lot now.'

Serena told me to stay where I was and that the solicitor for the Local Authority would now ask me some questions. Sam was on the attack from the outset.

She pointed me to Matt's statement, where he had described how he had scrubbed Andi's legs, back and arms. 'Why did you never tell the police this?' Sam accused.

As I had discussed with Serena, I told the truth, 'It only happened once or twice when she had pen marks on her. I hadn't given thought to it at the time.

'What do you think Andi's Dad would have thought about his daughter being in the bath with Matt?' Sam pushed.

'Don't know, he didn't care,' I replied tersely.

I again explained that Andi loved water. I didn't think anything of it when she jumped into the bath, when Matt was already in there. I thought it was because of her love of water and I was usually in the bathroom with them. Matt did sometimes say to me that he didn't want her in there because he wanted to be able to have a quick wash and get out. We were not fast enough to stop Andi.

Sam interrogated me about why I hadn't stopped this from happening.

Q: You knew she was going to do it because she had done it a few times.

A: Yes, I suppose.

Q: So why had you never thought of stopping it?

A: Once Andi had made her mind up on something, she would do it. No one could stop it.

The discussion then moved onto Matt's own history and the sexual abuse he had suffered. I admitted that I had not known anything at all about it until these proceedings.

When Andi was with us, we had stayed at Matt's parents' home on the odd occasion. It did send shivers down my spine, thinking back on that now. To be that close to a known predator and having not known it at that time. To be fair, Matt, never let Andi stay with his parents. Even when we popped to the shops, Matt never let Andi stay at his parents' house. I said, 'I thought it was strange at the time. Then I thought maybe it's because they weren't the actual grandparents.'

Sam then pressed the point about the work we had done around protective parenting. I acknowledged again that we had learnt a lot from that work and had done work around the children's bath routines. I again repeated that I now knew things needed to change.

'The thing I don't understand, Kelly and maybe you can help us here. Matt made sure he put his pyjamas on when Andi would come into your bed. That's right, isn't it?'

'Yes,' I replied.

'I mean, it was important to both of you that Andi did not get into bed with Matt unless he was wearing his pyjamas, right?'

'Yes.'

'In other words, Andi was not to be around Matt if Matt was naked in bed?'

'Yes, I have said that, yes,' I began to lose my temper.

'And yet, you did not even question why he let her come into the bath with him when he was completely naked.'

I had no words.

MATTHEW

As Kelly came back to take her seat next to me, I reached out for her hand, and she grasped it. We held onto each other tightly until court adjourned for the day.

When the Judge left the court room, Kelly whispered to me, 'I'm so sorry, Matt.'

'No, you have nothing to be sorry for,' I replied and pulled her into an embrace.

Serena turned and went to say something but stayed silent for a few seconds. She waited until we released, when she mumbled something about a quick catch up outside.

We scrambled out of the court room. We headed into one of the interview rooms for our usual debrief at the end of a session. Once away from prying ears, Serena did the best she could as always to reassure us.

Nothing could stop Kelly beat herself up. Kelly felt she had messed up at the end but couldn't see that she had come across as honest and thoughtful. There was nothing either Serena or I could say to ease Kelly's self-doubt.

'You did well, Kelly. You kept your cool and stayed calm throughout,' Serena reassured.

'I know I didn't,' Kel responded with tears in her eyes.

'Don't Kel, you did great,' I said as I squeezed her shoulders.

'I didn't Matt. I'm so sorry, I let you down.'

'You could never let me down, Kel.'

Serena tried to get us to think about tomorrow and the evidence I would need to give. Kelly and I were too mashed to be able to think straight or follow what Serena said.

We agreed that we would rest up for the day and go at it again afresh the next day. The aim was to meet at nine in the morning and go through what I would need to deal with. I told Serena that I would read through my statement tonight to save time in the morning. Hopefully that meant I would only need a quick breeze through it then.

I didn't spend much time with Kel that night

because I was distracted with thoughts of my evidence tomorrow.

Kel was preoccupied too. She kept asking me what I thought about what she had said in evidence. Whether she could have said that being in bed with a child was different to being in a bath with a child. Or, she could have said, she never saw it as an issue, the bed nor the bath, or she should have said no comment. She turned herself inside out and nothing I said alleviated her stresses. It got so bad that she went over every other part of what she had said and what she could have done differently.

Neither of us was any good to each other and needed time apart to think things through on our own.

We agreed that I would stay at our place that night, whilst Kel stayed at her dad's. When I was back there, I spent some time reading over my statement. I also looked over Kelly's statement and all the Local Authority witness statements.

I lost count of how many times I read them all and re-read them. I was a man obsessed and poured over the evidence, somehow willing it to fall our way.

The question that Kel got unstuck with played on my mind. Why was I okay with Andi getting in the bath with me when I never let her in our bed unless I put my pyjamas on? I saw the bath differently; its where you cleaned, and the bed was where you were intimate. I knew I couldn't explain it in this way, but that's how I had seen it.

I couldn't sleep and decided to go out for a walk. I didn't feel the February chill, but the midnight air cleared the cobwebs. Frosty steam exhaled out of me and reflected into my face. My nose was an ice tap, and my snorting was almost in tune with the beat of my steps.

I walked and walked, not even in any particular direction. Eventually, I somehow found myself back home. A few minutes later, I was sound asleep, but not for long and was soon up, reading those statements all over again.

When it was time to ready for the off, I was on autopilot, showered and dressed. I tried to make a bit more of an effort today than I have for the previous court hearings.

I decided to ditch my brother's suit and instead went for some smart trousers and shirt. I ironed my dressy, black trousers and my suit, plain white shirt. I grabbed the only tie I owned, a purple one with black dots in diamonds. I couldn't work out how to put it on and figured I'd get Kel to sort it out for me.

She sorted everything out. She was my rock and even though I didn't tell her enough, I don't know what I would do without her. Through all this, she had stuck by me without question, even when I pushed her away. I would show her what she meant after all this was over. I hoped I would redeem her faith in me, faith, that not even I had in me, at times.

I was not a breakfast person at all but did need a cup of tea first thing in the morning to get me going. I sat with my mug of tea and thought over what had gone on these past few days.

At times, I was completely bamboozled and out of

my depth with what was being said. I didn't always understand all the tricks and manoeuvrings in court, but I was hanging in there.

What was most concerning is that I didn't follow a line of questioning. I didn't know what the destination was at the start of the interrogation. That made me worry about getting tripped up but all I could do was deal with what I got asked, one step at a time. I had to focus on what was in front of me.

I drank my tea and tried to shake my nerves away. I pulled my jacket over me and darted out, stuffing my tie in my pocket as I went.

I made my way over to Kel's Dad's home and waited till Kel was dressed and good to go.

This was what it was all about, our kids and our family. Roddie was the most perfect baby boy I had ever seen but I knew I was biased. He was the spit of Kel and for that I was thankful. Whatever they threw at us, we had to keep Roddie and Andi in our hearts and minds as a way of getting through it. They were defenceless and depended on us to protect and love them. They needed us to be their parents. That was exactly what we would do.

As always, Kel knotted my tie for me and tidied me up before we made our familiar route back to court. Kel and I were back at court before Serena for a change. We found a room and holed up in there.

Serena was not far behind us and soon found us. She got comfortable exchanging her coat for our lever arch file in her suitcase. She wore her serious black skirt suit. We were most certainly now at the business end of things and Serena was about to close the deal.

I knew that I would either make or break this deal. I was not strong enough to carry that kind of weight but readied myself to throw everything I had at it. My legs fought against the current.

I waded through the quicksand towards my own personal torture chamber. Roddie and Andi beat inside me.

KELLY

I watched as Matt walked stiffly into the spotlight. The stress ached out of Matt, as he kept his head down and entered the witness box.

Matt is not religious at all. I'm sure he believes in a higher force, but he doesn't follow any particular belief system. Swearing on the Bible was never for Matt and so he affirmed that he would tell the truth. He spoke tautly and without any emotion, the words came out in stops and starts.

Matt confirmed that there had been a few occasions, about five to six times, when Andi jumped into the bath with him. There had never been an occasion when Andi would be in the bath first and that he would jump in. Matt was clear that he would be in the bath and then Andi jumped in.

He maintained eye contact with Serena and the Judge as fairly as he could. It was like umpiring a tennis game, when you were up there, giving your truth. His voice had more colour to it as he went on and he settled into this unreal situation.

Serena asked, 'When you cleaned Andi, where on her body did you clean her?'

'I would clean her face, arms, and legs. I never washed her genital area.' Matt replied.

'It has been said that you might have used a flannel to clean Andi in the genital areas. What do you say to that?'

'I never cleaned or touched Andi in the genital area. I never used a flannel to clean Andi in the genital areas. There would be times when Andi would wash her genital parts and I would be there.'

'Mr Barnett, can you tell us what you think about Andi saying that she washed you in your genital areas?' Serena questioned.

'Not true. I don't know that I even believe that Andi even said that. Andi would never wash me on any part of me, not even accidentally.'

I was so proud of Matt when he described how he would take a different view now about having baths with Andi. We had both learnt from the course we had completed.

Matt explained how we had undertaken work sheets about sexualised behaviour. Serena got him to talk about the changes in understanding sexual behaviour. He showed insight, how his attitude and approach had changed. It showed that the work had had the impact it needed. We could parent our children safely and protect them from sexual harm.

Sam stood up ready to put up the challenge for the Local Authority. The first line of attack was that Matt and I had colluded in what we said. Matt was firm that the reason our evidence was similar was because we were always together. So of course, we both knew what happened.

Matt said that he always worried that something like this would happen. That's why he always got me to come up so that I could verify what happened. I never knew this and had a newfound compassion for my Matt. He had carried a heavy burden all these years. I wasn't sure he even understood it entirely himself.

'Mr Barnett, can you turn to page E one hundred and sixteen, report from sexual offenders expert and look at paragraph sixteen?' Sam drew out.

'Yeah, I see it,' Matt confirmed.

'It says that your aunt had told you that your dad used 'to touch you up' and the others and used to do things with others.'

'I was only fifteen or sixteen years old, then,' Matt said.

I could see that he was more and more tense. The knots in his neck bulged. His eyes were icy. He grasped his hands together on the witness box, the tips of his fingers pressed down hard. I could sense that Matt was irritable. They threw this at him for exactly this reason; to get at him and it worked. I wanted them to stop but there was nothing I could do.

I had to sit there, still, and silent.

They moved onto the issue around Matt not letting Andi into our bed unless he was in his pyjamas. We had a stair gate in Andi's room, but she would often climb over this and come into our bedroom. Matt usually sleeps in the nude or in shorts. He said that he felt it was wrong to let Andi into bed if he was naked or wearing boxers.

Matt's gravelly intonation was unusually flat, and he tripped over his words from time to time. Matt's eyes darted all around the room. The problem was trying to explain why he let Andi jump in the bath with him when he was so strict about the bed situation.

'She would jump in when I was having a bath,' Matt stuttered.

'Why did you never call Kelly by the time Andi took her clothes off etc, it would have taken some time so why never call her?'

'I never thought of it at the time,' Matt replied sheepishly.

Sam threw a barrage of arrows at Matt for failing to tell the police about washing Andi. She revelled in painting a picture of Matt deliberately hiding it because he knew much worse had gone on. It was all part of the Local Authority synopsis that Matt had sexually abused Andi as his father had abused him.

Matt worked hard not to succumb to that. He desperately pleaded that he had just forgotten about it because it wasn't our usual routine. Matt frantically explained that if he had hidden it, he would still be hiding it now. His words tumbled over themselves and crashed into each other. I understood what he was saying but I was not sure that anyone else did; the point lost in the wilderness.

Sam then got into the nitty gritty of what Matt had been willing to accept.

Q: Why would you scrub her stomach?

A: She would have nail varnish and I would need to do it at times.

Q: What about her back?

A: Did her back because she couldn't do it.

Q: And her legs?

A: Washed legs with her flannel until three quarters up.

The Local Authority returned to Matt's history. They criticised him for not telling me about his history with his dad. Matt reddened, lowered his head even further. He hid behind his long floppy hair as he explained that he never told anyone. For a tall, bulky man, he shrunk before my eyes. It came out that he seemed to think that no one would want him, if they knew what had happened to him as a child.

'But Mr Barnett, Andi's mum didn't know what had happened to you. She didn't know if there were any concerns. You allowed her young child to get in the bath with you?' Sam highlighted.

'I didn't think it was wrong at the time. I've learnt through assessment and courses now.'

'But you did know it was a risky situation didn't you, given what your dad did to you at bath times. You repeated that same pattern of behaviour, didn't you, Mr Barnett?'

Sam threw her knockout blow.

MATTHEW

Here it was! I had read about my dad touching me when I was in the bath and knew that they would try to use that against me.

I couldn't remember it myself, but it made me feel sick when I first read it. It was like lightening on a clear day that struck me right in the stomach. I had had to rush to the toilet and threw up in the bathroom sink. It was diarrhoea from the wrong end. The pungent taste it left in my mouth lingered so much that it was there again now.

So, my dad had rubbed me down below and made me pull him until he came and that is what they believed I did to Andi. That was the whole thing with this case. They believed that I would sexually abuse my children as I had been abused. What had happened to me was used against me. I had suffered as a child and suffered again as an adult. My dad had abused me and now the system abused me all over again.

The sexual abuse victim was now the perpetrator. An inherited gene or something. I leaned forward and over the witness box, 'It wasn't risky for me. I'm not my dad,' I said.

We went over the bath issue again and again.

Q: She was in the bath with you?

A: Yes, she was.

Q: Any reason why she would say it nearly two years after?

A: She says a lot of things, she says she wants to see me as well.

Sam glossed over what I had said and pressed on with casting me as some sort of evil sexual predator.

I became frustrated that they were not listening to me. I was not my father. I was me, simply me. Serena had warned me that they would goad me and advised me to keep it at the same level throughout.

I had to remember that it was the Judge that would make the decision. It didn't matter what the Local Authority thought of me, only what the Judge thought of me. I tried to keep this uppermost in my mind as this inquisition continued. Sam's questions prodded at me relentlessly. She was the annoying bee that I wanted to swat away but it was so much more serious than that.

Sam threw questions about the specific allegations at me. 'What do you think about Miss Kaur's evidence?'

'Andi could have been pointing anywhere, it's misleading,' I answered.

'You touched Andi's genital areas,' Sam accused.

'I've never touched Andi anywhere,' I shouted back.

I immediately realised that I had broken one of the cardinal rules. Serena had been clear about this; not to show any anger. I looked down in embarrassment and didn't even dare glance in Serena's direction.

'And yet, you would have us believe that you touched her in all innocence, naked, in the bath. Like your dad!'

Sam got the winning point right there.

Something fell to the pit of my stomach, leaving my beating chest empty. I launched myself back into the seat, thrust my face into the open, cold, sweaty palms for a moment and released.

All eyes from the court room bore into me and I went to get up out of my seat. I was about to head back to my seat when Serena stopped me. She explained that the Guardian's Solicitor and the Judge might have questions for me, so I stayed put.

It turned out that Serena was right, and the Guardian's Solicitor did have things she wanted to raise with me.

The solicitor for the Guardian stood up for her turn at me.

Q: You told the sexual offenders expert that your aunt had told you what your dad had done to you.

A: Yeah, but I blocked it all out and didn't remember all the details.

Q: You told us earlier that if you were in bed, you would be wearing tight underwear. You wouldn't let Andi in and tell her to go to her own bed.

A: Yeah.

Q: Yet you had Andi in the bath.

A: I've accepted that I had Andi in the bath.

Q: You didn't let her in the bed when you had some clothes on so why did you let her in the bath when you would have had nothing on?

A: I know now it was daft.

Q: I can't understand why you didn't say, Andi, this is wrong, it is not on, when she came in the bath.

A: I didn't think about it then.

Margaret continued trying to put holes in the explanation Kelly and I had provided. Supposedly taking a neutral position, Margaret seemed to be very against us. She hadn't put up much of a challenge at all with the Local Authority witnesses. She was much more confrontational with me. 'I mean, come on, Matt, at the oldest she was three and half years old, baths are quite high.'

'Ours is pretty low,' I responded.

'Was she really able to jump in?'

'She held the side of the bath and jumped in. I was sat upright in the bath when she jumped in,' I explained.

'I would suggest that you had opportunity and you took it.'

'At the time I didn't think I was doing any harm, now I do. The boundaries were not in place at the time, and they should have been.'

That was it. Margaret was done, as was I.

I returned to my seat and Kel's hand reached over to me. It had been our thing throughout these days of the trial. Our way of being connected and finding our way through the ups and downs, twists and turns. It had been a rollercoaster and we were almost at the end, but I had made it a hundred time worse.

There was no coming back from the aggressive behaviour I had displayed. That was all the Judge would remember of me, violent and probably a sexual child abuser.

The Judge adjourned for the lunch break.

Kel, Serena and I managed to return to the same space we had had used earlier. A lot of times, they got taken up with other court users but this time, the timing seemed to work for us. I sank into one of the chairs and lay my head onto the table in front of me. I was fully spent.

Kel was by my side straight away and hugged me, 'Well done. I'm so proud of you.'

'I don't know,' I said, lifting myself back into my

seat. Kel sat in the chair next to me.

'You both have done your bit, now it's back to me,' Serena said.

'What do you mean?' Kel asked.

'All the evidence has been heard. Now each of the solicitors have the chance to make some oral submissions.'

'Oh right,' Kel said. 'So, do you need anything from us?'

'No, but you guys can go have some food and have a think about anything you want me to say on your behalf. Come back fifteen minutes before we need to head back into court, and we can go over it then. Does that sound okay?'

'Sure,' Kel replied. 'Do you want us to get you anything?'

'No, I'm all good, thanks. Matt don't worry about a thing, you did well. You spoke honestly and from the heart.'

'Thanks, Serena.' I needed that and somehow, I sensed, Serena knew it too.

Chapter Thirteen

KELLY

It was hard to think about what more we could say to the Judge. Our best had been the worst. We were both spent and feared that whatever we came up with would sabotage us as we had during our evidence.

My head throbbed and Matt was quieter than usual. Matt and I had given everything and there was nothing more we could say. We told Serena that she knew as much as we did about the case. Whatever the outcome, we had all done our best and there was nothing more anyone could have asked of us.

I saw that the Judge's pen was poised as Serena stood up to make her final submissions on the case. She patted the back of her suit as she stood and put her hands on the bench, steadying herself.

This had all been launched because of what Andi had supposedly said to her paternal grandmother and the reliance that had been placed on that. Matt had accepted that he was in the bath with Andi but that he was in there first when Andi jumped in. Serena asked the court to look at what Matt had said about being alone in the bath with Andi, pointing to the relevant section of Matt's statement, where he had said that he would call me up.

'Your Honour, in evidence he accepted he was alone in the bath with Andi by which point he had called Kelly up to the bath. It's difficult to judge the time that elapsed,' Serena pressed. She acknowledged that there had been poor boundaries in place; that we were not able to recognise what was appropriate at that time. At the crux of it, there had been no inappropriate touching and no sexual motivation.

The Judge wrote furiously, and I didn't know how he kept up with Serena. She was on a roll, and I could tell that she moved smoothly from one point to the next.

Having highlighted some of the aspects of our evidence, Serena then gave her take on Naeed's evidence. She did not hold back and went all out. She was scathing about Naeed's evidence and described her as 'wholly unsatisfactory and unreliable.'

I winced at times, thinking that maybe, Serena went a little too far and unsure how it would fall. I noticed the Judge raised his eyebrows, peered at Serena but did not stop her. He looked up from his notes, his pen on pause and seemed to listen even more intently. I hoped that these were all good signs.

I leaned forward and Matt leaned backwards, beside me. I looked back at him, he had his eyes closed, and I turned back to the front to hear what Serena was saying.

'The Local Authority evidence before the court is entirely defective. Starting with the initial visit the Social Workers made to Andi, this was very significant, particularly when considering what Andi said and she indicated by pointing. The questions asked were as important as answers given.

The topic of bath times and washing were introduced by the social worker and so there was no opportunity for Andi to give her own account. This fell far short of well-established good practice guidance. There was a complete lack of consideration of good practice.

There was no attempt to justify this departure, which evidences that it was not even on the radar. In fact, there seemed utter contempt for good practice.'

Serena explained that an interview with the child is essential. The Achieving Best Evidence guidance for police interviews with children applied to social work interviews in much the same way.

There ought to have been appropriate planning and Serena stressed the importance of this. Serena expanded on the dangers of not preparing and the consequence on compromising the evidence, effectively contaminating it. The result of this blatant disregard for good practice and haphazard planning was that the interview was an abject failure.

Serena continued tearing through the Social Worker's evidence and stressed how the Social Worker prompted Andi. She explained that the co-worker's notes using the word 'eventually' heavily implied that questioning went beyond the norm. Unfair pressure had been placed on Andi, perhaps to the extent that she had to say what they wanted to hear.

It was unclear what the truth was, whether Andi even said the things that are reported as it seems that the Social Workers were desperate to sell this story. If Andi did say these things, it was surely all the constant prompting that led Andi there. It was this that made the evidence so unreliable, that none of us knew what Andi genuinely wanted to say.

The Judge now made notes here and there, not with every point that Serena bulleted. It was hard to tell what this meant. Was he bored with what she said? Or was he sifting out what he felt would not help him in his considerations? Maybe, he was making notes of what he agreed with or what he didn't agree with. I couldn't take any cues from the pace or nature of note taking.

Serena asserted, 'It's impossible to recall now through passage of time exactly what words were used, in what order, to what question, so we need to look at the notes, but sadly, they too were woeful. The notes by Miss Collins include notes by Miss Kaur that she made in the car, but they were also not reliable, as she said, they were more an aide memoir to recall. Assessing the reliability of the evidence and what the child said was the problem here.'

On the issue of reliability, Serena pointed out that the social worker had told the court what Andi said to her about being touched in her genital areas, but this was through action and not words. We now knew that the allegations this father was facing was merely through pointing and through leading questions.

Serena neared the end of her submissions, 'Even if the Local Authority evidence was reliable, I ask the court where the evidence was that father's behaviour was sexually motivated? I remind myself that Andi said bath times were happy.

There was no suggestion, let alone evidence, that he touched her private parts. Sexual abuse was absent here. Unreliable evidence about the allegations from the Local Authority and not repeated in police interview. Complete conjecture and truth engineering at its worst.'

Matt and I had reversed our positions, I sat back into the bench and Matt had moved forward. What Serena had said was exactly the truth, but I didn't know if that was going to be enough.

My stomach pulled away from itself and turned on itself. My fingers were red raw from how much I squeezed at them. This was our life, our family and we no longer had any control, if we ever had any at all.

Serena was in the final straight. 'The parents' evidence was clear, consistent, and compelling. The weakness of parents' evidence, perhaps, was the admission by the parents that father and stepdaughter were in bath alone. Mother says she was always there. This was their routine, can't infer from that, that sexual abuse happened. What we would think was inappropriate can't be put on the parents, we can't infer that they think the same way.

The burden of proof should not be reversed. It was for the Local Authority to prove their allegation, not for Matt to prove his innocence,' Serena finished with a flourish. She looked back at us to check if we had anything else, we wanted her to say, there wasn't, she had summed it all up as best as anyone could.

That was our last throw of the dice.

NAEED
I have to say that there were times when Serena

even had me convinced, as frustrating as some of what she said was. Other times, my blood pumped with rage. My usually brown knuckles turned yellow and lined my punch ready fists. She denigrated me as a social worker.

All those years of study and fine tuning my work binned with household rubbish and the like. I knew in my heart that Andi had been sexually molested, but I had no way of proving it. I had tried my best to get the truth out there. Now it was over to Sam to make the court see it.

Sam started with reference to the Local Authority witnesses. She began with the paternal grandmother's evidence. She noted that it was clear that she loved her granddaughter. Nothing she said had been unreliable. She spoke with authority. She had a silvery voice shining through all the fog of this trial.

My yellow knuckles browned. My temperature fell as the anger seeped out of my flattened fingers. My hands sat a little more comfortably on my lap as Sam set out the case.

Sam pointed out, that if the police interview with Andi had yielded different results, my evidence was spot on. That, right there, was the irony of it all! 'Miss Kaur provided her recollections as best as she could. She accepted in her evidence, that no planning had been undertaken. Despite that, they used their best efforts.'

The fact was that Andi might have been happy with the baths. She had not shown any distress when talking about that, but that did not mean that she had not suffered. Andi wasn't worried about any moral context because she didn't have any moral context.

That was the failing of this mother and her partner.

Sam explained that there had been less than two feet between Andi and me when Andi shared what happened. 'Andi had pointed to her own genital areas and then at the social worker's as well as saying 'and behind'. If the court accepts that evidence, then only one sensible reason for that. That is that the child was telling the truth,' Sam asserted.

Next was Sam's spin on the parents' evidence. She submitted that it needed to be looked at within the totality of the evidence. The episodes where father said he had scrubbed Andi's back, stomach, and arms were not in his police station interview. That featured much later in proceedings. He had said that he had only washed her face in his police interview and there's a reason for that.

'Your Honour, when the police questioned mum, mum failed to mention these particulars. This is worrying. If she was around, when scrubbing took place, why did she fail to mention it to police? Why did they? And then why did they both admit it at the exact same moment, months later and very late in these proceedings? These are not mere coincidences. These are deliberate ploys to manipulate the system, very typical of an abuser!'

What had been missing in Serena's summation was the information about Matt's own history. An open net that begged for the own goal she masterfully avoided. This was something that Sam seized on and wanted to make sure she made this part of her winning points. She made much of the detailed evidence that the sexual offenders expert report provided. As Sam put it, 'That screams out alarm in this situation.'

Sam continued, 'He got into this, when he was supposedly concerned about Andi seeing him in bed. In those circumstances, that he didn't consider the risks is unfathomable. It does not make sense and it does not make sense because it is not credible. It is not credible, because it is a lie. He was alone in the bath with Andi. We only have dad's account for how long this was as mum says she can't remember. How very convenient that something as crucial as that, mum cannot remember.'

The rage I had felt a few moments earlier had now subsided like the molten lava of a volcano. I still had a simmering anger under the surface, but Sam had turned things back round.

Unfortunately, she then finished with what came across as defeat. 'If the court doesn't accept intentional sexual gratification, we ask the court to accept inappropriate touching.' It felt very much like a damp squib and was disappointing.

I could see that she tried to give the court all the possible ways of making findings against the parents. Either at a very high level of sexual abuse or at the lower end of inappropriate touching. The problem was that it came across as if our own solicitor did not believe our case. It was sexual abuse and needed to be found as such. Nothing less would do.

'Thank you, I will need some time to consider matters but I will be able to provide my judgment in a few hours. I will retire for deliberation,' His Honour

Judge Carter announced.

As always, he stood and bowed his head at all of us. The lawyers reciprocated with the dancing tilts of their own heads. With that, the Judge marched out of the court room. There was then the usual bustle of movement around us, papers brushed away, files collected, cases jostled out of the way and chatter between the lawyers as we trooped out.

My team manager, Lisa and I exchanged our thoughts on the case as we headed to an interview room. Sam met us there and said, 'Well, that's that. We have done all we can and now it's over to the Judge.'

'How do you think it will go?' Lisa asked.

'I don't know, but to be honest, I don't think we had enough.'

'How can it not be enough? The poor child told us that she had been touched in her genital areas and behind, how is that not sexual abuse?' I blurted out.

'Naeed, I'm afraid, your lack of objectivity in this case has gotten in the way of you doing what you needed to,' Sam replied.

'Well, your lack of understanding a child's perspective has gotten in the way of you doing what you needed to,' I retorted.

'Okay, okay. Let's all calm down. Sam is trying to tell us things from a legal point of view. Sam, Naeed has good instincts, which is what has helped her work with Andi,' Lisa intervened.

'I'm sorry, but I need to get out of here. I need a breather,' I said as I left the room.

I rushed to the lifts and saw Matt and Kelly waiting

there too. They clocked me and I dropped my head and turned towards the stairs instead.

I dashed down the stairs and out of the building.

I let the bitter wind hit my face, breathed it in slowly and then walked through the streets. I figured I had at least an hour and Lisa had my mobile number if anything happened in the meantime. Sam's words still rung loudly in my head. Was it my fault if all this came to nothing?

KELLY

The moment of truth was upon us. The clerk ushered us all back into the court with news that the Judge was ready to deliver his judgment.

Serena said that she knew we had put up a good fight but that she could never tell how these things would fall. She said that it was always impossible to know which way the Judge would go. She shattered the glass ceiling of illusion. The lawyers didn't share a secret language with the Judge. None of us knew what was coming.

The nervous tension pounded through me. I stepped to our seats, trying to force the adrenaline down.

The Judge walked stoically from the side entrance into the court room, taking up his throne. He was the masterful eagle ready to swoop and beyond reproach.

His Honour Judge Carter explained that this was a discreet fact-finding hearing. It had arisen from concern raised around Andi and the impact that that also had for Rodrigo. Further assessments were in hand

and were needed before matters could be finalised. An issue of fact had arisen and that had been his only remit. The Judge's voice boomed around the still room.

The issue of fact came about because of an older sibling, Andi. She now lived with her father and paternal grandparents. The Local Authority sought a finding of sexual abuse by father on his stepdaughter.

The Judge summed up the Local Authority evidence, 'The social worker asked what Andi had told her nan. The child seemed puzzled. The social worker felt it necessary to prompt. She prompted by telling her what nan had told her; that Matty had been in the bath with her. She asked the question about what he did. The answer seems to have been first, nothing and then I can't remember. Now the second part of the discussion took place upstairs. It involved only the social worker and Andi.

Before Andi had said anything more, the social worker took it upon herself to say she was going to have a bath later. She used scrubbing gestures. Andi joined in miming by scrubbing her tummy. This becomes the crucial part. Downstairs Miss Collins had been told to take notes. She didn't go up and so no contemporary notes there.

The social worker was thus in difficulty and took her own notes when she was back in the car. A few hours later, more detailed records and then days later, detailed evidence. In these circumstances, inconsistencies occur.'

His Honour Judge Carter continued with his analysis. 'The social worker recollects that she asked an open question about what happened in the bath. I have her notes from the car, which suggests more direct questions about what Matty did, was used. In the context of this inconsistency, I conclude that direct questions used. Whatever the question, Andi responded by indicating he scrubs me.

Then when asked where, it is this part of the case that is difficult. The social worker accompanied her question by gesturing washing herself, in her statement. She talks about washing upper parts in the statement. Typed written records says gesturing towards lower parts. More worryingly still, the notes from the car say that Andi asked where. The social worker said I scrub everywhere.

The social worker insists she asked an open question about where Matty had scrubbed her. The note in her car undermines that proposition. There is a real possibility that the social worker encouraged the form of answer. She mimed and pointed to her own body. She talked to Andi about her own preference of scrubbing everywhere.

The later dealings with the police didn't produce anything more. One answer the police obtained was the comment that Andi was washed all over by stepfather. This wasn't accompanied by any pointing let alone pointing to genital areas. Andi has not said anything more, not to anyone since these interviews and discussions.'

His Honour Judge Carter acknowledged that Andi seemed to be aware of sexual matters. Matt's evidence was summarised in brief. He accepted sharing of bath when he was in the bath. Andi had jumped into bath undressed. For short periods of time, they were alone until mother joined them. Father washed parts. None of the intimate parts, which he left for Andi herself or to her mother. Father denied any inappropriate touching.

The court asserted that we had minimised the situation. Then the Judge noted, 'I remind myself that it is not necessary for them to disprove the Local Authority allegation. It is more likely to be defensive when faced by allegations of troubling nature. It is the Local Authority that has the burden of proof.'

In conclusion, His Honour Judge Carter was critical of the Local Authority case. He dismissed their evidence as unreliable. It had been heavily reliant on memory, which was dangerous. It was inevitable that the lack of contemporaneous notes introduced doubt. It was clear that detail was woefully lacking.

'At no point was Andi asked about her knowledge of private parts. She was not asked what she has scrubbed with, no details of sexual element to behaviour in bath. Importance of these details, if present, enhances evidence, if missing, undermines the evidence. The detail here is lacking.

The truth is preparation was lacking. It seems to me that this social worker had no filter before speaking to Andi. The social worker must be careful in the circumstances. The social worker interview with Andi was contaminated and contents useless. Prompting formed a major part, which raises questions about what else was prompted.'

I had moved inch by inch more forward, gripping the edge of the bench. My palms were hot like coals. Matt was statuesque but his eyes widened and shiny. By now it was clear how the Judge determined the case. It was still very sweet to hear it.

'My task is to consider whether on a balance of probabilities, findings are made out. I drew attention to what I considered reliability of evidence problems. My conclusion is bound to be that there was no contact between father and child's genital or vice versa. Findings to include mother's knowledge. At the time both parents did not feel it inappropriate.

I urge the Local Authority to undertake its own internal review. There should be training around achieving best evidence guidance in interviews with children.'

I let out a gasp and broke down crying. 'Oh my God, oh my god, I don't believe it. Thank you, thank you,' I sobbed.

The Judge's face softened, and he closed his papers.

Serena turned round towards us and stretched her arm over the table. 'It's okay, it's okay,' she whispered over to me to try and quieten me.

Naeed glanced across at us. She turned away when I caught her eye.

Serena told us afterwards that she danced internally. She had wanted to give it a big old 'Whoop' but had to be restrained. She remained ever the professional, stony cold in her face and body. As soon as the formalities were complete and the Judge had left the court room, she turned right round and hugged us.

We did it!

NAEED

I looked across and saw the parents swallowed up in Serena's hug, whilst I was in my own headspace. The Judge had completely rebuked me for trying to protect these children. All the while, here were these parents that should have been admonished, celebrating.

I could not believe it and as I thought that I heard Matt say 'I daren't believe it. People like me never get a fair chance at anything.' He fell away from the embrace, back into his seat and broke down in tears. 'Matt, we did it, it's okay Matt, it's okay,' Kel said as she stroked his back.

'It was the right result, guys,' Serena said, excitement bubbling away in her throat.

'Yeah, come on, Matt, let's go and celebrate,' Kel urged.

'I want to go home,' Matt said. He seemed filled with a heady concoction of emotions.

'Matt, I know it's overwhelming and a lot to take in. Let's have one drink, a cup of good tea always does the job,' Serena encouraged.

'Yeah, okay,' he replied, and they all walked out together and united. They didn't say a word to any of us, not even a fleeting glance in our direction.

Lisa and Sam both said things to each other and to me, but I had tuned out. My mind was in overdrive, and I needed time to process. 'I'm sorry, but I need to get out of here,' I finally let out. I had not said anything since the judgment. I was a silent observer, though my head shouted all sorts of thoughts. It was a strange paradox, hearing all this noise from within me and yet emitting a harsh silence outside of me.

'That's fine, but we will need to discuss where we go next soon,' Lisa said.

'And we need to think about the ongoing personnel,' Sam added.

I was not going to discuss this right there and then but knew where they were going with this. They wanted to push me out.

I walked smoothly out of the court room. I was quite the expert at masking any sense of awkward humiliation and headed to my car. I wanted to get home but called Cynthia before starting the car. I wanted her to hear it from me rather than anyone else.

'Hi, Cynthia, its Naeed here.'

'Oh, hello, Naeed. Has it all finished?' Cynthia queried with quiet concern in her voice.

'Yes, I'm afraid it didn't go our way,' I replied.

'That bastard has got away with it, I could kill him,' Cynthia fumed.

'It's completely understandable for you to be angry, Cynthia. It is important to keep things under control.'

'I know, I know. I'll be fine in the morning,' Cynthia reassured.

'I mean it's important not to let this impact Andi and to keep her protected.'

'Of course, I know that' Cynthia snapped.

'Well, I wanted you to hear it from me. We can arrange one of our visits in the next week or so. I'll give you a call when I'm in the office tomorrow.'

'Yes, that's fine,' Cynthia replied, and we then said our goodbyes.

When I reached home, Alya was still up and greeted me with the warmest hugs. That little girl could clear out all the grime of the day with one of her hugs. She was the sweetest, most affectionate person I knew, and I prayed that she would always remain that way. I had arrived home in time to cuddle with her for a while on the sofa. We watched some cartoons before our bath and bedtime routines.

I went into the office unusually early the next day because I wanted to get some admin done before Lisa came in. I needed to get ahead of this by speaking to Lisa. I had to clear up what went wrong with the fact-finding hearing. I needed to stake my claim on continuing the Barnett case to its conclusion.

I recognised that I would have to eat some humble pie but also had to be careful to not overcompensate. I managed to get through half my emails before the other staff members arrived.

When Lisa walked in, I caught her attention and asked to chat to her when she could fit me in. We agreed on twelve noon and met up in one of the interview rooms off the side of the main office. 'Hi, Naeed, how are you feeling today?'

'Well, you know, it's difficult but it is, what it is.'

'It is important to reflect on it, to learn from it but also give yourself a break. We also cannot afford the mistakes of the fact finding to haunt us into the rest of the case. The court will say that your analysis in this case is now skewed.'

'Absolutely, but I want you to know that I am committed to this case like I am with all my cases. I will show the court that I have learnt from the errors of the fact finding.'

'I know that Naeed, but there have been some major mistakes in this case, and we cannot afford to have any more.'

My palms gripped each other, and my heartbeat fluttered. 'I get that, Lisa, and I know I should have handled the Andi situation so differently, but I will learn from that. I know that I need to put some distance so that I can act more objectively going forward,' I pleaded.

Lisa remained thoughtful. I knew she was conflicted. The lack of resources and heavy workload weighed on her mind. 'Let me have a think. I mean everyone is so pushed as it is. So, it would be better if you could stay with it but I need you to have a few days off from it. We can talk again next week and see where we go with it all.'

'Fair enough,' I resigned.

'I mean it, Naeed, no work at all on this Barnett matter. Nothing, got it!'

'I've got it, Lisa,' I said as I stood and turned out of the meeting room. I mean she meant nothing substantive, a few bits here and there would be okay, surely.

Lisa was right, of course but both she and I knew that I wouldn't resist it altogether. I had to have some distance from it for a few days at least. I hoped that that would in turn lead to a natural distance in the case for the rest of the proceedings. However, I had promised Cynthia that I would call her to arrange to meet up for one of the regular Social Work visits. Anyway, Andi, was not technically part of the Barnett case.

I arranged to go over the following week and Cynthia was calmer this time round. There was a little coolness there that hadn't been before. In time, we would overcome that after an honest conversation.

I then shot off an email response to the police, 'The court made no findings in respect of the parents.' I was sure that this would lead the police to determining no further action against the Barnetts. I guess that that would be the end of that, as Cynthia put it, 'He had got away with it!'

Chapter Fourteen

KELLY

Whilst we may have won the battle, the war still raged.

Serena explained that it was still not quite over. We still had to get through the assessment which would now resume at pace. Then we would have to look at what the final plans were. She stressed how intense these next few weeks would be and the fringes of dread crept in.

We celebrated this moment but still had a way to go yet. Serena was true to her word. Cups of tea were what we enjoyed in the old traditional English pub that we had stumbled upon.

It was quiet but there were pockets of people tucked away in different corners. We were all united in that we were in the same place together but all with our different agendas.

There was an old man in one corner. He had a pint of beer in front of him that he sipped on as he completed a crossword. Opposite us was a young couple that seemed to be rowing about something. The woman sulked, and the guy pleaded with her. On the other side of us, there was a group of men in suits, presumably at the end of a workday, letting off steam over drinks. We were quite the motley crew of revellers!

The pub itself was quite oldie worlde with caramel brown lounge sofas. Each sofa had different coloured cushions, some printed and others plain but bright. They all seemed to have their own stories to tell, and no doubt held secrets deep within them.

There was a stale smell of smoke around. The smoking ban had been in place for a few years now. Yet the previous decades of historical smoke were steeped in the walls. The paper peeled away in places and ripped in others. We sat in one corner, not far from the fireplace. Some embers burned away but not fully alight.

It started sinking in, what we had managed to achieve. We kept with the truth and forced the Local Authority's hand. Serena had been amazing and had pushed and pushed for justice and she had got it for us. I don't know how we found each other but she had been with us through all this. Sometimes, she was right alongside us. Sometimes she was behind us pushing us along and other times in front of us leading the way.

We talked over what had gone on, looked to the next steps of the case but also shared some jokes and laughs. Serena highlighted for us how critical the Judge had been of the Social Worker and her approach. 'It was as bad a telling off as it could be,' Serena observed.

'Serena, that's down to you and we can never say thank you enough but thank you,' Matt said.

'Wowser, Matty, I don't think I have ever heard you say so many words in one sentence.'

'And I don't think I have ever heard you say Matty,' he laughed back as I roared with laughter.

'I feel left out now, when will you ever call me Kel?' I giggled out.

Serena howled with laughter and managed to gasp, 'Oh Kel!'

A couple of hours later, we went in our different directions towards our respective homes. It had been a good evening in the end, a real moment of victory, even if it was only one little battle in the long war.

Matt and I headed back to dad's. We knew that he would have been waiting for the news and worried about what had happened. It was a chance for Matt and me to enjoy a proper analysis with my dad and give him the lowdown.

My dad was ecstatic and hugged me tight. He shook Matt's hand and patted him on the back, which was his way of showing his support to Matt. It had been a gruelling few months, the toughest we had been through and it felt good to be out the other side.

Matt and I hoped that Naeed would have nothing more to do with our case. Serena said that she felt that this might be a decision that the Local Authority would take. Otherwise, we would argue that she was biased and rely on this Judgment to support us. Serena said that it would be safer for a completely new social worker, but we couldn't demand it. It was something we could request but it did not mean it would happen that way.

We didn't want to come across as afraid of Naeed. So, we had already made up our minds that we would not request any change but inside we were desperately wishing it. It wasn't to be and Naeed was in touch with us a week or so later. The assessment was back on, full blown.

The small shot of confidence I had drunk in from the victory of the fact finding evaporated. In that one telephone call from Naeed, I was punctured and fading quickly. Naeed sounded so smug on the phone, like she had somehow gained the upper hand and was putting us back in our box. This woman was never going to let us go. She had her claws firmly stuck in our backs.

We had to focus on the assessment, which at least did not involve Naeed. The assessor was a lovely, round middle-aged woman. She spoke with a hot chocolate voice. Moments of the gentleness of melted marshmallows sprung out here and there. We drank up her guidance and suggestions with Roddie.

Matt was amazing with Roddie, so gentle and protective. It was great to see, and I loved watching their bond grow stronger and stronger. I watched as Matt threw Roddie up in the air, catching the laughing ball with confidence. I remembered the nervousness he had always held Roddie with in that awful prison, Crown House.

Midway through the assessment, we had Roddie all day at the centre. We were about to move into the last stage of having Roddie at home. I had felt achy and wasn't quite as energised with Roddie as I used to be. I let Matt take the lead. My furry mouth always carried a bitter after taste that I couldn't quite pinpoint. I was fatigued but put it down to the flu and soldiered on.

This had been going on for a few weeks. The lightbulb flashed in my mind, and it dawned on me that I had not had my period. Matt and I took the test together, which confirmed what I had by then worked out for myself; we were pregnant.

It was still the early stages, but Matt and I didn't know how to approach it with everyone. I called Serena.

'Hi Kelly, how are things? Is the assessment going okay?' Serena asked.

'Yeah, it's all good as far as we can tell.'

'Great, I guess time will tell and we should wait for the assessment to come through in due course.'

'So, the thing is, Serena, we are pregnant.' Before I could say anything else, Serena immediately was aghast. She fired all sorts of questions at me, and I was flustered and couldn't get my words out.

'So, you've done a home test and it's in the early stages, have I got that right?' Serena clarified.

'Yes,' I replied.

'You need to tell the social worker or the assessment workers before they find out from someone else. I mean you don't have to tell anyone right this second. I would say that you tell them before your first health appointment. Does that make sense?'

'Yes,' I said, even more quietly, 'but we will be able to keep the baby, won't we?'

SERENA

The assessment came through and as I was sure all lawyers did, I went straight to the back. I flipped the thirty odd pages and scanned the final page or so, 'Boom! We've got a shot here!' I said to myself.

I made myself a cup of tea, knowing now, that this would be a good read. I knew I had a grin sneaking across my face and a calmness now sat in the pit of my stomach. Champagne bubbles fizzed underneath that calmness. I was excited for reading this but held myself back so that I could savour it all the more. Sometimes, I had to take the time to appreciate a report as crucial to a case as this one was.

After a good read of the report, I got straight onto the phone to Matt and let him know the outcome of the assessment.

'They support a phased return of Roddie to the joint care of you and Kelly. I mean there will be ongoing monitoring. We will have to wait and see what the Local Authority's plan will now be, but it is good news.'

'Okay,' Matt replied. I had hoped for more of a reaction, but I got the sense that he was overwhelmed.

'Matt, did you hear me?'

'Yeah. I am not sure what to do.'

'You don't have to do anything yet. You do need to keep up with the counselling, and as I said, we wait to see what the Local Authority now say. When we have that, I will get you both in to work out your response.'

'Okay. Thank you, Serena.'

That was the best he could have said, and those few words made all the difference. For a man of such few words, his words so often hit the spot.

A couple of weeks later, we got the Local Authority final evidence and plan. By this time, they knew about Kelly's pregnancy but no plan was in place for the unborn yet. Kelly had not even got to her twelve weeks yet and so it was still quite premature to make plans. I hoped the Social Workers would work with Kelly and

Matt. They could plan together for the unborn child to remain with the parents. With any luck, they may also have Roddie back by then.

The Local Authority wanted a snail's paced, phased return with a care order. I did not understand their plan for the phased return. Naeed's statement was glowing of the parents and the work that they had completed. I heard her words creaking through gritted teeth. On the face of it, it was positive, maybe even overly so.

Whatever was going on, this seemed personal. This social worker had it in for these parents. Naeed suggested that they have daytime contact every weekday for a couple of weeks. Then they would introduce one overnight contact each week for a month.

Naeed wanted the overnight contact to increase by one night month by month. This meant that it would be more than 6 months before Roddie would be back with his parents full time. This plan was like water squeezed out of a folded hosepipe. That infuriated me. These parents had done everything asked of them and they should have their son back. Roddie deserved to have his parents back, full time, now.

Matt and Kelly came to see me about the Local Authority evidence. We needed to prepare their own evidence in response. They were the most relaxed I had seen them. Kelly chatted away in reception. Matt, still serious but occasionally letting slip to the faintest of smiles.

I called them through, and they stepped into my bat cave, but I was sure we all bounced in there. I explained that the Local Authority plan was for Roddie to return to their care but with a care order. This would mean that the Council would continue to share parental responsibility. The Local Authority's parental responsibility would trump theirs. If things went wrong, the Local Authority would be able to remove Roddie into care again.

The problem was the idea of the gradual return, Kelly felt apprehensive about it. 'I mean we don't want to go against them after getting this far, where they are now actually letting him come back home.'

'Yes, I get that but that doesn't mean that you have to take whatever they are offering,' I replied. 'You guys have worked hard, and it makes no sense to drag the return out like they are suggesting.'

'I mean, we definitely want him back as soon as but don't want to do anything to rock the boat now,' Kelly hesitated.

'Kel, we can't let them take the mick, though,' Matt interjected.

'Yeah, I know but I don't want us to do anything to put this in jeopardy now.'

'Listen, this must be a joint and agreed position. I am not saying that we have a big fight over it. We can express concern over the timing of their plan. We need to see if we can persuade them to progress things more quickly.'

We tossed this around quite a bit more. Backwards and forwards, side to side and finally agreed on a compromise position. We would make clear that we wanted to work with the Local Authority and that we would accept their plans. At the same time, we would highlight the need to minimise delay for a child. If there was to be a rehabilitation, we should work towards that as swiftly as possible.

We served our final evidence. We confirmed agreement with the overarching plan. We disputed the finer detail of that plan insofar as the timing was concerned. Then it was a matter of holding our breath. In this game of bluff, who would blink first?

The final document before the trial of a case like this was always the Guardian's report. The Guardian was the one voice the court relied on. The courts rarely decided a case against the Guardian's recommendation. The Guardian was the lynchpin of this case, well, every case. Unless we had the Guardian onside, we had to forget any pipe dreams of accelerating the tortoise of a plan.

Our Guardian had always seemed to be in cahoots with the dreaded social worker. They were a tag team constantly on the attack. They disappeared off together to the dark side to plot against us and so my expectations were low. Our Guardian's report was due in a couple of weeks.

Fortunately, we did not have to wait that long to get a clue to the way the wind blew. An email came through from the Guardian's solicitor copied and was the best of all prizes. The Guardian put pressure on the Local Authority to move their position. She agreed with us that the rehabilitation plan was far too painful and prolonged. I was shocked but had a little party inside of me.

The Local Authority finally relented.

They started the all-day contact every weekday immediately. They agreed that it would be two nights after a couple of weeks. It would rise by two nights two weeks later and then full time, two weeks after that. This was much more like it.

We were finally on our way.

Then another setback.

Matt had stayed overnight at his parents' home. The whole situation had to be re-considered.

NAEED

The final evidence had been filed on the Barnett case but one of the things I had not done was visit Matt's parents. Matt's dad was one of the major issues in the case, so I thought it would be good to touch base with him and Matt's mum.

I went over to their home on a pre-arranged visit, but the dad was not home. I suspected that he had an issue with anyone in authority. In some ways I was rather relieved that he wasn't there. I did not know what to make of him, being such a serial paedophile and continuing risk to children. It was in direct contrast to how I saw my role, that of protector of children.

I had been surprised by the Connect report and it jarred with me. I felt sure that the Connect workers had been hoodwinked but there was nothing I could do about it. We had to accept their assessment, or that was what both Lisa and Sam decided. I had wanted to write a different statement. Pursuing further assessment by the sexual offenders expert was the way to go. They overruled me.

I begrudgingly reconciled myself to supporting a return of Roddie to his parents. I didn't believe it was the right outcome for Roddie.

The risk of the paternal grandfather was still a significant issue. One that could not be underestimated. I wanted to ensure that the paternal grandparents understood the boundaries. I was uneasy with my final evidence. All I could do now, was to put in as many safety measures as possible.

Matt's mother, Barbara, was a rounded woman with short, wavy, dark hair. She seemed worn and stern. She was welcoming enough and took me through to the kitchen. We shared a pot of tea that she had brewed and some chocolate biscuits. We chatted and it was clear that she was in denial about her husband, his past and ongoing issues. 'They have him all wrong,' she explained.

'Yes, but your own children disclosed what he had done to them.'

'It's all very difficult but we have put it behind us now. All the kids visit and even their kids too,' Barbara continued.

'But they don't leave their kids alone with George, do they?' I asked.

'Well, I guess not but that's more because we don't have them over on their own. They come over as a family, if you know, what I mean?'

'And Matthew, Kelly and Andi, how often did they come?'

'Same as the rest, though Matt comes over at weekends sometimes. He stays over.'

'When you say that Matt stays over, do you mean, before?' I clarify.

'What do you mean? I mean he comes on a Saturday and stays over for the night before heading back home.'

'I'm sorry but I want to make sure I have got this right; do you mean that he still stays overnight at weekends?' I press.

'Erm... well, yes,' she replied. She was uncertain but also certain.

I returned to the office. After discussion with Lisa, I called the parents and arranged to see them at the office a couple of weeks later. It was Matt that I spoke with, and I told him what I needed to speak to them both about. Matt confirmed that he did stay over at his parents and did not understand why this was a concern for Roddie. Matt showed no insight at all and that put children in his care at risk.

I worried for Roddie, who spent all day with Matt and Kelly in the week. We had set them up to be reunited and now it seemed that all my worst fears about Matt and his past were all coming to pass. Matt did not seem able to break free of his family, particularly his parents and that could put Roddie at real risk.

I made enquiries with Connect. They confirmed that they were not aware of Matt staying overnight at his parents. They were horrified and rushed me off the phone. I assumed it was so that they could work out their response to this. This all added to my concern.

The parents were unable to work honestly with us and other professionals. This was a delicate situation and openness, above all else, was key to this working.

A darkness fell over me with a crawling sense that we had to keep Roddie away from this family. My head pounded with the conversation I was about to have with the parents. I rehearsed different approaches and none of it sounded adequate. These parents had been given every chance. More chances than most and they got themselves into this situation.

We found out in time before something devastating happened to Roddie. I was so close to placing this child in danger. A danger I had always foreseen, but somehow could not establish before. Surely, this was it, now!

Matt and Kelly waited in the office. I went out to greet them and take them through to one of the interview rooms for a chat. We had agreed that Kelly's nan would have Roddie whilst they came to see me. They looked like most other parents, fraught. They stepped on hot coals as they crossed the waiting area through to the private interview room.

I explained the information that I had and asked them what they felt about the situation.

'Yeah, I do stay over some weekends for football and to see Tommo but Roddie never has,' Matt confirmed.

'I don't ever stay, ever. It's easier. Matt's football is round there early on Sunday mornings,' Kelly added. She bit her lip and tapped her fingernails on her knee.

I tried to explain how this was a fear for Roddie for

two reasons. First the risk from paternal grandfather seemed still not to be understood. Second the lack of openness with us meant they were not able to work with us. I had always felt that Matt did not understand the risks from his dad. Also, that he had not processed everything about his dad.

It often felt like he said all the right things but not following through on it. He had given us lip service for what he thought we wanted to hear. I was also anxious that if Matt did not understand his dad's behaviour, there was a risk of cyclic repetition.

I felt for Kelly because she seemed to get it and she certainly did not like Matt's parents. She was under Matt's thumb and unable to stand up for herself or her children. Whilst I could empathise with Kelly, my priority had to be Roddie. 'Why didn't you let us know about these overnight visits?'

'We thought everyone knew,' Matt replied.

'Neither of you ever made it clear that your visits to your parents was overnight, Matt. You knew that we have huge concerns about your dad, and you never told us that you stayed there overnight.'

'I don't know... I thought you knew,' Matt repeated.

'Honestly, we never hid it or lied about it. We didn't think,' Kelly explained.

'This was important information that you both should have shared with us. You did not even tell Connect whilst they worked with you, and it comes across as something you were hiding.'

'We weren't doing that,' Kelly pleaded.

'We will have to review what we are going to do now but it does make things very difficult. We will leave it there for now.' I felt drained and my mind buzzed away.

I needed some time out and sensed that the parents felt the same. They walked away, heads down and in silence.

SERENA

'Serena, I've messed up,' Matt said. His despondence was deafening through the phone.

I grabbed my pen and scrap paper to jot down the notes of this conversation. 'What do you mean, what has happened?'

In a few words, Matt explained that Naeed pulled him up on staying overnight at his parents. He had not told anyone about it. Naeed, the 'headteacher', had called them into her office and lambasted both him and Kelly. The parents felt that they had blown it.

The fully grown man on the other end of this phone magically dwarfed to a little lost boy. The pain in the empty echo was tangible.

'Do you think I should move out; Kel might have a better chance without me in the picture?'

'Matt don't jump into anything yet. I know it's difficult, but we need to wait and see what the Local Authority actually say. If they are going to change their plans, they will have to let us know.' I steadied.

'Right, but if we separate now, that will help?'

'Listen, if you want to separate that's one thing. Don't do it because you think that it will be tactically advantageous. You need to fight this case on a true basis.' I advised.

The Local Authority served a further social work statement. The growing mould of dread filled inside me. It was pleasantly cleaned out as I browsed the conclusion. Despite the discovery that Matt stayed overnight at his parents' home, the Local Authority plan remained the same. This was the right call from the Local Authority.

'Now that is what I am talking about,' I said to myself, clicking my thumb and finger in the sweetest satisfaction. Maybe the parents made mistakes with the overnight stays at Matt's parents. It was not so serious that it should prevent Roddie from returning to his parents.

Roddie was not placed at risk and Matt's actions impacted only him, not any child. Matt was entitled to a relationship with his family. This included his parents, even a parent that is a paedophile. As an adult, Matt was entitled to make that decision for himself. What would have been alarming was if the parents had taken Roddie to Matt's parents' home. That would have justified a re-think on the care plan but this, Matt's visits, surely didn't?

I felt that the Local Authority should and could do more to support these parents. They needed everything spelt out to them and to be spoon fed. They didn't always understand the expectations on them.

A Working Agreement setting out all the boundaries would help. If the Local Authority wanted the parents to not stay overnight at Matt's parents, they needed to spell that out. If the Local Authority wanted to know when the parents stayed at Matt's parents' home, they needed to spell that out. If the Local Authority wanted to know where the parents stayed when not home, they needed to spell that out. Whatever it was that the Local Authority wanted, that needed to be spelt out.

The relief from the parents was palpable. I needed to get things finalised now. The sooner the final hearing came round, the better. We had to put this to bed before any more setbacks came along and threw this all under the train.

I headed home, feeling shattered. I kicked off my heels as soon as I got home, grabbed myself a glass of wine and headed straight to bed. I needed something stronger than tea tonight.

By the end of the week, we were back on the train tracks again. The Local Authority emailed to put the rehabilitation plan on hold. It was before the week in which overnight stays with Roddie was due to start. 'Imbeciles!' I shouted. 'Such idiots!'

The battle lines drawn again. My heart and head raced, my fists clenched and hit the desk once. I muttered nonsense to myself and pushed myself away from the desk to cool off. This was grossly unfair to the parents. They had had false hope and swiped the hope right away from under their noses.

A meeting was arranged for all the professionals in the case on Monday to discuss how to proceed.

I was the first to arrive at the Local Authority office in stamping stilettos. The Guardian with her solicitor arrived shortly after. The glass building towered high above with various Local Authority departments. We all had to sign in and were given security badges to wear. The Local Authority solicitor, Sam, came out to take us through to the meeting room.

We were taken through to a conference room, where Naeed and her team manager were already seated. Sam outlined the issue and the concern they had with regards to the rehabilitation plan.

The Guardian's solicitor, Margaret, empathised with the Local Authority. The Guardian also agreed that it did put the plan in difficulty. It started to feel like a witches' coven. I curbed all my natural instincts. I forced my fire of words down and wanted to take in the other parties' positions, but this could only go on for so long.

'So Naeed's recent statement was meaningless.' I said.

'No, but we have had to take stock since then. With the approach of the overnight stays with Roddie upon us, we had to review matters' Sam explained.

'That makes no sense. She referenced the discovery of Matt's stays at his parents. Despite that, she still supported rehabilitation. A few days later, it is all change. And you expect parents to roll with that.' My voice rose but still restrained.

'We accept that mistakes have been made. Now we need to work out a way we can move things forward,' Margaret tried to de-escalate.

'No. The Local Authority best work out how they are going to explain this whole debacle to the court.

You cannot change a care plan without referring it back to court. You have not even provided any evidence of the need to change the plan.' I retorted.

'That is a fair point,' Margaret accepted, 'but we do need to try and agree how we are going to resolve this. I am wondering whether we approach the sexual offenders' expert, Daniel Jones for a view?'

'That doesn't quite cut it, Margaret. You can't brush these parents away with nothingness. It will not do; I won't have it!'

'I hear what you are saying. We are where we are. The Local Authority has changed its position. So, we need to consider what we now need to do to enable the court to determine matters.'

'To be honest, you can all stick it. I have nothing more to say. I will listen to how you guys want to stitch these parents up so that I can challenge when I need to. So please, go right ahead.'

The room had a cold silence that blasted all around. Margaret and Sam exchanged awkward looks. Naeed and the Guardian looked down at their invisible notes.

After a thorny moment of unease, Margaret resumed her thoughts. She felt accessing the sexual offenders expert view was the way to go. Between them they suggested that we would do a joint letter of questions to Connect and Daniel Jones. I sat as the cynical observer.

Daniel Jones worked primarily with sexual offenders. He assessed their future risks and offering therapeutic work too. In fact, they had assessed Matt's dad and put him at very high risk. The report was damning and of course, Matt's dad was not willing to engage in any further work.

They had also assessed Matt and any risks he posed to children. Matt was placed in the low-risk category. The report was at pains to point out that everyone was assessed at low risk. They cannot guarantee no risk at all, so he was at the safest level possible.

We needed specific resource information about work on sexual abuse. We then required Connect's recommendation considering this new information. The others ironed out all the finer details. I did not actively involve myself in these discussions or agree anything. I knew that they were all inevitable steps. They were reasonable and appropriate, which the court would agree, even if I didn't. I knew there was no good ground to object.

Discussions came to a natural end. My quietness louder and punchier than anything I could have verbalised.

I had calmed by this point but still wanted to make my strong views felt in the room. I stood up and said 'I will be advising my clients to oppose any further renewals of the interim care order. We will seek the return of Roddie to their care,' and with that, I left the room.

Chapter Fifteen

NAEED

Here we go again, round two and technically, the final lap! The trial day had arrived, and we had heard from all the experts in the case. It was the end of the first day and I reflected on the expert evidence, as I was up the next day. I wanted to get my own thoughts together so that my evidence was coherent. I needed to make sure that I took account of the expert evidence and not be significantly in conflict with any of it.

Experience told me that the Magistrates would be more accepting of the professional evidence rather than the parents'. They had never decided against the Guardian's recommendation. So, I felt on very safe ground, to be honest but still wanted to make sure I played my part to the best. I pulled out my notes of the experts' evidence in the case and reviewed their written reports too.

Mr Daniel Jones confirmed that Matthew was enmeshed with his parents. This included his father. This heightened my fears. Matthew could not move beyond his father. He had normalised his predatory behaviour, without realising it for what it was. Mr Jones had talked about grooming behaviour being akin to normal affectionate behaviour. It was this subtlety that abusers employed. The difference is intention.

Mr Jones had hit the nail on the head when he described the parents as 'duplicitous'. He had also recommended protective parenting work for the parents. I did not believe in anything of the sort. These wishy-washy courses were exactly that. Nothing would convince me that these parents' behaviours could be changed.

Added to this was the fact that these parents had already been on some mickey mouse course as it was. They had had their chance. The parents had already had time to understand the very real risks of this sexual predator. Yet somehow still maintained a relationship with him. As adults they can make that choice, Roddie cannot and needed people that would protect him from that.

The Connect worker was consistent that parents' understanding had greatly increased. The expert was also clear about discussions with the parents. Considerable time had been exhausted about the relationship with Matthew's parents spent. At no point had the parents mentioned the overnight stays. This would have been a significant point of discussion if it had come up.

There had been an assumption from the Connect diary the parents kept. They had jotted down that Matthew had stayed overnight with family. Connect thought it did not mean Matthew's parents. They wrongly took this to mean other, wider family and not Matt's parents. Yes, Connect should have checked this out with Matthew and Kelly. That does not take away from the parents' obligation to have been more open. It seemed to me that the parents had been deliberately evasive.

It was clear to me that Roddie could not be safely returned to these parents. I felt for them all, but Roddie would not be safe around paternal grandfather. Matt was not strong enough to keep his dad away from Roddie. It wasn't about face-to-face contact between Roddie and the paternal grandfather. The risk of sexual abuse could permeate through whether there was any contact or not. That was what frightened me. Eloquently summarised by the sexual offenders expert and woven into his evidence. Matt did not get that.

I was sworn in on the Sikh religious book. I had been asked the questions already rehearsed with my solicitor. During the evidence in chief, I made clear that parents had deliberately misled us. Matthew was very entangled with his parents and both he and Kelly had regressed. Roddie could not wait any longer for final arrangements.

Parents needed to undertake the further recommended work for their unborn child. Roddie could not remain on the back burner. It was completely wrong for his needs to be secondary to these parents or anyone one else. Roddie had to come first.

My solicitor, Sam asked me to recap the concerns in the case. I replied, 'Kelly – First born. Extensive violent incidents in Andi's childhood and Local Authority involvement. Ongoing concerns about Kelly's ability to care for Andi during pregnancy with Roddie. There was domestic violence between Kelly and Matthew. It has been documented that Matthew punched Kelly in the eye. This followed a verbal assault. It was said that Andi was not present. Kelly said she told Andi and Andi saw aftermath.

Following that incident, Matthew himself approached the police. The Local Authority put in place a working agreement that Matthew not reside at the house. This was to ensure the children were safe. Matthew and Kelly breached Working Agreement and there was disengagement from professionals. This propelled the Local Authority to make application to court for an interim care order.'

I was prompted then to deal with Matthew's father's sexual offending history. This became a significant concern when it came to light. We moved onto the issue of overnight stays and the evidence went something like this:

Q: Did the discussions with parents include level of contact with paternal grandfather?

A: Focal point of discussions in January. Talked about level of contact. It was explained by Matthew that he stopped for a drink, left bike there. Happy with that. Asked if he wanted more, he said that that was level and could not envisage any more. Not weekly - every few weeks, have a drink and collect bike.

Q: Any sign of overnight?

A: No.

We moved onto the impact of this on my final analysis.

Q: What does it say about openness and honesty?

A: Absolutely key. It is the foundation – must be able to trust parents that they will share information, ask if any ambiguity, that they can make those decisions so close to rehabilitation of Roddie to their care raises huge concerns. After working with Connect, considered that they will seek guidance but clearly didn't.

Q: Timescales for Dennis Smith's work and impact on Roddie?

A: In my view, delay will have a detrimental effect on Roddie. We know about the impact of delay. Mum is pregnant and having a difficult pregnancy. Doesn't give me much confidence that they will work with us.

I felt confident by the end of my main evidence. That soon changed with first, Serena attacking me from mum's point of view and then from dad's. Serena pushed me to concede that mother had not done very much wrong. I stood firm that she would have known that Matt stayed overnight at his parents. Mother had not stayed overnight at Matt's parents' home and barely had any contact with them at all. Mother would never allow Roddie to be with Matt's parents and would always protect Roddie.

I was steadfast that mother was complicit. She kept this on the down low where the Local Authority was concerned. This made it impossible for us to have any confidence that she would work with us. In any event, she had failed the assessment at the Crown, the mother and baby unit last year.

Serena then laid into me about Matthew's own childhood and the Local Authority's failings with him. I was taken through Matthew's own Local Authority records. I acknowledged Matthew had displayed violent tendencies and sexualised behaviour in his childhood. Matthew's siblings also showed sexualised behaviour.

'It is a matter of great shame. Matthew was not given the support and professional help he should have had access to?'

'You are asking me to comment on colleagues' work,' I replied shakily.

'He should have had therapy.'

'At stage of disclosure, yes,' I tried to mitigate.

I was then grilled about the siblings and their families. It went something like this:

Q: Matthew's siblings returning home as adults. Normal and long before Matthew becomes an adult?

A: Yes

Q: Matthew's sister, Sarah has children?

A: Yes

Q: In care?

A: No

Q: Matthew's older brother, Paul has children?

A: Yes

Q: In care?

A: No

Q: Adopted?

A: No.

Q: Paul has children, Sarah has children and here we are with Matthew Barnett's. Matthew has shown signs of much work hasn't he?

A: Not a large part of work

Q: Highly specialised?

A: Yes

Q: Those who have been abused need specialist assessment?

A: Yes

Q: And yet, neither Sarah nor Paul undertook any such work. Their children see the paternal grandfather, right?

I accepted this quietly and wished I could disappear in that moment. I still believed in my view about Roddie, and I could only deal with him. I could not answer to the other children; I was responsible for this child, Roddie. He deserved a chance to live and thrive in a safe and happy environment. He could not be left in limbo any longer, it had already gone on for a year of his life and that was neither right nor just.

The Magistrates called for the lunch break, which was fortunate. I shrunk into my seat in the witness box. I needed to get out of here.

SERENA

I finished with Naeed with quite the flair. She had no choice but to concede that the turnabout in her position was not unexpected. It was a continuation of her persistent view that these parents would not manage the safe care of Roddie. Of course, it didn't quite come out as honestly as that, but I hoped that the Magistrates got the message.

Sadly, I remained sceptical of the Magistrates. Whatever the nuances of a case they would find a way to follow her guidance. It did not matter how serious the criticisms were. This was even more so when it was supported by the Guardian. This was what was so frustrating about these cases.

Naeed admitted she never believed that the parents

could protect Roddie. She went so far as to attack the Connect assessment. She regarded it as superficial and reliant on parents' self-reporting.

It was as much as I could have hoped for and put things very delicately balanced indeed. It should have put it firmly in the parents' court. Even if the Social Worker showed unquestionable bias, provided the Guardian agreed, that bias would disintegrate to dust. It would be swiftly brushed away as far as the Magistrates were concerned. As much as I railed against the wrongness of this, my hands remained tied.

During the break, I made sure to keep the parents on an even keel. Kelly, though, was worried. She asked me, 'Why do the Magistrates not pull the social worker up when it's obvious she has made mistakes?'

'They leave that to us to prove through the cross examination, I guess,' I replied. My shoulders lifted in a slight shrug, as I acted nonchalant. I hid my own angst about the Magistrates away from them.

'No. I mean, like when Naeed pretty much accepted she had never told us that Matt couldn't stay overnight at his parents. Why did the Magistrates not push her on that?'

'I guess because it's not their job to do that,' I apologised.

'It doesn't make sense. The Judge in the fact-finding hearing always asked questions. Whenever he thought something wasn't quite right, he hassled the witness.'

'Well, yes, there is a real difference between a qualified Judge and the Magistrates,' I conceded.

'It's like, Naeed's word is gospel. Her opinion is gold and can't be touched. They even seem annoyed with you for challenging her.'

'Do you think? I wasn't watching the Magistrates reactions because I was focused on Naeed. Whilst that is frustrating, that doesn't scare me and will not stop me.'

'Fair enough,' Kelly said.

The parents each gave evidence, mother and then father. Both came across as remorseful for not having been open as they could and should have been. They were honest. I could not have asked for any more from them. They held strong under cross-examination and stuck to the truth as they saw it. The last and perhaps, most important witness, was the Guardian.

The Guardian was quite a short, solid woman with wavy dark brown hair in a fluffy bob style. She wore a grey suit with a cream blouse. She rose from her seat and strode to the witness box. As she affirmed to tell the truth, the whole truth and nothing but the truth, she spoke earnestly. Her voice was crystalline. The whole courtroom held its breath.

The Guardian began with, 'It's very important I reflect to the worships how difficult it has been. This has not been a clear-cut case, gone in one direction one minute and then another. There was an obvious optimism to place Roddie with his parents. There was no hidden agenda there. We were pleased, very pleased indeed. It wasn't a case of complacency. Over a period of six to eight weeks, it was tested. It has been quite different in the last three months. The Local Authority had a very fine case to balance, being fair to parents couldn't be sufficient. I have gone through the same process. The lack of understanding made plain.'

The Guardian's solicitor asked the Guardian to explain balancing exercise. She replied as follows:

'In many ways, news of Kelly's pregnancy has made it harder. Delay for Roddie already clear. If there weren't other children, easier to say enough is enough. It is difficult because Roddie could be the odd one out. Andi is with her paternal grandmother. If baby ends up being cared for by parents, it is a difficult situation for me to contemplate for Roddie.

If we only had a crystal ball. If we could say that parents had completed the work and stayed together. There could be an argument for waiting. We don't have a crystal ball and the past is the predictor. It's very difficult to have confidence. Always difficult to come down on one side or another. I have a great deal of sympathy for the parents.'

The Guardian was clear that Roddie could not wait the test of time.

This was particularly the case where past evidence showed poor prospects of success. She urged parents to undertake the protective parenting work. She commended Matt on his counselling but emphasised that this was still in its infancy. There was much more to work through there.

It was then over to me to see if I could shake her in anyway. I probed with Matthew's history and how this had been entirely missed by the Local Authority.

Q: Sexualised behaviour at four, him and his

siblings all saying... asking for help. Matthew is the only one whose ability to care is being questioned?

A: Can't answer, don't know if any of the other children are in proceedings.

Q: Enquiries of your own.

A: I know that I made it clear that the other siblings should be informed.

The Guardian dodged the obvious, which I amplified. After more pushing, she conceded she had omitted making any enquiries herself.

The line of questioning continued.

Q: Bizarre, others can see them, children not to be left alone and yet, Matthew not allowed by himself?

A: Don't know the circumstances. I can see discrepancy... questioned about it.

Q: Worse, court has the idea of double standards?

Again, something to which the Guardian could not provide a satisfactory response.

This tete a tete went on. It was a delicate dance between landmines, with each of us careful to avoid setting off any of the waiting bombs.

'I know it is difficult. I am asking questions to help the court understand the issues that are important. Your take on them, as the independent voice for the child, is crucial. They are simple questions that require a yes or no, but it seems you are unwilling or unable to reply?' I said brusquely.

'Well, this is not a simple black or white case,' the Guardian replied. She looked to the Magistrates. Her open palms gestured outwards in complete exasperation with this line of questioning.

'The case might not be, but my questions are. With respect, your role here is to respond to those questions,' I replied going toe to toe with the Guardian.

I spotted from the corner of my eye, the Chairman of the Magistrates raise his eyebrow at me.

'Miss Sharma, we get the point, could we move on?' More of an annoyed directive than curious question.

I went on to press home that the Guardian had embarked on very little in this case by way of her own investigations.

Q: You hadn't insisted on seeing parents?

A: No.

Q: Why?

A: Don't want to give a long description. It used to be normal that we meet parents long ago. It's not the way to operate these days. When there are other assessments, we do not duplicate. We must check the assessments are sound, key points on track etc… Don't think there is anything further to be gained by repeating work already undertaken.

Q: That's all very good but how do you check assessments are sound without undertaking some work yourself?

A: I did do work but not the kind you are asking about.

Q: Meeting the parents you are judging, but hey, I am sure that is unnecessary work. Especially when you are ruling them out as parents.

A: I'm sorry was that a question?

I clocked one of the female Magistrates on the bench exchanged a smirk with the legal advisor. I pounded away at this closed door of the Guardian's, bolted and protected by these Magistrates. My fists were clenched, and my resentment burned. I hated how Guardians could do no wrong in the eyes of the Magistrates. They colluded with them in sheltering them from any stinging attack.

The Guardian accepted that the parents had completed encouraging work with Connect. She acknowledged that the non-disclosure of overnight contact did not impact Roddie. She refused to move from saying that the parents did not understand risks. In her opinion this meant they would not protect Roddie.

The time for parents to complete the protective parenting work and bed that in was too long. It did not fit Roddie's timescales for placement with his permanent family. The Guardian concluded by recommending adoption following a final care order.

My head hurt with the rush of exasperation that had boiled over. This coupled with the repeated punches it had taken was exhausting. This woman was an immovable, evasive, politician wannabe, stone of coldness. I had pushed and pushed till my whole body was bruised and battered but with no marks on my opponent. I had been in the boxing ring with myself. The Guardian strolled back to her spot next to her shield of a lawyer, who gave her a knowing smile.

The Magistrates wanted some time to consider their decision and draft their judgment. They invited written closing arguments from us. They would send us their decision two weeks later. In between my other cases, I read back through the notes of evidence. I tried to pull out all the points that helped our position.

The fact was that everyone accepted that there were positives in the parents' care of Roddie. It was well established that children should be with their parents, if, at all, possible. I genuinely believed that this was a case where Roddie should return to his parents.

I had to acknowledge that some further work with the parents was needed. The work would ensure that they understood the risks from paternal grandfather. The enmeshment between Matthew and his family had to be broken down. That work would take time, but it would save a lifetime of separation of Roddie being from his family.

I urged the court to grant Roddie and his family the time to be reunited. Severing those most primary of relationships for forever was a last resort. We still had a way to go before the last resort and we should try everything until then. Roddie relied on us to do everything for him and his family.

The closing submissions from the other parties did not hold any surprises. They were not particularly persuasive. They were kind to the parents but brought the court back to Roddie's need for immediate plans. The case had already gone on for well over a year. Everyone was sympathetic to the parents, but Roddie was the priority. Roddie deserved a permanent home and chance of a happy, safe family and he deserved that now.

NAEED

The Magistrates disappeared behind the veil of justice. The clamber and shuffle from the players and pieces moved in disjointed fashion. I looked over, as before, to the parents and their lawyer, they were muted and solemn as mourners by the graveside. Their heads were down, barely an exchange of a word between them and no celebrations today. Their family surely in tatters.

Our solicitor stood tall exuding confidence; we had done enough for the right result. We had got this over the line and wrapped with a stylish red bow!

Though it wasn't quite as simple as that and there would still be a long road ahead. We could then begin the search for Roddie's permanent family. I hated that we had a different team that looks after that part. I mean I understood why it was that way but felt cut off from full closure as a result.

I was at the coal face of the fire trying to save these children from often the most monstrous of situations. The permanency team were the true heroes. They found the perfect permanent homes for those children. It was an imperfect, perfect.

It was useful to have some fresh objectivity to seek out the right people for each child. You were so drawn into the case of removing the child from his birth family that you became jaded.

It helped to have that division of responsibility. Our priorities were very different. My role was to assess what was in the child's best interests. The placement team's role was to achieve the child's best interests.

I fired off the standard email, with Roddie's details and that we had finished the final hearing. The email was clear that we did not have a decision yet and that I would get back in touch when we did.

Life and work rolled on, whilst we waited for the court's determination. Statements, visits to other families, urgent referrals amongst everything else at work. My family needing me at home. I was often the comic juggler in a circus. The bright coloured plates whizzed above me, and I struggled to keep them all there.

We would need to consider the Barnett unborn child. We had time with that situation, and I needed to focus on my other cases.

At home, Alya struggled with her time with her daddy and in turn, I was more and more on edge.

Alya's dad had never stepped up for her the way I believed a father should, they seemed to have a fun relationship. Alya always seemed to enjoy time with her daddy. She usually came back with new toys and having been spoilt with junk food.

I was a little worried that there seemed to be a change, and something seemed to be upsetting Alya. The worry was like the unwanted creeping plant gripping the walls of a much loved and cared for home. It trickled through the crevices of the bricks. I needed to spend some time with my little one to try and get to the bottom of things.

Work was no easier. There wasn't any let up, so many children that needed our help, my help, and not enough hours in the day. We were pushed to the extreme with little support or reward. Everyone always turned on the social workers when things went wrong. It was little wonder that so many social workers exited the profession faster than Usain Bolt ran the Olympics.

I had been called out to a child yesterday that was admitted to hospital with a broken arm. The mother said it happened from him falling down a slide. The doctors seemed to doubt this story but also there were twenty odd, aged bruises all over his body. This poor kid was someone's punching bag. Angry red bruises, pained dirty blue bruises, and sadder faded brown stains patterned his thin body.

Sometimes this job got me. No matter what I did, I could not erase the past. No matter what we were able to do to stop abuse for the future, nothing eliminated the abuse in the first place. Nothing removed the impact it had already had for that young person. That stayed forever. A scar more permanent than an unwanted tattoo. Perhaps, a badge of honour.

I decided to spend some fun time with my Alya. My mum had arranged to visit one of her friends from back home who lived in the area. I wanted to stay at home with Alya.

I found that children can come out with all sorts of weird and wonderful on the one hand. Then searingly honest and earth shattering on the other when they are at their most relaxed. The trick was engaging them in something long enough for that to happen. I planned on some baking and whilst Alya's hands were busy in flour and water, her mouth might loosen and open.

My gleaming beamer sparkled under the shining

morning sun. My mum had readied Alya and I buckled her into the child car seat at the back of the car. I always struggled with the buckle on that car seat. I'm sure manufacturers made these things deliberately difficult to function. There was probably some marketing ploy behind it, but it was an everyday battle. As often happened, I caught my thumb in the clasp and let out a sharp 'Ouch.'

Alya was startled, 'Mummy?'

'Mummy is okay, don't you worry, baby!' I tapped the cute tip of her nose.

'Mummy is a silly billy, isn't she, beta?' My mum piped in and chuckled, making Alya chuckle back in return.

'Okay, okay, you two, stop ganging up on me,' I joked as I climbed into my car. My mum had joined us whilst I fought with that car seat and had belted herself in, in the front passenger seat. As I secured myself in behind the wheel, my mum did her quick prayer as she always did whenever we got in the car.

My mum's friend lived about ten minutes away and we all chatted and laughed together. Alya loved car trips and looking through the window as the world flew by.

We arrived at my mum's friend's house. She leaned across to me, placed her one hand on the top of my left shoulder and pecked me on the cheek. She then stepped out of the car.

I watched as she wobbled to the back of the car. She opened the door to Alya, gave her kisses and stroked her face saying, 'See you both later.'

She shut the car door and paddled towards her

friend's house. I watched her as she tottered to the front door and pressed the doorbell. Her friend swung the door wide open and with exaggerated movements welcomed my mum in. I gave a polite wave to them both before heading off.

Alya and I went on to Sainsbury's to get our ingredients. I grabbed a trolley, so I could seat Alya in there as we travelled around the aisles. Alya was singing to herself as I nipped her around.

I was fortunate that Alya's obsession was carrots rather than any sweet or chocolate. She never let me pass without grabbing a bunch and today was no different. 'Sweetie, we don't need these, we are going to have delicious cookies to make and eat.'

'Caotts, caotts,' Alya pleaded with her syrupy voice and a pout on her face that could melt ice.

'We already have some at home.'

'Puwearse, mummy, purwearse,' layering the syrup with some cream.

'Okay, here you go. Happy now,' I said as I poked her nose button again.

'Ove you, mummy,' my angel replied.

'I love you too, my baby girl.'

We picked up all the essentials for the cookies without any further interruptions. I got Alya to name each thing we picked up as we went round and eventually joined the queue at the cash desk.

I packed everything up, paid for my goodies and headed back to the car. On the way back home, Alya and I sang the Old MacDonald song. Alya's other obsession was animals, and she loved the song for that very reason.

We were home in no time at all. I put the carrots and some of the other bits away, whilst Alya played a while. Once that was out of the way, I shouted Alya through to the kitchen. She came running, her cute little butt swinging behind her.

We stood side by side mixing the ingredients together, Alya with a small bowl of mix for her little hands. I chatted to her about nursery. I heard all her garbled stories from there, in her squeaky little enchanting voice.

My ukulele giggled as she recounted her tales. She intermingled with not quite complete words, 'best fwend' and the 'choo choo' in place of train. It was clear that she was a very popular member of nursery, loved in equal measure by her peers and teachers. I swelled with pride as the mix formed a gooey, thick dough.

Next was rolling out the dough. Again, I let Alya do hers separately from mine. I wanted to give her that sense of responsibility and satisfaction.

As we cut out the different shapes we made, Alya said, 'Mummy, I don't like Uncle Mike.'

'Oh, who is Uncle Mike darling?' I immediately pricked.

'He's Kate's brudder, you know daddy's Kate, her brudder' she replied.

My insides flip flopped, and my ears were on alert. My mind raced and wild thoughts crashed around. Who was this Uncle Mike and what had he done to my little girl?

My hands massaging the flour concoction of butter,

chocolate chips and peanuts. My forehead scrunched inwards, and my temples throbbed. I was a human ball of worry, anger and confusion all kneaded in one like the cookie.

'Why don't you like him?' I asked. I was still cutting out some of the cookies. I had a deep in the gut sinking feeling, my head ticked over at breakneck speed.

'Mummy, look at this, it's a star,' she exclaimed in innocent wonderment. The moment gone.

SERENA

Some semblances of real life resumed. The Barnett family were on hold waiting for the court's decision. The problem with undertaking your own advocacy was that you got stuck at court for days at a time. When that happens, the paperwork on other matters was neglected. Work piled up like a sink full of dirty dishes.

In the digital age, things were easier but also more difficult. You could access emails wherever you were and were expected to respond immediately. Emails, by their nature, were a quicker form of communication. This wasn't always helpful when your head was elsewhere.

Many solicitors instruct barristers to do the court work. It was my favourite part of the job, and I only gave it up when I was on a sure-fire loser of a matter. I was happy to let the barristers take the glory in those matters!

I had had several new enquiries that I had to convert into new client matters. One was an estranged father, whose young son had been savagely beaten and removed into care. A new care case that would no doubt bring with it, its own twists, and turns. I had statements and negotiations to complete on pre-existing matters. I got my head down to clear through that forest of work.

I got everything up to date and was desperate for a holiday. We got the judgment date on the Barnett case, which was a couple of weeks away yet. So, I booked a last-minute holiday to Turkey for a week.

I didn't want to wait around to find someone to accompany me. I needed to get away. The day before the holiday I was in work tidying everything up as best as I could.

I knew it would be a long night so ordered some takeaway and got comfortable. It was always the way. Before and after any holiday, the amount of never-ending work seemed insurmountable.

The shutters were halfway down, and front door locked. Everyone else had gone home and the quiet lended itself to productivity not known in the daylight hours. It was light outside. The green of the village common splayed its blades and the emerald leaves rustled away in the light wind. Young people loitered, children on bikes and with footballs as they passed the office. The lightness of the day helped with the heaviness of the night ahead.

It was early evening and there was a knock on the front window. In anticipation of the Chinese, I rushed to the door. I could see through the windowpanes in the door that it was Matthew Barnett, not my Chinese takeaway!

I let Matthew in, saying, 'Matthew, what are you doing here at this time of night?'

'Could ask you the same,' he replied with a wry smile.

Matthew wore his signature cap, his uniform of blue jeans and white t shirt. He looked pensive.

Despite having cycled his way here, still composed and as if he had been a mere hop, skip and a jump away.

I walked Matthew through to my office and he made himself at home in one of the client chairs. He scribbled on scrap paper whilst I turned files on my desk over to preserve confidentiality.

I put those files I had finished with back in their homes. The cabinets were packed like London tubes at peak hours, as I squeezed, pushed, and pulled them in. Images of women forcing ill-fitting clothes over themselves flashed through my mind. Some of my files were so big that they split at the sides. Each one landed a further scratch on the wound of irritation inside me. I needed to speak to Janet and get her to tidy these all up. She was always usually so good in finding things that needed organising. I wasn't sure how this went under her radar, but I knew she would have it ship shape in no time.

'Are you okay there? I will be with you in a second or several. I have to put these away.'

'Yeah, yeah, I'm good,' Matthew answered not moving his eyes from his doodling.

I squashed more of my files in these grey, army like filing cabinets. The Barnett case included, as I continued to struggle to shove those files down. I was on the last file when I felt my index fingernail bend and pulled back. There went my beautiful equal shaped nails but at least, the nail snapped evenly. I left that rogue file on top of the cabinet rather than continue with the risk of further war wounds.

I was about to sit back at my desk when there was another knock on the front door. This time, it had to be the food. I was a little more cautious as I went to the front door, followed closely behind by Matthew.

'It's okay, Matthew, you can wait in there.'

'Hmmm...,' he mumbled and stayed with me.

It was the takeaway, which I gladly took from the delivery guy. Matthew and I re-traced our steps back to my office. I grabbed some forks from the back and shared out the food with Matthew, as we finally chatted, 'So what's going on?' I asked.

'Nothing much,' Matt said taking a forkful of noodles and chicken.

'Come on, there is obviously something on your mind. I mean, I get it, it's your family, after all.'

'Yeah,' and another mouthful went down.

'I mean, you usually have so much to say for yourself that I am not sure I can cope with this verbal diarrhoea of yours!' I joked. It fell flat.

'Yeah,' more food went down the hatch.

'Okay, if you don't want to talk, I'll talk instead.'

I went on to tell Matthew about my holiday. I told him that I tried to put things in order at work. There were holiday preparations waiting for me at home including the packing. I rambled on and on, with Matthew making enough polite sounds to keep me going, well to keep us both going.

I scooped up the rest of my Chinese and enjoyed every bite. Matthew finished his lot in quick time. Considering he had said he was not hungry and had already had his dinner or tea as he had put it, he gobbled it up. I jested with him about that. I saw a glimmer of a smile, but a glimmer was all it was, it disappeared as fast as it had appeared.

'We lost,' Matthew burst in.

'We need to wait for the judgment. We don't have to wait long now.'

'We lost,' Matthew repeated.

'Listen, I can't control how you feel and what you think but I am going to wait until I hear it for myself from the court.'

'We lost and I can't let Kel go on losing.'

'What do you mean? You are both in this together.'

'Not if I split.'

'Matthew, you don't need to do that. You have a shot with the unborn and we still don't know what will happen with Roddie. You can't split for the case, I've told you before, split if you want to for yourselves but not the case.'

'If we lose Roddie, I'm out. Kel will be better off without me.'

'I don't think that is how Kelly will see it.'

'That's because she is too sweet, but it is down to me to do the right thing.'

'Kelly has a right to decide what she wants for herself. You would not be doing anything noble or right by taking that choice away from her.'

'It's what I have to do for Kel, our babies and for me.'

With that, Matthew stood up and marched out of the office. I sat back in my chair, lost for words, lost for thoughts even. Thoughts of whether I should tell Kelly thrashed about in my head. She was my client too and had a right to know everything about her case but then Matthew wasn't talking to me as a client. What Matthew had shared with me had nothing at all to do with his case.

My brain was wiped out. A tidal wave of tiredness swept over me. I wasn't sure that I could finish up the last few dregs of work. I hoped a cup of tea would fix me up and tried to put Matt's revelation to the back of my mind. I kicked back with my tea and some trashy YouTube video. A half hour later and I knew I needed to head home.

When I got home, I packed my suitcase, threw whatever I could lay my hands on and hoped for the best. Whilst I was away, I thought about the Barnett case. It was on my mind, and I worried about how things would pan out. Success or failure would have lasting consequences for the whole Barnett family.

Whether they remained a family or splintered forever. I tried to convince myself that justice would be served. I had my doubts, but I hoped that I was wrong. I wasn't.

Chapter Sixteen

The Magistrates were in position. The parties took their places with their respective lawyers with them. They had all been waiting on this moment. The air was loaded, there was no return, this was it. An oppressive silence fell over them all. The lawyers' pens poised to note the Magistrates' words.

The Bench was a shuffle of papers and looming authority. The Chairman pressed down on his papers. He peered ahead without warming in any particular direction. He maintained an icy glazed stare into the distance.

With a quick re-set of his black, plastic glasses and clearing of the throat, the Chair kicked off. 'It seems to us that, in that balancing exercise, the certainty of damage to Roddie through further, on any view, significant delay with no certainty of a successful outcome, outweighs the damage and the loss to him of separation from his birth family... We share the view of the Guardian. This was a finely balanced case. It is a case to which we have given much anxious thought. On balance we have concluded that the Guardian is right. We have decided that the stage has been reached in this case where only care and placement orders will do...'

KELLY

I could barely take in what else they said.

My heart pulled out of me, where there had seconds before been hope and dreams was now an emptiness and anguish. I dropped as a ball of weightlessness leadened with pain. I fell to my knees, right there on the court room floor. The benches in front of me were oak hardened. The cinema type seats harsh and uncomfortable, but the wooden floor was cold and gloomy.

Tears rolled down my face uncontrollably without my even realising it. My baby, Rod, was being taken away from me and there was nothing I could do about it. I didn't know how to breathe any more without him.

Matthew grabbed me and curled himself around me. Serena tried to quieten and comfort me from her seat in front of our row whilst trying to listen to the judgment. The chairman spluttered through the rest of it, which I heard between my sobs but couldn't listen to. I heard the sharp screeches of chairs and feet rushing away.

Serena came round to us and as a rarity reached over and hugged us, 'Come on guys, let's get out of here.' Gradually, she encouraged us onto our feet and out of the courtroom, with me sobbing along the way.

We huddled up in one of the interview rooms, for one last time. There were words around me, but my head leaked any brain cells it contained slowly. It was mushy and tears streamed down my face. My nose was a running tap that I could not turn off and the remnants snuck into my mouth.

Matt was sitting next to me with his thick set arm over my back as I stretched across the interview room table. The tables in these rooms were flimsy. Still, they were strong enough to hold the weight of clients in distress when things went wrong.

Serena talked in long sentences and tried her best, I heard Matt making cursory grunts here and there. Eventually, Serena seemed to run out of steam, and she bid us farewell.

Matt had telephoned for a taxi to get us home, neither of us in any fit state to get on the bus.

I went to the toilet before heading out with Matt to wait for our taxi. I tidied my nose a little, having come to a natural stop with the crying. My eyes were red and puffy. I threw some cold water onto my face and then joined Matt.

We stood against the brick wall of the court waiting for our ride. My eyes stung and tears flowed afresh. Matt still hadn't said a word or made any sign of anything of what had happened.

Our taxi pulled up and we climbed into the back seats. I sat by the one side of the car and Matt sat next to me with his arm around my shoulders, but rage infused with my sadness. I moved forwards and away from Matt's hold and edged even closer to the door. I wasn't angry with Matt, but I wanted to be alone. I didn't want his comfort. I didn't want anything from anyone. I wanted Roddie.

The journey continued in silence. Matt inched to the other side of the car, staring out of the window.

When we returned home, Matt took me to the

living room and put me on the sofa. I was numb, my tears having finally dried up.

There was a hollowness that crushed me from the inside out. My throat was scratchy and dry. I could hear Matt, but I couldn't listen. I curled up on the sofa and lay rolled into myself for the rest of the night. Matt tried to talk to me, but I didn't listen or respond.

'It might not be the end,' Matt said.

'Mmm... yup, okay,' I replied.

'I mean Serena said she would have a look at whether we can appeal.'

'Yeah, okay.'

'I'm sure Serena will do her best.'

'Yep, okay,' I said.

'I mean she will find something, right, what do you think?'

'Yeah, sure.'

'I guess we need to focus on baby to be,' Matt tried.

'Yup, okay.'

'Kel, are you listening?'

'Uh-hu, yep, got it.'

'You need to snap out of this,' Matt urged.

I had no idea what he had said but I heard that, 'Snap out of it, snap out if. I've lost my son, that isn't something I am going to snap out of today or any day,' I yelled and broke down in tears again.

I wanted to disappear but knew I was stuck with this reality. I had to find a way to live this and fight on for our unborn child. It was another contest waiting to happen and I didn't know if I had any warfare left in me.

I had dozed off and Matt woke me with a bowl of comfort soup. I wasn't much up for eating or doing anything.

He sat on the floor beside me and fed me one spoon at a time. Neither of us said anything to one another.

NAEED

My mind had shooting stars of thoughts whizzing around and criss crossing. I feared that history was repeating and that my little girl had been exposed to some form of sexual abuse. My whole being a fully charged antenna.

I reported the matter to the police, but they were useless. There was nothing disclosed of a criminal nature. I knew where they came from, but it did not lessen my resentment over it.

I was stuck and didn't know what to do to protect my little girl. My sleep was disrupted with flashes of a nightmare almost nightly. The nights were the worst, but I struggled with my appetite too. I steeled myself and broached Lisa with it. I had felt shameful embarrassment to have to turn to Lisa over this.

This was my daughter. Yet I had no clue how to help and protect her, me with all my social work qualifications and experience.

Here I was, saving all these other random children, but unable to offer my own sweet angel anything at all. Lisa was magnanimous, put me at ease and kindly offered to speak with Alya to find out more.

I had to recognise that Lisa had years of

experience ahead of me. Kids seemed to want to open up to her, so I was grateful to her. We organised her to come on a Saturday afternoon and I had already prepared Alya for the visit. Alya knew it was my boss coming over and that she would spend a little bit of time with us.

On the day, my mum had agreed to make herself scarce and went off out. As great as mum is, I couldn't tell her what had plagued me all these weeks. So, whilst I hadn't gone into any detail, I had let my mum know that I had worried about Alya. I told her that I had asked my boss over to speak to Alya. I hadn't asked my mum to disappear out of the house but wanted her to let us have some time with Lisa.

Mum was concerned. She wanted a distraction, even though she didn't know anything. Sometimes that's even worse because your mind goes to the worst places. I wasn't sure I would tell mum anything if I turned out to be right but also wasn't sure that I could keep it to myself. It's different when it's your daughter.

Lisa arrived promptly at two in the afternoon, and we did a little work talk. I made us tea and gave Alya some juice in her cup.

My mum and I had arranged for her to call me, which she duly did, and I excused myself to speak more with her. I went into the kitchen, and I let mum carry on. My mum rang off and I crept to the open kitchen door, straining my ears to hear Alya and Lisa.

Lisa was sat cross legged on the middle of the floor and Alya played with her train set and tracks. She was obsessed with Thomas the Tank Engine. 'Choo, choo, twain is coming,' Alya giggled out.

'Oooooh, careful, don't run me over now. Can I jump on?' Lisa joined in.

'How?'

'Watch and see. My brother and I used to love playing trains when I was small like you,' Lisa replied. I, then heard, the heavenly sound of my girl's twinkly laughs.

'My daddy plays twains with me,' Alya said.

'Wow, mummy told me that you like seeing daddy,' Lisa said.

'Yeah,' Alya replied.

I couldn't make out if she said something else. Then I caught the end when I heard my girl say, 'but I can't say anything, it's our secret.' This was atypical of sexual abuse, I was going to kill this Uncle Mike, my brain ticked over the next steps.

I would ask Lisa to stay with Alya whilst I would go and confront my ex. He was a useless dad and let our daughter become easy prey for this predator. I already planned what I would say. It would be something like, 'You bastard! You were a useless husband and now you have gone one better and become a deadbeat dad!'

My rage bubbled away inside the pit of my stomach and rose, heating my whole body.

A little while later, Lisa came into the kitchen with her cup and Alya's cup.

'Naeed, you have nothing to worry about with the sexual abuse,' Lisa reassured.

'What, but I heard her...' I started.

'I'm not sure what you heard, but trust me, there is no sexual abuse. Nor any other direct abuse, though there are concerns you need to address.'

'I don't get it, Alya said about it being a secret, that's standard for sexual abuse.'

'It's a secret in that her dad told her not to let you know. She wasn't told in a sexual abuse sense of intimacy or anything.'

'Oh my God, that is such a relief,' I sighed. I felt my whole body ease back into itself.

'Yeah, that is not the problem at all. Apparently, this uncle drinks a lot and Alya struggles with that when he is around in that state.'

I had stopped listening, I mean, I knew that I would still have to tackle that, but I was overcome with emotion. All that weight I had carried, released. I sank to the floor sobbing with my head resting on my bent arms placed heavily on my bent knees. Lisa crouched down next to me and put her arm around me but then Alya ran into the kitchen. 'Please, Lisa, please get Alya out of here,' I managed to gulp out.

I grabbed at air between sobs but tried to force them down. My instinctive leap to sexual abuse banged inside my head. It had been my go-to straightaway. I had been far, far too quick to rule out the Barnetts for exactly that same reason.

The dawning realisation that I had not come to terms with my own past was suffocating. I had not processed any of it and it pervaded everything I did now. It had had such a toxic impact. I had made a huge mistake. I'd torn apart the Barnett family for no good reason other than my own very damaged insecurities. What had I done!

SERENA

I was sure that an almighty gasp escaped from deep within me and at about the same time, I heard the wailing from behind me. I whizzed around and saw Kelly as she fell to the ground. I patted down on the table behind me in some vain attempt to comfort Kelly.

The Magistrates had not quite finished but accelerated through their judgment. I dropped my pen to the long, wooden table in front of me but gripped it to steady myself. I refused to show my true face here and reshaped myself to the ice queen.

It was devastating and worsened my sense of injustice in cases like these that gets right under my skin. Right now, though, an emptiness.

I went through the motions. I stood tall, all five feet of me, packed my papers away in my matted black bag that frayed at the ends. I turned and saw Kelly and Matt huddled together, unmoved but Kel pumping up and down with her pained sobs.

My heart slowed, I was a hollow shell, barely breathing or hearing anything outside of us. I reached over the table between us and cajoled them out. I tried out some words of comfort. 'I'm sorry,' I thought of saying or 'It will be okay' but each word pricked the insides of my throat. My voice was a growing cactus in my mouth that was only dissolvable with silence.

I guided them into a vacant interview room. Kelly

was lost to me, and Matt worked hard to keep it together. I needed to try some words again and some ideas floated in my head. The thinking time became a painful silence settled between Kelly's audible distress.

'I'm sorry, guys,' I attempted. 'It's completely unfair what has happened. You are not bad parents and did not do anything wrong. I wish it could be different, but it is the system we have. I'm so sorry and wish it could have gone our way. It's not over, though. I mean, I am going to look into everything and speak to a barrister to see if there is any way we can challenge this. I'm not going to leave it but also you have your unborn to think about.'

'Uh-huh,' Matt responded whilst still trying to comfort Kelly, his arm reached over her.

'I'm not giving up on Roddie, but we need to look to the future and the future is right there for you guys to grasp. You must do the further work that they were talking about. We will need to push the Local Authority to get that sorted out as soon as so that you keep your newborn baby from birth. We have to work with them, and you both need to tell them everything. If you go to the toilet, tell the social worker, if you even pass wind, tell the social worker. I don't mean that, but you do have to tell them every little thing as well as the big things. Don't think about whether you should tell them or not, just tell them. Do you get it?'

'Serena, we need to get out of here,' Matt replied. Matt wanted to bundle Kelly home. Well probably he wanted to whisk her away to some exotic destination. Then, I remembered our conversation the night after the trial.

'Matt,' I called out, but Matt waved me away needing to get Kel settled. We exchanged knowing looks. I feared he would carry out his promise, but it was his life, it was his family and his dreams.

I was shattered at the end of each day but didn't have time to even realise it, no more so than at the end of this trial. I hadn't had time or energy to meet with much family or friends. I spent most evenings and weekends in the office juggling everything. My only regular social visit was with my parents every Tuesday.

As a Hindu, I should be a vegetarian but enjoyed meat and fish far too much to be vegetarian full-time. To compensate, I did my bit by being vegetarian every Tuesday.

If I didn't drop by my parents, I would most likely have not eaten anything every Tuesday. They knew I had this 'big' case on but not any of the details. They let me witter on about whatever nonsense might come to me as my way of releasing all that pent up emotion.

'I managed to finally mow the lawn last Sunday,' I rattled on. 'I was meant to do it on Saturday so that I could clear the weeding in the patio. Also, I have so much trimming and weeding to do in the front.'

'Darling, you need to spend more time at home, and I don't mean your office, I mean your home, home,' my mum replied.

'Aaah, mum, it's all good and anyway, it is more fun in a jungle than a manicured garden,' I giggled and so it continued.

It was good to hear about whatever had been going

on for them too to take my mind off things. The food was as delicious as it could be for non-meat food.

I could not shake the disappointment of this case for some time. It lay somewhere deep within me. It was an invisible scar that surfaced when I least expected.

The persistent itch from the Magistrates' ignorance to my submissions. Their abject failure to address that in their paltry judgment. It came to mind more often than it should, that's what happens when justice was cheated. I could not bear it and yet, it motivated me to power on. I became a tornado on a mission to destroy that injustice. Injustice in justice was an authorised evil.

This case was over, and I had to focus on all the future cases that would come my way. I piled onto this steamroller, ploughing through to continue to strive for justice. It drove me harder than before. I was even more scrupulous with my cases. I checked, double checked and cross referenced everything to secure justice. For the Matts and Kels of the future. For me.

MATTHEW
'I'm sorry, Kel,' I said.
'What for?' Kelly asked, bemused.
'It's my fault all this has happened.'
'We both made mistakes,' Kelly responded dejectedly.
'I guess.'
'I can't do this anymore. I can't lose Andi. I can't lose Roddie. I can't lose another child. I can't go on like

this.'

'I'm the problem,' I insisted.

'I don't know. I don't know...'

'It is and I'm so, so sorry. I will make things right.'

'Uh-hum, okay,' Kel replied. She looked off into the distance.

I had been strong at court when the damning judgment was delivered. I never thought my stupidity in visiting my brother on weekends would have this impact. That was my problem; I never thought.

My stupid parents and brother were more important than Kelly, Roddie, Andi and our unborn. It had torn our family apart, that innocent mistake blew our family to smithereens. I had not caused either of our children any harm and had tried hard to do the best I could, and my best was not good enough. It would never be good enough.

My past would always hold me back and there was no chance I would be allowed to have a family of my own. I didn't deserve a family of my own.

Whilst Kelly napped, I blocked my parents' numbers on my phone. I couldn't cut myself off from my brothers and sister. I might not see them anymore, but I couldn't completely let them go, not yet anyway.

Then I gathered up anything around the house that reminded me of them and piled it all up. I ransacked the cupboards around the house like a mad man. I threw everything in the drawers out and picked out every last thing that was connected to them. My anger thrashed against every storage space as I cleared it all out. I left the bedroom wardrobes last.

By the time I got to the bedroom, the rage had subsided a little. It was still right there under the outer skin, still simmering away. I crept into the bedroom and as quietly as I could, opened my side of the wardrobe. Rather than pulling everything out, I looked through the packed clothes.

I pulled out gifts and borrowings from family. My mum's favourite top on me. Even the trousers with the ketchup stain from when my dad accidentally knocked it. It all joined the reject collection.

'What on earth are you doing?' Kelly asked.

I spun round and saw Kelly perched up in bed looking across at me. There was a deep furrow in her forehead, her eyebrows scrunched, and eyes narrowed.

'Having a clear out, need to get rid of my parents.'

'Matt...' Kel started but then didn't seem to quite know where to go with that.

I pressed on and Kel laid back down in bed. I pulled out the folded clothes and went through that same ruthless process.

A few hours later, I had piled all my old family stuff in the back yard. I soaked it all with oil and set it alight. As the fire raged in front of me, the hot flames mocked me. I stared out the dancing flares and tears silently rolled down my cheeks. I glanced up at the house and saw Kelly watching down at me, but she moved slowly away when our eyes crossed.

I could not and would not let Kel suffer this because of me. I still had Serena's words beating in my heart, but I had to squash that, she was wrong. She was wrong with this case, and she was wrong about me.

A week or so later, Kel was still very broken and desolate. We were completely disconnected, and it was not hard to push Kel to spend the day at her dad's.

It had almost become an obligation to stay together in this miserable house, where it had all gone wrong. So, any chance of respite was grabbed.

As soon as Kel left, I immediately packed up what clothes I could manage. I was empty and felt dehydrated. I pushed past this and kept on. My head was heavy and throbbed as I pushed things into my rucksack. A couple of hours was all it took to collect my worldly goods and was ready for the off.

This would give Kel the best chance for a family and find a way to get Andi and Roddie back, as remote as that might be.

Family life and I were not a match. I had to learn to accept that. My dad had ruined me. The engagement ring burnt my soul as I fumbled with it in between my fingers, in my trouser pocket.

ONE YEAR LATER

'We won!' Serena sung down the phone.

'What do you mean? We get Roddie back?'

'No, not quite,' Serena explained, 'but it means that you still get a shot at it.'

Serena confirmed that there would be another trial. That would decide the long-term arrangements for Roddie. We met Serena at court the next morning,

Amelia, our newborn being left with Kel's dad for

the day. Serena talked to us about the Appeal again, 'So Roddie can come home?' I asked.

'Like I tried to explain yesterday, it's not quite as simple as that.'

'So, we lost,' I pressed.

'No, we won but we won the right to have the matter re-considered afresh.'

'I don't get it. I mean if they were wrong, then surely that means we were right and that Roddie should come home.'

'You know at the trial, we said there should be a further assessment. We argued that this should have been after the protective parenting work.' Serena said.

'Okay,' Kel and I said in unison.

'Well, the Local Authority was saying that that was wrong and that Roddie should be adopted.' Serena continued.

'Right,' I said, and Kel nodded.

'Well, the Court of Appeal has in effect said that the Local Authority's approach was wrong. They said that you guys could not be ruled out. That's not to say that you won't be ruled out properly at a re-hearing.

'Okay,' I said, 'Well we have to make sure that we are ruled in.'

The Court of Appeal was scathing about the lower court, the Local Authority and the Guardian. Justice was not just ice; it had a beating heart and a probing soul. In our case, justice had been long, meandering but in the end, justice.

On the day I left Kelly, I arrived at Sarah's house. She ushered me in, and my stuff thudded to the ground.

I fell into her embrace and blocked everything else out. She had tried to persuade me to talk things through with Kel. I had called ahead, 'Hiya, do you think I can crash with you for a while?'

'What's happened?'

'I need somewhere until I can sort something else.'

'What is going on? Where's Kel?'

'Can I stay or not?'

'Whatever has happened, you can work this out.

'Forget it.'

'Wait, wait. Obviously, you can stay.'

'Thanks, I'm on my way.'

I ended up staying with Sarah, which was ironic, because her kids were allowed to stay with me when my own kid wasn't. Their sofa became my friend but on weekends, I tried to give it back to them to use as a family. I pounded the streets. Drowned in tea in cafes. Lounged in libraries and generally watched as time passed by.

I was packing my things away for the start of another weekend when there was a knock on the door. 'Hello?' I said.

'Morning, you off out again,' Sarah said as she came in.

'Yup.'

'What is planned today?'

I shrugged my shoulders and placed the folded sheets on the beanbag. I folded my pyjamas and placed them on top of the sheets.

'This cannot go on. You have to sort yourself out.'

'I don't know what you mean.'

'It's been over a month now. Do you want your life to be on our couch!'

'You want me out. I'll sort it.'

'Oh yeah, how exactly will you sort it? With that amazing job of yours, I'm sure you've saved up your deposit and first month's rent, right!'

'Whatever.'

'Real grown up! No wonder they wouldn't let you have Roddie!'

'What the hell! Get out of my way.' I tried to push past Sarah, but she stood firm blocking the door.

'I'm sorry, you know I didn't mean that the way it sounded but why are you so determined to prove them right! Why are you so determined to be as rubbish a father as our mother was a mother!'

I retreated and sat down on my friend of a sofa.

Sarah sat next to me and stretched her arm across my shoulders and leaned into me, her head resting on me. 'You know I love you but that means I'm allowed to say these things to you.'

'Mmm… you get a kick out of digging me out,' I half-joked.

'That is an added bonus,' she winked. 'I'm serious though, I know you can be a great dad but being a great dad is being a dad all the time. Even when the kids are not there. Everything you do should be about how it will make things better for them. Do you know what I mean?'

'I suppose. I don't know where to start.' I sighed.

'That's a good place as any.'

'I don't get it.'

'Start by working out what you need to do to help Kel and the kids.'

'I've got to forget Kel but yeah, I do have to start coming up with a plan.'

'Stay in this weekend and work on that.'

'Are you sure?'

'Of course. Have you been disappearing because you thought we wanted you out?'

'Well, yeah. I thought Robert and the kids wanted you to themselves for the weekend.'

'Don't be daft! You're part of the family. Robert and the kids get that, we only need you to get it, now!' Sarah said as she punched me lightly in the shoulder.

The wheels were in motion. I managed to get a factory job as a supervisor and enjoyed it strangely. The lads looked up to me and came to me when the machines ground to a halt. They watched as I got in and around the power tower. I knew those machines better than people. Often it was an easy fix but other times it would take longer but I revelled in the puzzle. The grime and solidity were my happy place.

I re-started the counselling, which was gruelling. Elizabeth always wore her blond hair in a low bun, with a few wispy strands loose around her porcelain face. She spoke with a husky rasp but used it rarely. Her favourite three words seemed to be, 'Tell me more.' My favourite words in response, 'Don't know,' but that wasn't enough for Elizabeth. It wasn't enough for me.

Over time, with Elizabeth's persistence, I talked about Roddie's removal and the slap. I also took up the protective parenting work around sexual abuse. I'm not sure doing it all in one go was the best idea.

The protective parenting happened on Tuesdays and my counselling was on Fridays. I was talked out after these sessions, which were at the end of a workday. I went back to Sarah's, ate, and crashed out on the sofa. The weeks went by, and this was my life.

'Matt, Kel has called,' Sarah said through the phone.

'What's happened?'

'She's in labour.'

'I'm on my way. Thanks, Sare!'

My boss gave me the all clear to head out and I called for a taxi. Blood rushed up to my head and my heart throbbed. My palms were sticky and my throat dry. I didn't know how Kel would respond. I was excited about our newborn but scared that I would never know them. My head was full of mashed potato and when the car arrived, my words spilled out, 'Hospital, go, Stafford, I, please.'

'Yo, slow down man, slow down.'

'Sorry, I'm having a baby. I mean, my girlfriend, well never mind. Please hurry.'

The taxi dropped me right outside the hospital entrance. I ran the corridors to reception, and they pointed me in the right direction. I found Kelly's room and tapped the door.

'Come in.'

I skulked in, keeping my eyes averted. 'Hi, Kel. How are you doing?'

'No, get out.'

'Kel, I'm sorry. Let me be here for you.'

'But you are not here for me. Get out. Aaaaah. Damn it.'

'I'll get a nurse.'

'GET OUT! GET OUT! GET OUT!'

Kel's explosions got the nurse running in. 'What is going on here?'

'This man needs to leave.'

'I don't know what is going on here but young man, you heard her.'

'I still love you,' I mumbled.

I shuffled out of the room and waited outside in the corridor. The nurse told me that there would be a wait still. A few hours later, they took Kel to the delivery room and one of the nurses came looking for me. 'Come on, dad, we need you in there.'

I rushed behind the nurse and went straight to Kel, I rubbed her back and did my best at encouraging words. 'You're doing great, Kel. So great!'

'I still hate you.'

'Keep going on, you are amazing.'

'Aaaaaaaarghhhhh. I can't.'

'You can, you are. She's almost here.'

'I HATE YOU!'

Our baby girl soon arrived and let out her first most beautiful sound. Her cry pierced the tensions of the room. Her little hands and legs waved around as she was mummied in a fluffy wrap. They placed her onto Kel's chest and tears streamed down Kel's cheeks, as she held our baby girl close.

Kelly and our baby girl were taken back onto the maternity ward. It was late and so they were staying there for the night. The hospital said I could stay for a couple of hours. They were both sound asleep.

I cradled our baby girl, memorising every part of her. The thin wisps of hair crowning her head, the fleshy eyelids, the heart shaped lips and scrunched up nose. Kel stirred and reached out for something. I grabbed a glass of water and placed it in Kel's hands. I laid our baby girl back in the cot.

'What are you doing here?' Kel whispered.

'Let me explain,' I started.

'You left us. What is there to explain? You left when I needed you the most.'

'You can get the kids back without me. I'm the problem here.'

'Get out, Matt. I cannot do this.' Muted, I left.

Serena had negotiated that our baby girl stay at home with Kel. This was conditional on Kel living with her dad and me staying elsewhere. I was able to see our baby girl as much as I wanted but not overnight. They were still heading to court for her but at least this was something.

Serena hadn't told anyone that Kel and I were over, but she would have to at the first hearing. I went every evening in the week and in the day on weekends to see Kel and newbie. Kel always seemed busy with something or other. I couldn't blame her, but I wanted us to be civil with each other and hopefully friendly in time to come. Kel didn't want anything to do with me.

Ahead of the first hearing, Serena staged an intervention. She arranged an appointment with me to discuss strategy. She needed to know what we would present at court about my relationship status. We were chatting it through. She had an emergency call she had to take from another room. For confidentiality purposes, she said. Shortly after, Kel ambled in, 'They told me to come... what are you doing here?'

'We have been set up,' I replied.

'Guys, you two need to talk and work out what you want. So, I am going to leave you here in my office for half an hour. I won't be far away but after that, I need to know what you want to say to everyone about your plans for your children.' Serena intervened. She had snuck up behind Kel.

'So, why did you leave us?'

'I knew you would have a better chance without me.'

'That's rubbish. I deserve the truth.'

'That is the truth. I'm ruined, can't you see. I don't deserve a family; I don't deserve you.'

'You are a coward! That is the truth.'

'Yup.'

'For God's sake, can't you fight for us? Don't you want to fight for us?'

'This is for us. You are a good mum; the kids should be with you, but they will never let that happen while I am around.'

'You talk about love, but you don't know what it means. You don't love anyone but yourself. Well, I hope you'll be happy.'

'I don't know what else I can say. I thought this would make things easier.'

'Leaving me all alone with three children, yeah, so

much easier! Stop with the excuses. If you have fallen out of love, be man enough to say it. If the reality of taking care of three children is too much, be man enough to say it. Be a man!'

'I'm screwed! Don't you get it?

Apparently, I don't!'

'My dad, he, he, you know. Don't make me say it.'

Kel reached out to me and held my hands. Neither of us said anything and yet somehow, the wall of silence between us fell away piece by piece.

We lived separately until I worked through the counselling. Kelly had completed the protective parenting work. I was still working through that. For the purposes of the proceedings, we presented a united front.

It was a long and windy road, but every family has its ups and downs. Ours had been pulled apart and we fought our way back. The heartbeat of life is family.

Serena went onto become a Judge a few years later. She told us that our case made her determined to root out injustice and pursue justice for all, not just the few.

Naeed fell out of our case, thankfully, but she continued as a social worker. She remained Andi's social worker. That made it near impossible to get anywhere close to having Andi back at home with us. I knew that this burned a hole in Kel. There was a strange perfection in imperfection. Kel still had regular contact with Andi. Now it was community based and not supervised, so some slow progress was being made.

It became clear that Roddie and our baby girl, Amelia would be with us. The night before the final hearing, I told Kel that I would sort dinner out for us. By that, I meant I would get us takeaway. As we tucked into our pizza, I took a moment to get down on one knee and pulled out the ring.

'Oh my God, Matt! Yes, yes, yes,' Kel said with tears rolling down her cheeks.

'I haven't asked the question yet,' I chuckled as we leaned in for a kiss, cementing our family. Whatever the future held, we would face it together.